A VEIL OF STARDUST AND SAVAGERY

ANALEIGH FORD

A Veil of Stardust and Savagery

Analeigh Ford

A Veil of Stardust and Savagery by Analeigh Ford

For permissions contact:

analeighfordauthor@gmail.com

For all those still looking.

You're in the right place.

A VEIL
of
STARDUST
and
Savagery

LAND OF AVARATH

AVARATH
SEA

MOUNTAIN COURT
THE PLAINS
THE VALLEY
WOODLAND COURT

1
DELPHINE

THEY SAID THE STARLIGHT FAE WERE THE GREATEST TRICKSTERS of all.

But when the Starlight Fae came for me, it wasn't a trick.

The sound of the two realms colliding echoed in my ears even long after they'd once again split. I heard the ringing in the quiet moments, the crash of broken rock, the screams of bodies and souls blinking out of existence.

Caldamir and the other fae princes did not awaken the king from his imprisoned slumber. They did not rouse him from his grave.

Caldamir, Nyx, Armene, and Tethys—the four princes of Avarath—had failed in their quest. They'd not returned the magic to the realm. Instead, they'd lost something.

They'd lost me.

Because I was not in Avarath anymore.

True to their word, the fae whose blood ran through my veins had taken me away from there, alive. What they'd not done, however, was take me back to Alderia.

There was one brief moment where I thought they had,

where I thought the hand tugging me toward the warped wall of light and blurred figures was taking me back to the village I'd once called home. Back to Sol.

I swore I saw the sunshine catching on his golden curls, the late summer heat sticking his shirt to the back of his neck as he ran my stepmother, Nerys, in circles round the front garden. It was like a dream, and like a dream, it faded before I even had the chance to fully grasp it. It slipped from my fingers; the colors draining from my vision to be replaced with the sharp contrast of white against black.

I felt the shift as much as I saw it. Cold air slammed into me, igniting me and dousing me like its own kind of flame. I looked back once in that moment, seeing for the last time the cavernous expanse of the tomb I'd left behind—and with it, the faces of those once determined it would be the last thing I'd see.

Nyx.

Armene.

Tethys.

Caldamir.

Rocks rained down on them in a shower of silver stone, but not one of them moved. The momentary battle that had raged behind them was stilled, the shivering form of soldiers halted as they looked up with bent necks from where they lay, scattered and shaken to the floor by the earth-shattering crash of the two realms. It was as if, in that moment, I could hear the heartbeat of all of Avarath. I could feel it racing, pulsing ever faster, even as the whole world held a collective breath.

I was suspended once more as I had been in the pool. All around me, the world moved more slowly until it almost stilled, allowing me to look between the faces behind me and take each one of them in. The world was quickly flickering out of sight, but what I found before it was swallowed whole left my own heart stuttering. In those faces before me, I expected to find anger. Disappointment. Sorrow, even.

Instead, I saw relief.

Joy.

Hope, even.

All of that, with one exception.

Caldamir glared at me with an indescribable fury. Unlike the other princes, whose jaws fell slack with surprise and shock, the Mountain Court's leader stared forward with a piercing gaze fixed steadily in place.

At me.

Through me.

It cut into me, tearing through the little places inside me that had ever once wondered if he might care for me in the slightest. For a moment, the dream around me flickered to a moment in the past, to the moment when the two of us had stood chest to chest, angry words heavy between the shrinking space between us. Not as heavy as the thrill of emotion had alit inside me in that moment, and not as heavy as the one that dragged me back out of it again and into the present.

Into the moment when Caldamir was the only prince looking at me with all the rage an immortal soul could muster.

In that moment, he alone seemed able to break the spell that had fallen over the rest of his companions. His mouth dropped open, not in surprise, but in a battle cry. His sword lifted from his side to plunge forward, a new kind of determination flashing in his eyes—not of due vengeance or the righteous exchange he'd nearly convinced me my own sacrifice would be—but of pure, unbridled hatred. The point of the sword drew close, nearly slicing through the billow of fabric swimming suspended between my ankles. Fear flashed up my spine as I tried to move away, but found I was still caught in that in-between. I moved too slowly as the world behind me faded back to normal. My hair swirled in a curtain before my eyes, creating a halo of white through which the prince's eyes seemed to flash even darker.

Nearly as dark as mine.

He would have me. He would end me. He would succeed.

If it was up to him.

In the moment before his sword could catch on more than fabric, before it could even graze the tender skin of my calves, another sword flashed between us. In one final act of treason, his personal guard, Tallulah, protected me once more from her princes. From *her* prince. The only one that really mattered.

I might have remained frozen there forever suspended between the two realms, slowly falling apart just as the world seemed to be around us, if it weren't for the hand that once again guided me forward. The grip on my fingers tightened ever so slightly, pulling me forward in the moment that I faltered. I looked at the back of my savior's ashen hair.

He'd not once looked back. Not once turned to see the chaos and destruction that fetching me had wrought.

But once my gaze shifted down, and I saw what it was he was looking at instead, I understood. Once I turned away from Avarath, really turned away, it was impossible to turn back. All above me, the lights sharpened until I was looking up into a world of stars like I'd never imagined before. The stars were not cold, unfeeling pinpricks of light clustered in far-off galaxies, they were close.

They were *here*.

They surrounded us completely, their light shining in the blackness of the sky as they moved around us in a clockwork dance. Their paths left shimmering trails across the expanse, like glitter cascading across the dark. For a moment we were inside them, swimming up toward them, and then suddenly they were tilting overhead. Together, my savior and I broke through the surface of a pool and rose effortlessly to stand at its edge. All around us, shining black pillars rose up to cage us in as we did. They formed a long hallway to either side, stretching above and overhead in an open lattice through which the stars danced in and out.

That was the moment I left Avarath, the moment I'd been promised.

Why then didn't I feel the same confusing mix of emotions I'd seen on three of my four prince's faces? Why was there no relief, no joy?

Why then was the only thing that I felt … dread?

Six figures rose into view at the base of the pool, their faces turned up to watch as we stepped in a kiss of cold air to the top of the steps surrounding it. I felt my hair finally flutter down around my shoulders and the press of my skirts as the heavy fabric returned to resting against my flesh. A slight dizziness overtook me, but the fae holding my hand kept his footing steady, as if to adjust to the shift in mine. For the first time, I looked up at him and saw him for who he was. He was not just a fae-shaped shadow whispering promises in the dark. Not anymore.

The fae beside me stood a hair's-breadth taller than Caldamir, but the sweep of his shoulders and the tilt of his chin made him appear to tower above me. His sharp jaw came to a soft point aligned with cheekbones that cast deadly shadows across the planes of his face. It was a severe look softened by the tumble of silver-white hair falling in a pin-straight sheet down his back.

And then, of course, there were the eyes.

My eyes.

He was awe-inspiring and terrifying all at once. He was

beautiful, but not in the way Nyx was. Where Nyx drew you in, mesmerized and entrapped you, this new fae's beauty made it impossible to look too long. His face was a perfect mask, and if I gazed too long, I feared what I might see simmering beneath those impossible features. Or worse, what he might see in mine.

But when I looked back down at the figures gathered before me, I quickly realized he wasn't what I should have been afraid of. Something pulled at an inner part of me I'd never felt before. Something stirred. Something awakened. I had no words to put to it, and yet somehow, I knew in every fiber of my being that for the first time in my life, I was in the very place that my bones and blood belonged.

And I hated the feeling just as keenly with every one of those same fibers, even before the woman in the center stepped forward and hissed an accusation between her lips.

"Seren—what have you done?"

2
DELPHINE

It felt as if it wasn't just the fae gathered before us that watched too close. It was the very stars, too.

Every pair of eyes was on us, but only the woman who had spoken stepped forward. Her silver robes swirled around her feet with an elegance that didn't match the frown creasing her otherwise perfect forehead.

Seren—the fae still holding my hand as he guided me down the next step on the stairs—wasn't fazed by her in the slightest.

"Is that really how you greet one of the fae returned to us?"

Something close to joy teased on the back of his words. They caused a sparkle to alight in the eyes of the six other figures looking on, even the woman who'd just accused Seren of committing some kind of terrible mistake. They craned their necks to look around the woman, who was now rushing up the steps, as curiosity got the better of the other five and they tried to get a better look at me. Instinctively, I shrank back, but Seren felt it almost before I did and pulled me forward again.

He dropped his voice a little and tilted his head down, so it was clear he was speaking only to me.

"There's no need to hide here."

He'd barely straightened back up and had time to reset the slight twitch of his jaw before the female finally came to an abrupt halt one step below us. Only then did Seren stop, steadying me again. He didn't incline his head, but rather looked down at the fae with her heaving breaths through hooded eyelids.

"How could you? The pool hasn't been used in centuries. Not since …" She trailed off, air hissing between her teeth as if she couldn't bring herself to put her accusation into words. "You of all fae know the dangers, Seren."

Seren just lifted his gaze upwards, slowly, his eyes sparkling with the reflected light from above.

"Has the world shattered?"

She followed his gaze to the heavens all around us, where the glowing stars continued along their ever-steady paths. When the two of them lowered their heads, an intense look briefly flashed between the joining of their gaze.

"That's right, because I stopped it," Seren said, matter-of-fact. He leaned closer, but kept his voice loud enough for the other fae in the room to hear this time. "Like you said, I *of all fae* know the dangers. They were going to awaken the sleeping court's king."

"The …" Her eyes widened and flickered over to me, registering for the first time the trickle of blood trailing down the center of my chest. She stared on for a moment as if it was a foreign sight before mutters broke out behind her and she finally registered why. "Why didn't you tell me this sooner? Why didn't you tell any of us?"

Her words made silence fall again, all eyes falling on Seren this time.

"Would it have changed anything?"

She went to argue again, but Seren caught her arm not-so-gently. "I'm the Seeker. Or have you forgotten?"

Those words made the other five fae straighten. A couple of them nodded in agreement, and at least one of them shot the fae standing in front of us annoyed glances.

She pressed her lips tight in her own response, and though a thousand thoughts flashed across her face, she didn't argue. "So you are, brother," she said, reverence returning to her voice.

"Besides," Seren continued. "I didn't do it alone. Tarrack saw the girl first."

One of the fae in the half circle at the base of the stairs made a small, surprised sound. "This is her? This is the girl?"

Seren nodded, but there was something in his face that stopped the other fae, Tarrack, from saying anything more—not that it was easy for him. Despite my near delirious state, I could see him itching to say more, to ask more. His lips practically quivered with all his unasked questions.

And he wasn't the only one.

The female fae, the one still standing between us, seemed to be the only one uninterested in hearing more about just *why* Seren had brought me here. A hardness had turned down the corners of her mouth and creased into that ever-deepening frown on her forehead. Whatever Seren had meant by reminding her he was this "Seeker," however, kept her from arguing, too.

She dipped her head ever so slightly, arms sweeping out to either side. "I'll go make the proper arrangements."

"Thank you, Itris," Seren said, once again taking hold of her arm, if only for a second. There was a sincerity in his voice that she met with a nod of her own. Her face finally smoothed at his reassuring voice, only for that frown to return full force when he added, "But that won't be necessary. I already have."

"You and I are going to have to talk," she hissed back at him, after a moment. "Later. For now, I'll excuse myself."

Her tone was as clear as the way her tongue pressed into her cheek. *Before I say something I regret.*

She managed to smooth away the contempt on her face so that the only hint of her displeasure that remained was when she cast one last look at me over her shoulder before she left through an arched doorway at the end of the hall. Her eyes narrowed first at me, and then at the pool from whence we'd stepped.

Trouble, that was what we were to her.

There was a good chance, I knew, that she was right.

The moment the fae, Itris, left, it was as if a seal was broken. A breath escaped the fae standing before me as color began to flush their cheeks, the weight of their gaze once again falling to hungrily devour me.

Out of the five of them, three were male and two female.

The one called Tarrack stepped forward, his head turning down as his features softened. "You've no idea how long we've waited for you," he breathed. "It's been too long since one of our own was called home."

I had no idea how to respond to that. My head was still reeling, as was my stomach, at the immensity of everything around me. My heart still beat like thunder, but my own buzzing mind still managed to drown it out.

To add to the overwhelming sensation, Tarrack reached out and clasped one of my hands in his. For a moment, his eyes widened, but then he let out another breath.

"This is going to be interesting. I so look forward to getting to know you better ..."

He paused, all faces just as suddenly turning from me back to Seren.

"Delphine," he said, in response, "of Alderia."

"Alderia."

It was one of the women who stepped forward next. Her eyes had taken on a glossy look, catching the tiny sparkle of lights even more than before. "It's been so long since I saw that place. I was starting to think it all might've been a dream."

She reached out for me too, but that hunger in her eyes sparked too and I found myself wanting to shrink back again.

All of the fae before me leaned in, intrigued even further by the revelation of Seren's words.

They all shared the same silver-white hair and dark eyes, but more than that, they shared a searching look that seemed to see past my shaken exterior to my very core. They were looking for something, that same thing that they were undoubtedly about to ask me, before Seren took a turn stepping between us.

"There will be plenty of time for questions, but give the girl some time to adjust before the entirety of the court descends on her."

He swept me after his sister, and with one last glance behind me at the pool at the top of the steps, I followed. Except we didn't step through to the hallway after Itris. The world tilted once more the moment I stepped through the archway, and I found myself standing in a rounded tower room. All the walls were made of a soft white stone, the windows wide and paned with crystal-cut glass that looked up at the black and silver pinpricks of the starry sky.

Behind me, Seren's body briefly pressed into mine, and I froze at the touch. I caught the flash of his face in the reflection of one of the windows, and the way the corner of his mouth turning up. It was the closest thing yet to a smile that I'd seen from him, but somehow, it did nothing to soothe the ever-growing ache inside me.

"Whatever shall you do now that I've saved you?"

I wasn't standing on a dais, preparing to be sacrificed. I wasn't dead.

I should have felt some sort of gratitude. If not quite gratefulness, then at least relief. I should have been able to share that, at least, with three of the princes I'd left behind.

But instead, my earlier dread had begun to mingle with a new, even heavier feeling.

Loss.

For one moment, however brief, I'd believed I was going home. To Alderia. To my brother. To safety. But instead, I'd been brought here—to another damned fae court.

Seren was no savior. He was just another kidnapper.

For the first time since I stepped through the portal with Seren, I felt the rush of air pour into my lungs with the rising of my chest—and with it, I was flooded with the blinding heat of anger. His words twisted my mouth into a snarl that spilled from my lips as I whirled on him. It was as if all the warring emotions in me had been frozen in the pool, only to suddenly rush in now that the shock had begun to wear off.

I lifted the fiend-blade dagger from my skirts, still glistening with the glow of my red blood, and gripped it tight between my fingers.

"I'm going to kill you, and then I'm going to escape."

"Ah good, finally, I was starting to worry that I might have been wrong about you."

I blinked back my surprise, searching his face for sarcasm or mockery that wasn't there either. Still, his words made me pause, at least long enough that I *didn't* immediately plunge the dagger into his heart like I'd briefly considered.

More than considered.

"Aren't you worried?" I asked.

For a moment Seren's face searched mine. "About which part?"

I let out an exasperated breath, my hand gripping the dagger tighter. "I'm no damsel in distress. The threats I make, I mean."

He looked over me then in a way that he'd not before, his eyes raking over me all too slowly. It made a new kind of heat awaken in me at the base of my spine. It was all I could do to stop from returning the favor. It would be easy to get lost imagining what lay beneath the soft drape of his robes. There was something ethereal to him, serpentine almost, a sort of energy humming beneath the surface of his skin that screamed for me to reach out and touch him.

When his eyes finally lifted to mine, they shone with a satisfaction that made me have to fight off a shiver.

"Spoken like a true fae."

I was about to ask him what he meant, but I felt my resolve start to slip as his eyes dropped down to my lips for the briefest of seconds. It was so short that I might have imagined it, but it didn't stop the way my thundering heart skipped enough beats to make my head swim.

"I agree with Tarrack," he said, slowly. Carefully. "I'm looking forward to getting to know you better."

The way he said it was decidedly *not* the same as the fae earlier. It made that heat inside me bloom hotter, made it spread to my core where it wrapped around a forbidden part of me that was better left ignored.

"Stop trying to distract me," I snapped out, swallowing hard and then shook my head, inching ever so closer to Seren with the dagger pressed between us. Still, he didn't so much as flinch away. In fact, he leaned closer, his head dipping so his breath rustled the stray hairs at my temple as his lips parted.

"Oh, that would be a crime." His voice had dropped low, too

low. And then, all too suddenly, it returned to normal. So did he, to his full—and considerable—height.

The dagger still pressed between us, but he regarded it with the same interest he might a wooden spoon. One finger reached down to play with the pointed tip, and I found myself having to resist my own urge to flinch back, or warn him of the fiend's deadly poison that tipped it.

"To answer the first part of your declaration earlier, Delphine, no. I'm not worried you're going to kill me, not today. It's not in fate's cards for a fae in this court to die for some time yet."

His words elicited a thousand new questions of my own, but I was too focused on the way his finger continued to swirl around the pointed edge of my blade to force any one of them to form more than a flickering thought. My stomach clenched at the smudge of red that appeared on his fingertips, and for a moment, I was unable to stop the way my breath caught in my throat.

But it was my own blood, not his.

I realized that the same moment he did, the same moment he lifted the red stain to his lips and slowly, all too slowly, inserted the two afflicted fingertips into his mouth. He let out a soft moan, eyes closing for a second as he drew his fingers out again. They glistened, but no longer with blood, and once again, my throat tightened.

"And to answer the second," he continued, as if he hadn't just displayed the nearly orgasmic experience of tasting my blood, "I have a better idea than escape."

"And what is that?" I asked, unable to hide my own breathlessness. It was all I could do to hold the dagger steady between us. The power of it seemed to have waned, feeling more and more like that wooden spoon than a deadly immortal-murdering weapon.

"You walk right out. No escape needed."

As if to prove it, he stepped to the side and flung the door open behind him. A staircase curved to either side, its narrow steps echoing with far off footsteps.

"Take your first right at the bottom of the stairs, then a left when you exit the palace. No one will stop you." He leaned back into the room for a moment, eyes peering out the window as he studied something in the heavens above. "If you're quick about it, you might be able to see tonight's conjunction."

I had no idea what a conjunction was, but I wasn't about to give him the satisfaction of asking.

"So, what are you waiting for? You're not a prisoner, Delphine. How could you be when you're finally home?"

3
DELPHINE

You're finally home.

Those were words I'd so longed to hear, but hearing them now was like poison in my veins. Home wasn't cold and grey, with no sun to light the sky. Home wasn't in an unfeeling palace with strangers waiting down below to prod me with questions. Home wasn't here.

Home was complicated. Home was cruel at times.

But home was with Sol, and nowhere else.

Seren still stood before me, his eyes boring into mine, eyebrows raised as if in challenge.

I knew the fae was baiting me, but I didn't care. I took one last look down at the dagger, considering, then tucked it back into the sheath still buried beneath my skirts. I was more than a little annoyed by the fact that not a single shred of relief showed on Seren's face.

I fought back the urge to test that further and instead crossed through the threshold to the curve of the stairs, my eyes still locked on Seren's until I heard the echo of my own breaths in the narrow corridor. There was no tilt, no trick, no secret portal placed to carry me to a dungeon.

I took a step down, and then another.

Nothing happened.

They were just stairs.

And in that moment of realization, something took hold of me and suddenly I was taking more steps, then more still. My movements grew quicker, more fevered by the second until I was racing down the steps so quickly that I had to hoist my skirts up to keep them from tangling between my legs. I nearly ran into a servant at the bottom of the stairs, my footsteps faltering as I skittered to press myself up against the wall. I waited for the telltale look when she noticed me, when she looked up and saw the fae-marked human and recoiled in shock or horror.

But she barely looked at me. She barely glanced my way before moving on, unfazed.

The encounter should have emboldened me, but instead, it shook me to some deep part of my core.

It wasn't right.

It felt as if all the world had conspired together to get me here, and suddenly, in the blink of an eye, I was completely insignificant. It was like I didn't even exist.

I followed Seren's instructions, taking the door to my right at the bottom more carefully now. I fought back the growing feeling that this was all some sort of set up, that at any moment someone was going to jump out and tell me this was all another act. Another trick.

But stranger still was the empty space the door opened into. A long courtyard spread out before me, a pool of black water stretching out through the center until it reached a pair of large wooden gates at the end. No guards stood at the doors, though they were open, looking out on the sweep of a city far below, with mountains rising on the other side. The only sign of fae was the flicker of more grey silks through the columned walkways surrounding the courtyard, its arches disappearing into dark doorways that honeycombed off through the spiraling towers overhead.

These figures moved like ghosts about me, shifting between the stones with nothing more than the faint echo of footsteps that seemed to fall a moment too late, a moment after they were already gone.

That ache inside me grew with each one of my own ever-faltering footsteps. A nagging feeling pulled at the back of my mind and a dreamlike sensation began to take hold of me. As the black pool passed beside me, I caught sight of the stars reflected inwards, but something about it seemed off. The water seemed to reach for me even as it stretched endlessly down. It called to me with a familiar call, but this time I ignored it—as much as it could be ignored when it seemed to tug at that same place deep within my soul that had drawn me to the Starlight Fae's gift when I first arrived in Avarath.

Tonight, though, I made it past the draw of the dark water and to the gates, but that was where I stopped.

A balcony stretched out from the gates, a set of stairs curling down on either side in long, wide pathways cutting down the sides of a cliff as they reached toward the city below. The entire city was encased inside these cliff walls that the palace had been built into and around, as if in a giant, sheer-edged bowl. No guards stood on the balcony outside the doors, either. A hesitant step forward, hand lifting to test the air before me revealed no hidden wall or enchantment either.

I'd half expected to find some kind of magical barrier or another portal that would send me spinning back to my tower room, but there was nothing.

The only thing that greeted me when I took those next hesitant steps forward to rest my hands on the balcony rail was the surprisingly sweet waft of air carried up the side of the cliff. It caressed my skin and brushed the tangled strands of hair back from my face, moving with a near life of its own. Each tendril of air moved with purpose, both independent from the others and intertwining with them at the same time.

It passed by me with a final kiss of warmth across my shoulders, its fluttering movement drawing my eye back toward the sweeping expense in front of me.

The view spread out before me in a pattern of elegant, winding footpaths carved in stone. Homes and shops sprung up in clusters of tall, sharp towers above them as if everything here was constantly reaching for the stars, trying to draw them nearer even as the stars did the same. Across the valley, another massive building rose above the rest. Rather than reaching spires, a large glass dome caught the light of the stars above. A strange metal instrument turned above it, curved glass planes within it twisting the light to send it scattering across the roofs of the city below.

Beyond the city, beyond the mountains … there was no beyond.

Stars reached in at all sides, fading into the edges of the city and stone it was carved from until they became one.

The breeze gusted up to meet me once more and as it returned to make its journey up into the sky, and this time, it carried all the fire from within me. It left me pressing hard into the rail for support, a darkness plunging through me even as I gazed down at this city of light.

Escape? Where was I even going to escape to?

This was the trick.

This was why Seren had told me to go free. To leave.

There was no point in locking me up when there was nowhere for me to go.

At least in Avarath, I'd had a place to picture, the bridge in the forest, a crossing point—not that I'd be able to actually cross it. But that hadn't mattered. Just knowing it existed gave me hope, however small that spark of hope might be.

Here … here …

Here, the last of those embers had drifted off with the breeze.

I was trapped in the fae realm still, deeper now than ever before.

The echo of footsteps carried out of the courtyard a moment too late. The soft fabric of Seren's sleeve grazed against my arm as he came to rest beside me. My heart seized a moment as his hand reached for mine, but as soon as our hands met, I stiffened and brushed him away.

His gaze flickered down and the slightest smile drew on his pale lips, as if I'd amused him.

"At least it seems you're not so keen to draw that dagger now as you were earlier."

I pursed my own lips. "Don't test your luck. I could change my mind."

"Just as I intend to change yours."

I looked up at him then, his silver hair framed against a night of stars. As much as I felt the tug to look away, I forced myself not to this time. He looked softer here, away from the court. Away from the watchful, waiting eyes that had weighed just as heavily on him as they had on me.

That tugging sensation changed, drawing me to him this time, instead of making me look away.

Seren was undeniably gorgeous, not only in the way that all fae were, but in his own right.

I forced my thoughts away from him, and instead to the empty doorway at our backs.

"Why are there no guards at the gate?"

"Why would there be? We have no enemies here. Not anymore."

His hand reached out, stopping before it could caress mine this time. "*You* have no enemies here, Delphine."

I felt the space between our fingers as keenly as I had the touch I'd cast aside. It made my skin tingle, my smallest finger almost itching to reach back and close the gap.

Instead, I asked the most burning question that had been haunting me from the moment I crossed through the realms with him. "Why didn't you take me back to Alderia?"

"I took you to the place you belong."

He must have seen the way I set my jaw, because he didn't leave time for me to interrupt him.

"This is where you belong, Delphine," he said, more urgently this time. "Here, in Elysia. In faerie. Even in Avarath. I didn't take you here to be my prisoner. I took you here to give you your freedom. True freedom. To let you see what you are. What you *can be,* if only you're willing to try. I want to show you what it is to be fae—to be a Starlight Fae."

He nudged me, cold fabric rustling against my skin.

"Look up. Look up and tell me that doesn't call to your very soul, to that spark within you that you never before knew you had. Tell me you don't feel it, Delphine."

But, of course, I couldn't.

Because I did. I felt it.

I felt it in every vein in my body.

Far above our heads, two moons began to eclipse each other in the sky. Rather than growing darker, their light grew brighter and brighter until they were completely laid one on top of the other, shining like a great beacon in the middle of the sky. The brighter they shone, the brighter the other stars seemed to shine, too. For several long minutes—though minutes that still somehow felt too short—all the stars seemed to draw a little closer.

The light had to dim, eventually, however. The moons continued on their paths across the sky, and with it, I felt myself drifting further too—from Seren, from the edge of the balcony, from the brief moment of companionship we'd shared with our heads tilted upwards.

Seren could claim I was no prisoner, he could throw open every door in the palace, in the whole realm, but so long as I was here and not on my way back to Alderia, I was a prisoner still, and he my captor.

"You'll soon come around. I promise you, once you know what it is to be fae, you'll feel differently."

"Is that a bet?" I asked.

Instead of comforting me, his words had made me feel ill. Not at first, not until Seren offered me next what I'd somehow known was coming all along.

"Not quite … but we could make it a deal."

4
CALDAMIR

WE, THE PRINCES OF AVARATH, HAD FAILED.

Or so they thought.

The arrival of the Starlight Court had only presented us with a new challenge. We found our Starlight Fae once, we could do it again. This time, the second time, we'd know better. We'd awaken the king before anyone had the chance to step in again.

Admittedly, the other princes hadn't remained quite as… optimistic…about our prospects as I would have liked, but they always let me be their leader anyway. They always left the hard decisions up to me when it came down to it. There in the end, I'd started to think that if I hadn't insisted that we go through with the ritual that one of them might have freed Delphine.

But that was then, that was *before*. The havoc wreaked by our failed quest left a sour bite in all our mouths. We needed to get the glamour back more than ever before the rest of Avarath descended into chaos.

What was left of it, anyway.

In the last weeks since the realms collided, what semblance of order we'd managed to maintain over the last half-millennia had completely fallen to ruin, and not just in my court. When we saw the destruction of Nyx's forest, we should have seen it for what it was. It was a harbinger of what was coming for all of us. It had gotten to the point that none of us princes accepted mail from our advisors any longer unless it was carried by urgent messenger. We just couldn't handle any more news of plague, famine, or disappearing orders of the lower fae—and that's wasn't even the worst of it.

The Sand Court had fallen into fighting amongst themselves. The Sear Court was considering packing up altogether and leaving Avarath for good. The Woodland Court, well, there wasn't much *woodland* left for them to inhabit. More and more of Nyx's court arrived each day here for shelter—those who survived the increasingly brutal attacks of the fiends on their way here, that is.

Fiend attacks had increased tenfold since the forests—and all the other natural fauna of this realm—started to fade, truly fade. With nowhere else to go, the bloodthirsty creatures had grown bold, too bold. It wouldn't be long before even *I* would be wary to journey outside the castle walls.

Armene had threatened to leave soon if we didn't make headway with our plan to find Delphine again. We had yet another meeting scheduled in the once-abandoned war rooms, and while my footsteps were already carrying me towards it, I had to admit to myself that even *I* was growing tired of looking at the inside of it again. How much longer did this have to go on? It took years to find out about Delphine's existence in the first place, then months more to find her, but it all felt somehow *easier* than it did this second time—and now, we even knew where she was.

We just didn't have a way to get there.

For all we knew, there was no way to get to the Starlight Fae unless their court came for you, first.

It was a sign of just how distracted I'd become that I didn't hear the fae following me until her voice called out over the clatter of my footsteps.

"Caldamir! My prince."

For one, brief second, I let my eyes close in annoyance. I didn't have time for this, but it was my own fault for not figuring out how to escape her sooner.

"Lilliope."

I must not have smoothed the emotions from my face as well as I thought, because when I turned to face her and greet her with a nod of my head, she drew back—if only a little.

"Come, now, Caldamir…" she purred, "It's been months since you called for me."

"Yes, well, I wasn't here, was I?"

"And you've been back for weeks now. It's not like you. That's all I'm saying."

I would have turned away, made another excuse to make it to the war room with the other princes, if she hadn't reached out then and taken my arm. It was a presumptuous motion, one that few in my court would dare, but she was one of the few.

Or at least, she had been once.

Her touch made me pause, and that was all she needed.

The fae grabbed me by the lapels of my jacket and, with one glance down the corridor to make sure no one important was watching, she pulled me into the nearest room. Lucky for her—or both of us, I supposed as she began tugging off the various layers of her jewel-toned gown—it was a bedroom, and it was abandoned.

Or, if not abandoned completely, at least in the meantime it was empty.

And that was all we needed.

There was no false foreplay, no stolen kisses or heated passion. It had never been that way with Lilliope.

It wasn't long before she was climbing atop me, dressed down to straddle me in her loosened stays and petticoats.

"Close your eyes," she instructed me, reaching forward to trace one finger down the middle of my chest. "You're worrying too much. You need to remember how to relax."

I had to force my eyes to close, to do as she instructed as she fumbled with the last of the drawstrings that held up my trousers, but my mind still reeled with the same thoughts that had consumed me these past weeks. What was our next step? Where would the fiends strike? Was it worth staying in Avarath at all, worth even fighting?

But then, if we didn't stay, where would we go?

"You're not relaxing," Lilliope tried to purr again, but it came out too sharp. "Just…just think about something less awful. It doesn't have to be me. Think about, I don't know what you princes like. Swords? Daggers? Duels?"

She let out a small, satisfied sigh before saying, "Never mind. I'd like to see you try *not* to relax now."

She'd finally undone the last of the laces. Her hand reached into my trouser and pulled out my cock, still impressive despite the fact it was hardly standing at attention. As much as my mind didn't want to quiet, the feel of the female fae as she began stroking the length of me in gentle, precise motions…it did make my mind start to at least wander in a new direction. Soon, beneath her practiced touch, I finally felt some of the tension start to leave my shoulders.

I fell back into the bed a bit, eyes closed again as I tried to focus on the feel in my hardening member instead of everything else. Instead of the war. Instead of the fiends. Instead of…

"Delphine…"

Fuck.

The name had slipped from my lips before I knew I was thinking it. My eyes flew open to look into the eyes of a fae so very different from the one that had slipped into my fantasies, and just as quickly, she was suddenly scrambling off of me.

She didn't look at me as I sat up too, my hands reaching to fumble with the strings at my waist.

"I'm sorry, Lilli—"

"No need," she said, holding up a hand, though she still didn't look me in the eye. "I knew there was a reason you hadn't called for me. Now, at least, I know what it is."

"Lilli—"

She didn't stay to hear my weak excuses, and maybe it was a good thing…since I didn't have any.

She was right.

As much as I hated to admit it to myself, I think I'd known it all along. It wasn't the war that had consumed me these last weeks.

It was *her.*

It had never been a romance between us, me and Lilliope, more of a…mutually beneficial arrangement. That arrangement, however, was over the moment I moaned that half-human's name. It was obvious not only in the disgust on Lilliope's face as she finally finished dressing to flee, but in my own. I didn't let it mar my face, but that didn't stop it from seeping deep inside me.

What was wrong with me?

I was the prince of the Mountain Court and I bowed to no one. Why then was I unable to get a single half-human out of my goddamned mind?

I stormed out of my rooms and back towards the war room. I'd had enough. We had to find Delphine—we *would* find her—if it was the last thing we ever did. Sacrifices had to be made. I, for one, was willing to give anything. It was time the other princes pledged the same.

We would find Delphine and at long last, we'd put this all to rest.

5
DELPHINE

Let me make you a deal.

Let me show you who you are. Who the Starlight Fae are. Let me show you what it is to be fae.

And if the time comes and you still don't feel like you belong, then I will take you back to the human realm.

If there was one thing I'd learned from my short time in faerie, it was not to make a deal with a fae. Caldamir had warned me of the rules of Avarath, warned me to trust no one, not even the realm itself, but he'd neglected that one most important thing. It was the fae that were dangerous. I could handle the realm. I could handle even the fiends.

It was *his* kind that I had to watch out for. His kind didn't act on instinct. The high fae were more than that. They were cunning and cruel.

He more than the rest, because he'd pretended to warn me, but had neglected to warn me of himself.

Morning came with a strange kind of glory. No sunlight streamed through the window to wake me, because, of course, there was no sun. Instead, it was as if the stars themselves shone a little more brightly, the air moved a little more warmly. It coaxed me out of a slumber too deep for what I deserved.

I knew where I was the moment I awoke. There was no way I could forget.

That, I remembered, and more important still, I remembered the choice I made before sleep took me.

I did *not* accept Seren's offer of a deal. As compelling as the night air was, as tightly as I was wrapped in the cold of the night sky and the warmth of the cliff-face wind, as much as the stars themselves seemed to whisper, begging for me to take it, I didn't.

But I didn't completely refuse it, either.

Maybe I was a fool still, but I had to have something to cling to. I had to have something to tether me to Alderia, to the human realm. It was more important than ever now that, with each passing day, I slipped further and further into faerie. Further and further away from home. The more time that passed, the more this place began to feel real and what came before … that was what felt like the dream.

That was what terrified me the most, what kept me from turning Seren down the moment I should have.

That was what made me vulnerable, and I hated myself for it.

If I was going to survive in faerie—whether it be Avarath or Elysia or any other goddamned faerie realm they hadn't bothered to tell me about yet—I had to be strong. I couldn't keep my heart plastered to my sleeve, couldn't let my desires bubble to the surface with the slightest brush of skin.

The memory of that moment with Seren made heat rise in my skin, though this time mostly from shame. What was wrong with me? Hadn't I already toed that line enough? It was just the glamour, just more of the fae's magic trickery. I couldn't deny what I felt, no matter how much I wanted to, so I had to focus on what it was. It wasn't me, it was this place.

It was the magic.

Except, I had a sneaking suspicion it wasn't, only I wasn't ready to face that truth.

I had to remember what the fae were *really* like, what the fae really wanted. I had to keep that knowledge firmly planted in my brain, or else it—like everything seemed to do in faerie—would slowly slip away, fade and dull until I was faded and dull too. I had to stay sharp. It was all I could do to protect myself.

That and, of course, try and stab a few fae with my fiend blade.

I'd resisted so far, but only because I knew it was a temporary solution. There were many fae, and there was only one me. The blade might come in handy if I was cornered in a cave somewhere again, but not in a place where any number of fae could come running the next minute. I had no illusions of overpowering a whole court. I'd be lucky enough to overpower *one* fae enough to stab them in the first place.

If there was one fae I should have stabbed already, that fae was Caldamir.

The Mountain Prince had paid me an unwanted visit in my dreams, a visit that left me drowning in a cold sweat atop the sheets of my tower bed. My mind kept returning to the moment the realms collided, to the looks on his and the other princes' faces when they thought they'd lost me. All of them had surprised me. All but his.

Caldamir's face was the one that stuck on the inside of my mind long after I woke. His was the face that haunted me even as I stumbled to the basin of water, placed on the dresser in the night by an unseen servant, to splash the remnants of sleep from my eyes.

The unbridled rage on Caldamir's face—that I could understand. It was the others, the sorrow I saw there on the other prince's faces, that I could not. What were they so sorry for? Not for me, surely. Not because I was being taken from them. They'd made their choice. They'd *chosen* to sacrifice me. I'd already been taken from them the moment they'd made that decision.

Their sorrow had to come from somewhere else.

Most likely, from the loss of their glamour.

Or then again ... maybe it wasn't sorrow at all. Maybe I had misunderstood what I saw. It wouldn't be the first time I'd assumed to know them better than I actually did.

A strange sort of quiet hung over the palace. No birds twittered outside the window. No carts rumbled past downstairs. The only sound preventing silence was that ever-present humming of the stars, and the distant echo of feet on far-off cobble. Not that I could exactly call the gemstone-laden flagstones *cobble.*

There was no way for me to tell the time. The moons that had met in conjunction the night before were long since vanished from the sky, replaced instead by a smattering of smaller ones in their stead. They moved slowly across the sky in their opposing routes, making the world below feel as if it was the inside of some gigantic cog, looking out.

It was stranger still to creep out onto the staircase, my stained gown from the day before pulled back over my shoulders, only to once again find no one waiting outside. Seren had promised me I was no prisoner, but I'd yet to fully believe him. I doubted still that I ever would. Every day I'd reach for those doors expecting to find them locked, or better yet, for guards and gleaming weapons to wait on the other side. For now, however, Seren's words held true.

The palace halls seemed too quiet, quieter even than in the

minutes leading up to Elysia's form of midnight. I got the feeling as I crept down the steps and out into the courtyard—the only familiar path I knew to follow in this place—that it was either very early still, or the Starlight Fae preferred to spend their waking hours when the black of the sky pulled harder down toward the realm.

A single figure sat hunched at the pool in the center of the courtyard when I reached it. At first, I ignored him, pausing just long enough to peer down the many branching corridors but not long enough to make up my mind on whether I should explore them or venture back out the still open gates on the other side. I was stopped from having to make that decision when a voice carried over to me. It was quiet, scratchy, spoken in tones and words I'd never heard before. The sound of it was both familiar and foreign, the soft-spoken echo catching in the courtyard stones so that it took me a minute to realize the sound was, indeed, coming from the fae by the pool.

From the way he sat, shoulders pulled forward and hood draped over his face, he clearly wanted to be left undisturbed, but curiosity got the better of me and I moved closer, the foreign words itching at the back of my mind, as if I'd once known them but had now forgot. I didn't stop until my shadow passed over him, a soft thing cast in odd shapes by the many sources of starlight overhead.

I wasn't the only one who stopped. So, did he, the last syllables of his muttered chant ending in a strangled cry a moment before I realized my mistake. I knew it before the fae turned around, even before his pupils grew wide and it was all he could do to keep drool from dribbling down his pointed chin out of excitement.

It was a face I recognized looking back at me from the inside of the dark hood.

"What luck! I didn't think Seren would let me near you so soon as this."

It was Tarrack, the most over-eager of the fae that had greeted us on our arrival to Elysia yesterday. He was practically panting with excitement as his head tilted up, eyes scanning the heavens as he made calculations that caused his eyebrows to shoot up into his forehead.

"By the stars, you're up early. Are you feeling alright?"

I opened my mouth to respond, but he just continued, leaping up to his feet with surprising agility and taking my hand in his to pull me closer. His motions were too fast, too abrupt. I'd be more worried about him dislocating my shoulder if I wasn't more presently worried that he might accidentally kiss me, he was putting his face so close to mine in unsettling scrutiny.

"Not that it matters. Even if you were ill, it wouldn't be anything serious. No deaths today."

"That's the second time someone's mentioned that to me,"

"And I doubt it'll be the last," he said, eyes somehow widening even more as he looked me over. "Now that you're here, there's much to learn."

His next words were spoken more to himself than to me. "To think ... a new Starlight Fae amongst us for the first time in so long."

I got the keen impression that I was some kind of specimen under a lens, that he was trying to figure me out in a way that made my heart take on an irregular beat. If it were up to Tarrak, I had a feeling he would have hauled me off to a proper laboratory to continue his investigation, only with a lot more unwanted poking and prodding.

Thankfully, it was not left up to him.

Not when Itris chose that opportune moment to come barreling out of one of the corridors, two young fae practically scuttling at her feet to keep up. They were the closest thing I'd seen yet to fae children, the only evidence that these creatures—creatures supposedly like *me*—actually procreated instead of simply springing from some foul pit somewhere born of black glamour.

Of course, they could *still* be born of dark magic, but something about the innocence in this pair's wide eyes when they looked over me would make even the most skeptical of humans pause.

Just as Itris paused then, her eyes narrowing as she scanned the fae pressing in a bit too close by the pool.

6
DELPHINE

There was a look in Seren's sister's eyes that was a little too close to rage. It made me shiver in my own skin, despite the fact that it was aimed at the man slinking back from me ever so slightly, even before her voice boomed out across the courtyard.

"Tarrak, are you harassing the poor girl already?"

"I'd hardly call it—"

"Call it whatever you like," she cut him off, the tone of her voice making the two fae at her heels duck behind her further. "But don't forget she's Starlight Fae. She's not one of your *experiments* to be toyed with."

If I thought her words made the last bit of color drain from my cheeks, I was wrong. That happened when she turned to me, instead, and I was suddenly the object of the sparking fury in those eyes.

"Does Seren know you're out here?"

Somehow, I didn't completely collapse under the weight of her gaze despite the shaking in my knees. I had no doubt that this woman, fae or not, could destroy me if she wanted to.

It took every muscle in my body to simply shake my head from side to side. "Seren told me I'm free to go where I please."

Those weren't his exact words, of course. If I could really go where I pleased, then I'd already be back in Alderia—or at least well on my way there.

Itris bowed her head to look at me a little more closely.

"Do you even know where you are?"

"The Starlight Court," I answered too quickly, knowing immediately how stupid I sounded.

"No," she said. "Do you know where you are, right now? Here and now?" She nods once, a curt, jerky motion toward the black water over Tarrack's shoulder. "If you fall into that pool without a tether, you'll never come out. You'll be lost forever." She turned back to me, that spark returned to her eyes. "And let me tell you, speaking from an immortal's standpoint, forever is much longer than you imagine."

The two fae behind her chose that moment to peek their heads back out, eyes scanning the dark water with as much interest as they did a certain kind of unmistakable fear. They weren't quite as young as I thought at first glance. They looked like they could be only a few years younger than me in human years, it was just compared to Itris that they might as well have just crawled out of the cradle.

A coldness wrapped around my body, reaching its pointed tendrils beneath the surface of my skin until my teeth threatened to chatter.

"I thought I was safe here."

"From what? The fae or the court itself?"

Her question struck me dumb.

"Once again, my brother has somehow managed not to think this through." Itris chewed on the inside of her lip for a moment, lost in thought. Though she stood still, there was a restless quality to her that made it obvious she itched to be long gone from here already.

Her head tilted up, reading something in the starlit sky.

Tarrack picked up on this too, and took his opportunity to add, "I'll be happy to show her around. I was just thinking …"

"You already have enough business to attend to. Unless, of course, you've grown tired of your position?" she asked, the question making Tarrack's mouth draw into a tight line.

"She'll be fine with me. I hardly bite. Besides, as we both know, no fae is dying today."

Her jaw worked, eyes flickering between me and Tarrack for a moment.

"Death isn't the worst fate that can befall you here, or do I need to remind you of that?"

I half expected one of them to look back at the pool, but when neither of them did, another chill raced up my spine. I hated to imagine what could be worse than that. Worse than death. Worse than an eternity trapped in endless night.

Tarrack, it seemed, couldn't argue with that … or he wasn't willing to.

"Come with me," Itris said, her voice turned sharper than ever as her attention returned to me. "I have no time to babysit you."

"You don't need to."

"Yes, well, we'll see what Seren has to say. If something is to happen to you in this court, it'll not be under my watch. Not, at least, until we figure out if you matter."

I had no idea what to think of her words. There was something there, something more she meant by the words, *not until we figure out if you matter,* and I didn't like it. I knew what it was to matter in the fae realm, and I'd already had enough of it.

Still, since I didn't want to figure out what kind of fates

might befall me in Elysia that could be worse than death, at least not on my own and without some sort of prior warning, I followed her. Not that I had much of a choice. Not when staying here, with Tarrack, sounded as close to one of those other fates as I was willing to imagine.

THE WINDING CASTLE corridors didn't lead the way they were supposed to. Straight corridors seemed to take us around curves in the castle. Paths veering left took us to the right side of a turret. It was hard enough keeping up with these other fae's strides. For all their talk of my being one of them, I was a good head and a half shorter than Itris, and at least half that of the two young fae keeping up decidedly better than me despite the fact that their heads were craned back to stare at me more often than they were actually looking where we were going.

I was just starting to think I was going mad, that I was imagining the strange, twisting nature of the corridors, when a long, winding trek up a tall tower staircase finally dropped us at the entrance to the castle gardens—right at the very bottom of the imposing gemstone-encrusted structure.

Like the gardens at the Mountain Court, these were hardly like the gardens in Lord Otto's estate back in the human realm. For starters, the flowers of this place didn't appear to *bloom* so much as they *crystalized.* There was a shining, gemstone quality to even the most lifelike of the flowers drooping over pathways and climbing up the carved walls. The garden was perfectly manicured in only the way a garden made of crystal could be, with each flower falling in perfect alignment to catch the light of the ever-shifting stars above. The effect was mesmerizing, enchanting enough to nearly make me stumble from Itris' side in favor of exploring the gardens winding in and out of the nearby archways on one side, and turning down the side of the mountain in the other, their crystal facets lighting another narrow, winding path leading away from the Starlight palace.

This entrance was unguarded, of course, like all the others.

Even in times of peace, I'd never have imagined a palace like this in the human realm. It was as if the Starlight Court couldn't even *imagine* danger creeping up on them. It should have been reassuring, but like everything else here, it seemed instead to elicit a nagging worry in the back of my mind.

Maybe it was my fault, but something seemed wrong with letting your guard down in faerie, for even a second. It didn't matter if it was Avarath or Elysia, they were the same to me. I had a feeling Itris, if no one else, would agree with me—but the last thing I cared to admit, especially to her, was that we actually might agree on something.

Not when every time I caught her looking at me, it wasn't with the rapt curiosity of the fae at her heels, but rather something closer to disgust.

The lack of guards didn't mean we were alone in the garden.

There were other fae strolling through the paths as well, and though their glances toward us lingered no longer than a passing moment, I still felt a lump rise at the back of my throat at the thought of being left alone with them. Seren could promise me all he wanted that I was safe here, that I was amongst my kind, but I'd had enough experience with the fae in my short time since being kidnapped by one to know that was never true.

Once more across the grounds at Itris' tail, and the final doorway led into a large, circular room overlooking the whole of Elysia.

My head swam for a moment as my body tried to reconcile the sudden change in height, from feet firmly planted—or at least as firmly planted as they could be in a faerie realm—to suddenly standing amidst a circle of open archways perfect for throwing yourself off, if your wish was certain death.

It made the view from the balcony last night pale in comparison. From up here, the stars truly were closer, so close I was sure if I leaned out over the rail-less edge of the tower, I might just be able to reach out and touch one.

Right before I fell to my death, which at the moment, I was ranking a little higher up on the ways to die in Elysia than lost in an eternal pool of night.

From the center of the room, a silk sheet of water poured like perfect glass from a sliver cut in the ceiling. Black water frothed at its base before running in a narrow rivulet cleaving the room in two. It eventually trickled down the edge of the tower toward the city far below. I'd seen no sign of it last night, though from this height there was a good chance any remnants of the stream would have turned to dark mist before it reached the rooftops below.

For the first time, I was able to see out past the edges of the city. I expected Elysia to stretch out the way Avarath had, into plains and hills and rivers and valleys that would all eventually lead to the sea in the end, much like my own world. Instead, no sea crashed against the rocks at the base of the towering mountains surrounding the city. The only sea was that same darkness, that endless void glittering with stars that pressed in from all sides.

Though *pressed* wasn't the right word for it.

It expanded out, dragging out the corners of this world until the two melted seamlessly together, even from this height.

No, *especially* from this height.

Aside from the trickle of the waterfall, the room was eerily silent. Empty.

Our breath was all that broke the quiet rhythm, right up until Itris marched to that glassy sheet of water and stuck one arm elbow deep, only for her to pull it back out with another arm now attached. I looked on in awe as she pulled her brother seemingly from nothing, until he loomed over the rest of us with his brows furrowed and eyes set defensively on the fae woman still clutching his wrinkled grey robes.

"I hope you have good reason for interrupting me. You know I wouldn't allow it from anyone else."

Seren's voice was deep, as close to holding gravel as its smooth tone would allow. There was more than a little threat in the sound, but though it made the hair on the back of my neck stand up, it seemed to have the opposite effect on his sister.

Itris let out something close to a snort. "As if anyone else would dare try."

Seren shook her off, and once again the folds of his silken clothes slid back into perfect cascading lines, much like the waterfall he was just pulled from. His skin and hair shone with a glittering residue left from the stream.

"Just because you're the Seeker doesn't mean you can leave me to clean up your messes."

Seren shot her a strange look then, his full lips parting for a second before his sister turned her head to motion at me. His gaze flickered over to me then, softening ever so slightly, unless I imagined it.

I had to have imagined it.

The words he was going to speak died somewhere in his throat with a small sigh. The sound of it made my heart feel as if it squeezed a little too tight, if only for a second.

"Ah, Delph, I hardly expected to find you here so soon."

"You should be surprised to find her here at all," Itris said, voice stern enough to make me fidget—to say nothing of the two fae still standing at the doorway. They hadn't dared follow us inside. "I found her with Tarrack of all people."

"Is that really a surprise?" he asked, one brow lifting. "You know it's only a matter of time before he has his way with her."

"As he does all of us," she growled. She, unlike Seren, was able to conjure the broken, throaty sound easily. "What was she doing out on her own?"

"She's not a prisoner, Itris. I can hardly control her."

I barely had time to warm at the words before Itris continued on. "But she'll soon end up as a prisoner or worse if you don't at least offer her some guidance. How old is she, anyway? She doesn't look a day over a hundred and fifty."

I blanched at her words, but it was nothing compared to Itris when Seren responded, casually, "Twenty-one, actually."

"Twenty-one?" There was so much outrage in Itris' voice that I was surprised she hadn't popped a blood vessel yet. "And you're just leaving her to her own devices? Letting her wander around the court is asking for trouble."

"I thought you might—"

"No." Itris' response was so quick, it was obvious she'd expected this, just as it was obvious she'd prepared her answer. "This is *your* doing, Seren. I might not be anxious to sit back and watch as this toddler you brought here accidentally slips into oblivion, but I happily will if only to spite you for it."

"So gracious, as always, sister."

"Speaking of graciousness, have you taken a look at her? That wound isn't healing."

There was a slight pause before Seren replied, "Wound?"

"Yes," his sister said, her voice growing tired. "The one that leaves her dress—the same one she arrived in, no less—bleeding redder by the day?"

All four sets of eyes were on me now, their eyes trailing

down the front of me to rest at the place my breasts met in the middle. Sure, it was also where—true to Itris' words—blood had stained a dark maroon down the middle of the jewel toned fabric, but it still made a distracting blush stain my cheeks, too.

I lifted one hand to press over the spot, trying to shield myself from their gaze, but only managed to brush the wound and make myself flinch. Seren flinched too, though only enough that I noticed. Everyone else was still staring at the stain of blood across my bosom.

"Something will have to be done about that," Itris said, decidedly. "It may have been some time since we had a guest, but it can't be so long that you've completely forgotten how to be a host? If not a good one, then at least an acceptable one."

"Maybe I have forgotten."

Itris' lips pressed together into a thin line. "Well then, take this as a good opportunity to remember. As much as we'd like for things to remain as they have the last five hundred years, I think we both know they can't. Delph won't be the last new fae we welcome to Elysia. As much as we've tried, you can count on that."

"You're overreacting, Itris."

Itris just fixed him with that hard glare. "But am I, brother? It was only ever a matter of time. You might not see it, but you mark my words—you've set into motion something that can't be undone. You only see Delphine, but I see so much more. Maybe all this time as the Seeker has made you blind to everything else. You might be blind, the rest of this court might be blind, too, but I … I am not."

7
DELPHINE

ITRIS' WORDS HUNG LIKE THE WARNING THEY WERE, HEAVY AND stinging, in the thin air of the tower.

Seren's tongue darted out ever so slowly, brushing across his lips as his thoughts flickered silently behind his dark eyes.

"Tell me, sister, what it really is you're trying to say."

For the first time, I saw uncertainty flicker across Itris' face. She held her brother's gaze for a moment before Seren motioned toward the doorway we'd just come from. The next moment I was left alone with the two young fae, both sets of their eyes turned to stare decidedly, unblinkingly, at me. It was curiosity, not contempt, that washed over me, however, and I was all too happy to return the gesture.

Upon better examination, the duo looked to be about fifteen in human years, though what that meant in fae years I had no idea, especially given Itris' most recent reaction to learning my own age.

"So, are you really part human?" the girl finally blurted out, eyes growing even wider as if she was shocked she'd actually said it out loud. "You don't look human to me. I've never actually seen one, but I've always imagined them looking much more ... grisly."

The boy beside her nodded his head enthusiastically. "Like a bear, or a boar."

"Not that we've actually seen one of those, either."

I let out a small snort, and the girl furrowed her brow.

"Have we said something wrong?"

"No," I said, a small smile threatening what's become something of a perpetual scowl on my face. "I've met my fair share of boarish humans. Grisly seems the right term for them."

The image of Raful, the old head of the servants at the estate where I worked, came to mind—only for it to conjure up a second face that I'd rather banish from my thoughts altogether. It was the face of the man who killed Raful for laying his hands on me.

I was eager to keep my mind from returning to that dark place that remembered him, so I shook it from my head and asked a question of my own. "How old are you, anyway?"

"A hundred and twelve."

The two of them spoke together, their words tumbling over each other in a way that made my mind work for a moment before understanding crashed over me, and with it, a wave of light-headedness.

"But we've been that way for a while."

That did nothing to stop my head from feeling like it was going to turn all the way around and snap my neck in the process.

"What do you mean?" I asked, glancing between the two of them. I knew they were older than they looked, they had to be. But a hundred and twelve? They looked so young, *so young*.

The boy cocked his head at me. "You really have no idea about anything, do you?"

"Shut up, Alder," the girl hissed at him, before looking up apologetically to me. "He's worse than Seren. He never got to leave Elysia before the war."

The boy, Alder, rolled his eyes at her side. "As if leaving it for all of ten minutes counts, *Elvie.*"

Elvie pursed her lips and tilted her shoulder away from the boy at her side. "Ignore my brother. He still hasn't gotten over that age where boys think the best way to get to their crushes is to pull on their pigtails. And since you don't have pigtails, I think he's chosen a more verbally abusive route."

The redness of Alder's face against his short-cropped hair was unmistakable. He muttered something indecipherable and stalked off behind the wall of water, his feet scuffing with every step. I watched him for a second out of the corner of my eye, my stomach twisting at the thought of moving one step closer to the unprotected drop from the tower edges.

I caught one more look of Alder as he glanced back at me, face reddening some more, before he ducked conspicuously behind one of the arched columns.

Elvie was looking smug when I turned back to her.

"Are you …"

"Twins," she answered for me, nodding with more of her earlier enthusiasm. "Itris is our grandmother, but she's been raising us since the war broke out. It was just our luck to get stuck like this when the realms separated."

She motioned down to her body, a slight thing despite the fact that she was well over a century old.

"And that was?"

"About five hundred years ago, in human years, anyway. Time doesn't exactly pass here now."

If I thought I blanched earlier …

Not over a century old—over *six.*

"That's why your cut hasn't healed. Healing magic takes time, which … you know … doesn't pass here."

We both looked down at the stain across my front, and I was instantly glad I'd never gotten past a small pinprick before Seren finally arrived. Still, I had to shake my head again as I looked back up at the fae girl in front of me.

Elvie must have seen the look on my face, because a sly smile overtook her and she moved over to nudge me ever so slightly. I expected to hate the touch, but I didn't. Something about this fae disarmed me.

"Don't look at me like that," she said, a small blush rising in her own cheeks. "We're closer in age than you might think. At least, you're the closest fae in age to me that I've met yet. Everyone else here is practically ancient."

"*Literally* ancient," Alder called from the other side of the archways, announcing in a way, that he was still listening in … even if he was still in hiding.

"It's not that. It's … it's that Alder's right. I really know nothing about this world." Or about my own, for that matter. At the moment, I felt like I didn't know anything at all.

I glanced over once more at Elvie's twin pretending not to peek out at us from across the room, and I felt that knot twist tighter in my stomach. Alder looked nothing like my own brother, with his pale skin and white hair, but the mere presence of him made me ache for Sol. I'd left him in Alderia thinking I was never going back, but as much as I tried to resign myself to that, it felt impossible. I was tricked into thinking I was protecting him by leaving. Now, I knew better. Now I knew I'd only damned him further, and it was becoming more and more impossible by the day to think I'd ever get to lay eyes on him again. I might be a danger to him in Alderia, but I was even more of a danger to him here.

The closer I got to fae, to Avarath, the closer I was to being used to hurt him again.

Whatever Itris and Seren had spoken about had left them with a similar kind of soberness upon their return. Itris called for her grandchildren to follow, which they did dutifully, but not before each of them sent me their own kind of surreptitious glance—a glance that didn't go unnoticed, and only served to make Itris' footsteps stomp a little harder as they retreated out the door.

Seren moved as if he hadn't noticed me for a moment. His footsteps carried him back to the dark waterfall, one hand reaching out but stopping just before one of his fingers could actually brush against it. In that moment, and only for a moment, I swore I saw a flickering face inside the black facets of the water. As quickly as it was there, however, it was gone.

Any thoughts of dwelling on it were banished when Seren finally spoke, his voice cool and calculating enough to make a small chill race up my spine.

"Itris has insisted I take a more active role in what she calls *rehabilitating* you."

I shuddered at the comment. "I thought you said—"

"I still stand by what I said."

Seren finally looked at me then, and I felt a breath of relief escape me—not just at the words he seemed to still be mulling over on his tongue, but the look on his face. Only a day freed from Avarath, and already I'd grown used to at least the pretense of freedom, however small.

"But Itris does have a point," he adds, eyes drifting back down to my chest for only the flicker of a second, but still enough to keep me from getting too comfortable. "I'm out of practice. We all are. I've neglected you—something I plan to remedy right away."

This time his fingers did touch the edge of the black water, but it was only his face I saw reflected in it. Small bits of mist sprayed out, dotting his face with more glistening droplets. He leaned forward then, pressing his face into the water just far enough that I couldn't hear the words he spoke for whoever waited on the other side, only knew that he was speaking at all from the working on his jaw. I shifted on my feet, leaning far enough back to catch a glimpse at the other side of the thin sheet of water. Just as I suspected, there was no sign of Seren's face peering through, let alone another fae. Whoever he was speaking to, wherever he was speaking it, it wasn't here.

It wasn't until he reemerged, eyes sliding over to me with a self-satisfied expression, that I realized how soaked through he was. Everything from his silver hair to the matching clothes were drenched to the point of clinging to his body, and had been ever since his sister interrupted him earlier. The silk offered little in the way of privacy. Every sharp edge, every curve, every muscle was on display more prominently than had he been wearing nothing at all. I was too distracted to notice earlier, but now, it was all I could do to come up with a new distraction to force myself to look away.

Seren, meanwhile, seemed completely oblivious to the way my gaze had shifted so carefully away from him.

"Tarrack," I came up with, finally. "What would he have done to me? Itris seemed determined to get me away from him."

"Oh, he's harmless, really. He's more likely to bore you to death than he is to actually kill you. Though, when you live as long as we do …"

"Itris already warned me," I muttered. "Fates worse than death and all that."

Out of the corner of my eye, deft fingers had begun to unlace the back and sides of Seren's robe until it fell open, allowing him to peel the swathes of soaked silk from where they clung to his skin.

There was a marble-like quality to the fae's body beneath. It was all hard, smooth lines like the planes that made up his face. Each muscle of his body seemed to have been carved with the same care as the cheekbones that turned up at the corners of his eyes. Try as I might to keep my eyes peeled forward, it was impossible to *not* look at him.

It felt like looking at something forbidden. He was so perfect, every muscle moving methodically as he carefully pulled the layers of silver silk down off his shoulders, past the hard, defined lines of his abs, only stopping when the dripping fabric slung so low over his waist that it was a small miracle it didn't slip down of its own accord to pool on the floor like another puddle. A sharp v drew my eyes further down, but I was rewarded with nothing more than the bundled fabric covering the length of him that had been all too visible a moment before … had I been looking.

Which I wasn't.

Not purposefully, anyway.

It wasn't until he turned away, his exposed back facing me for the first time, that I did look. Really look. I wasn't able to help it.

Long silver scars tattooed the length of his shoulders, stretching down from his broad, muscled back to the narrow taper of his waist. I couldn't decide if they were purposeful, marks inflicted by his own making or from some long-healed accident. There was a careful pattern to them, a symmetry just chaotic enough to drag my eyes across them in question.

The tips of my fingers ached to reach out and touch them, to see if the scars were raised enough to trace, or if the faint pink lines that peeked beneath the silver would make Seren flinch at their touch. The draw if it was strong enough to almost make me do it. I felt my fingers twitching forward, my hands fighting the sensation to follow this strange new urge.

Seren, meanwhile, was oblivious to his effect over me. He stretched his arms over his head, pushing back the long strands of his hair away from where some of them had begun to cling to the sides of his face. His hands, smooth and glittering still, slicked back his hair until the fingers began to tangle in the strands at the nape of his neck. They worked beneath the sheet of his hair in practiced movements, lifting and twisting the locks into a single long, rope-like strand. He gave the twisted form a soft wring, nothing sharp enough to break the hair, and I watched as dark water dripped from the ends. It left his hair even more white and glowing than before, the dark rivulets carving across the chiseled line of his stomach as he turned to walk toward the edge of the tower. The water, though dark, didn't look dirty. It simply looked like shadow, the kind of shadow that didn't make the world darker, but rather made the light seem brighter.

And, in this case, made my breath suddenly feel more difficult to find and my words catch as I forced myself to break the spell I was quickly succumbing to.

"What does it mean to be the Seeker?" I asked as Seren moved to pass the wall of water still trickling from the ceiling, flinching at the hitch in my own voice. It was a genuine question, despite the fact I was using it as a means to distract myself from the pounding of my own heart in my ears. I'd heard Itris mention it twice now, the weight of the title almost as sharp as the way she liked to use it to lash out at her brother.

Seren, still oblivious, spared only the smallest glance toward the sheen of water as he passed.

"As one of the seven rulers of Elysia, I've been tasked with the protection and use of the gates," he says, casually. "Portals. Pools. Arches. We've many forms of them."

"Like the pool you pulled me out of."

"Like that pool. And the one my sister was so anxious to warn you off of."

A slight chill managed to cool some of the curling heat at the base of my spine.

"She said I'd be lost forever in it without a tether."

A small, strangled sound came from the back of Seren's throat. "You *could* be. It's not a definite. Plenty of fae have entered that pool without a tether and come out unscathed. Just as many have entered with one, and never come out at all."

The words meant to be a reassurance to me had somehow issued more of a threat than before. As with most of the things I've come to learn about faerie, even this couldn't be so simple. I made a mental note to stay away from *all* the pools, portals, and any concerning-looking archways, just to be safe.

"So, you have the glamour here still then? The same one as Avarath?"

"Glamour yes. The same as Avarath? Not quite so much," Seren said. "Like Avarath, the glamour chose to carve paths within the fae of our realm. While we all share a common connection to the glamour, each family line holds certain … strengths … compared to the others."

"So Itris and her grandchildren …"

Finally, Seren's gaze cut back over to me.

"Why all the sudden questions? I thought from our last conversation that you weren't interested in learning what it was to be a Starlight Fae?"

The blush raging under my skin was enough to make a self-satisfied smile start to creep up Seren's face. Knowing he saw it only made the blush deepen as much as my own self-loathing.

"I … I just figured it'd be best to learn about my enemy if I have no choice to be trapped here with him."

"Strange choice of words," Seren said, his voice dropping a tone into something smooth as honey, "when the way you're looking at me now is hardly how you're supposed to look at an enemy."

If my calling him that offended him in any way, he didn't show it.

No, the only thing he was showing was the same insufferable heat still clawing up my spine and into my head where it swam with unholy thoughts.

There was no looking away from him now, not even pretending to. My gaze raked over every inch of him, taking in every hard edge of him from his slicing cheekbones to the deadly v once again drawing my eye away from abs that would better be suited to a palace's marble statue than one of its rulers. The sheen of the water had begun to dry from his skin, but it still tugged heavily on the bunched fabric nearly slipping from his hips. The drape shifted so that it no longer hid him from me, slung low, so low that I was able to more than make out the shape of his length beneath that thin, clinging fabric.

And what it told me was that my desire, the one raging up inside me like an untamable beast, was not unshared by the fae standing in front of me.

The fae that I should hate as much as the others, *more* than the others, even, but it isn't hate that was commanding my thoughts in that moment.

I'd felt this draw to the fae before. I felt it first with Caldamir, but he wasn't the prince I first succumbed to. It was unmistakable then, but then, it was different. Then, I could overcome it. I could see it for what it was.

But now … here. I couldn't write this off as the product of

exhaustion, of dying adrenaline still lingering in my veins. My panting breaths, growing faster with every inhale, filled me with the fear that I might no longer be so strong as I was before. I might not be strong enough to resist it.

Seren moved toward me, drawn I knew from the look in his matching eyes, by the same thing that made it impossible for me to move away. Even as he stepped so close that I could feel the heat from his skin, I didn't shrink back. I couldn't shrink back.

All I wanted was to reach out and take hold of him, to draw him to me, into me, to let him consume me.

And that terrified me more than anything else.

"What's wrong with me?" I finally managed to whisper, lips parting as his drew ever more dangerously close to mine. My heart had begun to beat so furiously that I couldn't decide which I was more afraid of—dropping dead here and now of a heart attack, or how it would actually feel if Seren closed this ever-shortening gap between us.

"Nothing is wrong with you, Delphine," Seren said, his voice as low as my whisper but carrying in it something so deep, so primal, that it might as well have been shouted. "You're fae. This is what it is to be fae. For the first time, you're feeling it."

This is what it is to be fae.

His words took hold of me and for the first time in what felt like an eon, breath rushed back into my lungs. I knew immediately what he meant. What it was I was feeling. I'd been feeling it for days now, ever since my transformation in the Mountain Court. I hadn't been able to put my finger on it, not with all the circumstances surrounding the moments that followed.

It was more than my appearance that had changed, and though the transition was more subtle at first, I now felt the racing of it through every part of my body.

"But to answer your earlier question ..." Seren continued,

slowly. His body, so close to mine, had made me completely forget how we'd gotten in this position in the first place. "Yes, Delph. Itris and her grandchildren, my niece and nephew in a fashion, share the same affinity for the portal magic as I do. Just as you might."

It took me a moment to understand what he meant, but when the meaning of it began to sink in, I finally found the strength to break from the spell that had fallen between the two of us.

"Wait, are you saying we might be related?"

"You're a Starlight Fae."

The way he answered was so casual, it infuriated me.

"What does that even mean?" I snapped, the unquenched heat in me quick to lash out in any way it could.

"All fae are related, eventually. We're all created of the same stardust. But if you want any more answers tonight, you're going to have to give me something in return."

He finally reached out and touched me, his hand grazing my temple so briefly as he pulled back a strand of my hair, and the rush of his touch was almost enough to make me melt into him again.

Almost.

But not quite enough, not now that I knew the true danger of my draw to him.

"What exactly are you suggesting?" I asked, clenching my jaw as I looked back up into Seren's dark eyes.

"I'm talking about a deal. Though …" his words trailed off as his eyes broke from mine just long enough to follow the curves of my body. "I might be open to an alternative, if you ask nicely enough."

A moment ago, I'd have been putty in his hands. I had no doubt I would have happily fallen into his arms and damned the consequences. Now, not so much.

Not when my head was now reeling with the idea that the fae standing before me, however strong my attraction to him, may be my great-great-great-grandfather—or something close enough along that line to make my blush run cold.

My skin paled and I visibly stumbled back from Seren's touch.

I felt an ache at the growing space between us, but that only served to make the rising nausea in my stomach worsen.

Seren noticed this, and thankfully his thoughts weren't quite so dark as mine. He tilted his head to one side, features twisting from one of lust to one of concern instead.

"It'll take a while for your body to adjust. Human bodies always do. It'd be a lot easier to manage if you just gave up your humanity altogether."

This time, his words make my stomach twist for an altogether different reason.

"What?"

That smug smile returned to Seren's lips. He pressed them together for a moment, eyes narrowing as he looked me over with an air that told me he thought he'd caught me at some kind of game.

"I see what you're doing," he said, slyly. "But I've already told you, if you want answers, you have to make a deal."

"Well, I'm not making a deal," I said, forcing my mind to still as I straightened up. My body might be trying to betray me in a myriad of ways, but at least of that, I was certain.

Seren saw my resolve, but instead of disappointment flickering across his face as I might have expected, that smile of his only somehow grew more smug.

"I'm not going to force one on you, don't worry," he said. "I'll not ask you again. But if you change your mind, Delphine, you're going to have to beg for it."

He waved an arm dismissively toward the door, where I spotted a fae female waiting in the shadow of its frame. From the way she was staring at me, and from what looked like a bundle of wash clothes in her arms, I knew right away that she was here for me—one of the servants I'd caught sight of darting between the palace shadows.

I had nothing more to say to Seren, not when I knew whatever it was, I'd come to regret one way or another. He, on the other hand, was not finished.

I left him with his parting words still ringing in my ears.

"After all, if I am going to be your enemy, I might as well start acting like it."

8
DELPHINE

THE FAE SERVANT LED ME DUTIFULLY BACK THROUGH THE honeycombing labyrinth of hallways to my own tower room—if a little *too* dutifully. She moved so quickly through the winding passages that I would have thought there was something supernatural to it if it weren't for the way she herself seemed to be struggling to keep from tripping on the drooping fabric in her arms.

I would have offered to help carry them if I'd had any breath left from trying to keep up in the first place.

I was breathless for more than one reason, not just the incessant pace that left my ears ringing with the sound of too many uneven footsteps. My encounter with Seren had left me shaken. I was too many things at once. My lust, now cooled, had solidified into something too dense and syrupy in the pit of my stomach.

It was more than the fact that he might be a distant relative of mine that gave the attraction I felt an all-too-sour aftertaste. It was the fact that I might have relatives at all.

Somehow, in learning I was part fae, that thought had never occurred to me.

But of course, for me to be part fae, that meant there had to be a fae somewhere in my family tree—and because of how long their lives spanned, there was a good chance that whoever this fae was, he might still be alive.

I assumed it was a *he,* because I couldn't imagine a female abandoning her baby to the human realm, knowing that the fact it was fae would have almost certainly meant it would be killed. At least if the human in question had been a woman, then she could have passed the pregnancy off as another's far more easily. I'd seen enough hasty marriages between the girls that were far too loose with their love in my village to know how easy that would be.

But a strange, fae-marked infant simply showing up on a man's door one night?

I knew firsthand how the village would have come for its blood. They came for mine despite my human parents. If there had been nothing to prove I wasn't a changeling as I'd been accused, I had no doubt I would have ended up being left outside for the wild animals as I'd once been threatened.

I was still so absorbed with these thoughts that it took me altogether too long to realize how strange the servant was behaving. It wasn't until I heard a loud clanging followed by a muttered swear that I even realized what it was she'd been doing.

She stood halfway across the room, hands braced against a giant metal tub she'd been dragging across the crystal floor to draw it closer to the fire. That same fire was barely spluttering, as if it wasn't used to being lit, to say nothing of the small metal pot haphazardly hung above it—presumably for boiling water for killing a hapless frog, because there was no way on earth the combination of the pot size and that tiny fire were ever going to actually heat a human-sized tub of water.

It certainly wasn't going to heat a tub the size of the one the fae girl had gone back to gruntingly tugging across the floor in a manner that made me utterly surprised it hadn't left a long line of permanent scrapes etched through the sparkling floor.

"What … what are you even doing?"

She stopped only long enough to look at me as if *I* was the dumb one here. "Drawing you a bath. Humans do know what baths are, don't they?"

I ignored the slight in her words and the far more offending once-over she gave me. In my current state, I could hardly be offended without being the worst kind of hypocrite. Instead, I nodded my head toward the shining basin in her hands. It gleamed a perfect, bright copper in the waning starlight. Not so much as a fingerprint marred its perfect surface despite the way the fae's hands had been splayed over its surface in her rough attempt to move it from the cold corner into the only slightly less cold middle of the room.

That was the problem with whole palaces made of gem and stone.

"Has that thing ever been used?" I asked.

"Not in—"

"At least a century, I'm guessing," I cut her off, eyes roaming over the glistening surface.

She finished tugging the heavy bath the last couple inches, then stood up to wipe a hand across her brow. She made a motion with her hand, frowned, and then let out a small annoyed sound as she moved over to the fire to pick up the hot pot with her bare hands.

I was surprised they didn't burn until I saw not a single curl of steam lift from the dark water she poured into the bottom of the tub. The lukewarm water was barely enough to line the bottom with a solid film.

The both of us stared in silent disappointment at the empty basin for a moment.

"Itris insisted," she finally said, another sigh escaping her lips.

"Why's that?" I asked, instantly suspicious.

"She didn't want to make a spectacle of you by taking you to the public bathhouse."

That suspicion I'd felt moments earlier soured a little into something more like guilt. Why was I so quick to judge Seren's sister? She might be abrasive, but so far, she hadn't actually done anything to make me mistrust her so. If I should be mistrusting anyone, it should be her brother.

The same brother that made two very different kinds of shivers race down my spine at the very thought of him.

The servant left me alone with the instructions to strip and didn't return until long after the last of my soiled garments were peeled and pulled to pile on the floor at my feet. Still, it wasn't until I stood, shivering slightly in the cool air as she dropped the last of a half-dozen cold buckets of water into the tub, any attempt of heating it long forgotten, that I realized what it was about her that really seemed off. It wasn't the bath, the pot, or even the images of amphibians slowly boiling to death that turned over incessantly behind my eyelids.

It was her.

"You're not Starlight, are you?"

She paused where she stood directly before me, a cloth dipped in ointment in one hand, and a bandage in the other. She'd already cleaned the bit of blood from my sternum. Upon getting a better look at the cut, I was relieved to find it was really barely more than a paper cut, just enough to leave a slow, if incessant, drop of blood to pool upon my skin, but not enough to threaten to bleed me dry in the coming days if what Elvie said about healing in this realm was true.

The servant worked in silence, making me wince with the ointment, and then fixing cotton and bandages to my chest so that the blood had somewhere to go that didn't leave me looking more and more like the victim of a failed murder in every gown I wore.

The one I'd brought with me from the Mountain Court already laid in a heap on the ground, the stained bodice layered with dried and fresh blood so that there was a good chance—even aside from the rips it incurred in the last battle—it was more likely to be retired than worn again.

It was kind of a shame. It was a beautiful dress, the finest thing I'd ever worn—even if it did now remind me also of the worst moments of my entire life.

The servant didn't answer my question about what kind of fae she was, not until she was able to step back and admire her handiwork with the bandages. It was sloppy at best, the work of someone who'd never had to tie a bandage before in her life, but it also would do.

I didn't have the heart to tell her that it would all have to be re-done as soon as I got into the bathtub, and was a little relieved when she left the extra supplies for me to fix it myself, so I didn't have to tell her at all.

"So, Starlight?" I reminded her.

Her nose wrinkled in annoyance. "You really are chatty. No wonder Seren refused to answer any more of your silly questions."

She'd given up entirely on the bath after she'd made enough trips out into the hall to make me think there was another magic doorway somewhere nearby that brought her to wherever they drew the water here. That or I'd so entirely lost track of time that it would be better off not knowing.

The servant started laying out the bundle of clothes she'd carried with us on the first trip up the tower that we took together instead. I barely paid any attention to the individual garments, each one in a silvery shade of the Starlight Court's colors.

I was too busy paying attention to her.

"So?" I asked again, making her pause where she stood, straightening out a lace-trimmed chemise. "Are you?"

She let out a small sigh and for a second, her carefully drawn back shoulders slumped forward ever so slightly as she answered the question despite her snappish reply. "No," she said, "I'm not. I'm a Mountain Court fae. Or I was, once."

I looked over her once more, finally understanding what it was about her that had been nagging at the back of my mind. Of all the fae that were the most similar to the Starlight Court, the Mountain Court would be it. It was why it took me a minute to realize it, despite the fact that the fae in front of me was the only one I'd seen without the telltale white hair and black eyes since I arrived.

But as soon as I thought it, I knew that wasn't entirely true.

I'd seen plenty of fae from other courts since I'd gotten here, they all just moved so quickly in and out of servant's passages that I'd barely taken any notice. Now, as I reached back through my blurry memories of the many winding passages of the palace, I began to remember glimpsing many such fae that were also clearly not Starlight Fae.

Though, unlike many of the others I'd seen, the servant in front of me could have passed as Starlight with a quick glance. Her hair was still fair, her body tall and shoulders broader than that of another court, like Nyx's Woodland Court. But it was her face, the stony way she cut her eyes to me with no mirth in them at all, that truly drew her resemblance back to the court with a prince like Caldamir on its throne.

Knowing this, I finally understood what it was that made her movements seem so strange before. It wasn't that she was doing anything particularly unusual … for a human. But for a fae?

Even in Avarath, the fae hadn't worked like her. They'd grown used to the dying glamour long enough to learn how to work their kingdoms with a grace like the magic had never left. Here, where the threads of glamour still practically shimmered just out of sight, her lack of magic stood out like a beacon.

"Is that why you aren't using magic? Is it tied to Avarath and that whole glamour fiasco?"

"Actually, no," she said, her voice for the first time taking on a dark edge. "It's because of this."

She held up her arm, but it took me a second to see what it was she was trying to show me. The most delicate of silver bracelets encircled her wrist.

"*This* is why I'm left dragging basins of water and lugging pots of water instead of using glamour to do the work for me. My sentence wouldn't be half so bad if they'd left my glamour intact. But the judges have their ways, and once they've made up their minds, there's no changing it."

"Sentence, like … like you're a prisoner?"

"When you say it like that, you make me sound like the victim."

She was nearly out the door when I stopped her one last time.

"Are you telling me you're not?"

She didn't turn back from where she was picking up my stained and tattered gown, or what was left of it, anyway. "Let's just say that remaining here, as a servant to the Starlight Court for all eternity, was a mercy. I didn't deserve it. Not after what I did."

She would have left me there, with that, if I let her.

"What's your name?"

She paused long enough to make me wonder if she was debating withholding that from me after all she'd already shared.

"Ayre."

Somehow, knowing her name did nothing to banish the chill that had settled in my spine with an intent to stay—and not just from the freezing cold water taunting me from the tub.

9
DELPHINE

WHAT COULD A FAE DO THAT WAS SO BAD THEY WOULD GLADLY accept eternal servitude?

Or, if not gladly, then at least not so begrudgingly that they wouldn't try to murder their eternal masters. Unless, of course, that was got Ayre her sentence in the first place.

A hot bath might have banished the chill, but the cold one only served to settle it more firmly into my bones. If I'd had any notions to explore more of the palace that night, they were banished the moment I dragged my freezing body back under the covers on my bed. I'd done my best with the cold water, but there was only so much scrubbing cold water could do.

I scrubbed until I was worried any more would rub me raw, but still I felt dirty beneath the sheets. Maybe they were too soft, the threads of fabric softer than the threads of me so that my skin felt rough and wrong beneath them. No matter how cold the touch of air on my damp skin, I couldn't convince myself to stay beneath them.

Sleep was close enough not to evade me still, despite my shivering form. I found sleep curled in a ball, the cold air wrapping around me in a steady current. It was a form of punishment, almost. I didn't deserve to slip beneath the opulent sheets. I was a stranger here, as I'd always been, and it was better that way. Try as they might to make me feel like something more, I couldn't let myself be convinced to be comfortable here. So far, the only fae who'd treated me like myself was Ayre, and our brief encounter had left nightmares flashing before my closed eyes.

As it should.

The fae were my enemies. I had to remember that. In a world where my captors were as silken as the sheets they laid out on my bed, I had to remember what they really were … or I too would become like Ayre, a slave to their desires forever.

I'd let myself forget before, become entangled with the fae who'd brought me to the faerie realm to begin with. I saw their faces in my nightmares the most, the swimming image of Tethys, Nyx, and Armene's pained expressions turning gaunt in the dark shadows. Even in sleep, their faces made my stomach lurch and something treacherous pull at my heart. I wanted to quell the pain I saw there. I wanted to let them know I was okay, that the fae that had stolen me away hadn't subjected me to the same fate they'd once tried to.

At least when Caldamir's face resurfaced, I could understand his rage.

I sank into it, letting it warm me. For once, I focused on his face until it stoked the flames inside me, spreading my own rage through my icy veins.

Heat curled around me in the morning. It slunk around my shoulders, twitched across my back in warm brushes, soft across my skin. A freezing ache had built between my muscles, especially where my hands had furled into balls in front of my face, my fingers fisting into the fabric that still made my skin prickle at its silky touch. In my dreamlike state, I felt my lips forming a name—though I wasn't entirely sure which one before the last bleariness of sleep sent me bolting up in bed instead of pressing further into the warmth.

The sudden movement sent something skittering across the bed and into the corner of the room so quickly that it took me a moment further still to understand who it was—or rather what it was—that had really been keeping me company in my bed. I busied myself in distracting myself from the blushing disappointment in my cheeks.

The moment I realized the heat was coming not from my own internal rage, but from something in my bed, my thoughts had immediately gone to thoughts of a well-muscled fae at my side. A high fae, and not whatever creature was still casting flickering shadows as it slunk around beneath the furniture pushed up against the rounded walls.

The thought should have had me reaching for the dagger hidden beneath my mattress, not pushing my ass up in search of something to press further into. It certainly shouldn't have left my lips parting and a soft, breathy sigh escaping between them like an invitation.

More certainly still, it shouldn't have made more heat pool slick between my thighs.

It was just my new fae senses still adjusting. It had to be. It was one more thing for me to watch out for, a betrayal of my own body and not just the fae around me.

The creature shifted again, reminding me of the very real fae threat that presented itself at present. I had no idea how it had gotten in since I'd at least had the foresight to close the windows in the night. I found myself stiffening, mind reeling as I tried to get a better look at what it was. I'd only had a few encounters with the lower fae of the faerie realm, and in

Avarath, those encounters had turned out to be with fiends rather than friends.

I was wary to discover which one this was.

It was a creature not unlike a cat but nearly twice the size of any cat I'd seen in Alderia. It wasn't the size, however, that marked it as a faerie beast so much as the eyes. They were strangely human looking, or fae-looking I supposed. Intelligence burned within, lids opened wide as the creature tried to read me at the same time I was trying to read him. They were a reflecting sort of green with dark rims, contrasting against the white and silver stripes of its fur.

I was so mesmerized by them, lost in the golden flecks that seemed to swirl with a life of their own, that I didn't hear Ayre come in. I didn't know the servant was in the room at all until a broom suddenly shot out into the corner and started swatting at the creature crouched beneath.

My own shriek of surprise was drowned out by that of the creature, whose snarls rang in my ears a second before it lurched from beneath the legs of the table. It wasn't just so much larger than a normal cat, but it had the claws to match. It darted straight at me and I froze, but it skirted around my legs dangling over the edge of the bed. Before it could scrabble underneath, Ayre was at it again, the long handle of the broom wielded like a sword to jab at it again.

The creature hissed as it narrowly avoided her and headed for the wall, only to be blocked again. I shouldn't have been surprised by how quickly Ayre moved after the way I was barely able to keep up with her yesterday. Everywhere the creature turned to hide, Ayre was a step ahead of it, the back of her throat letting out a half snarl of her own with every swing.

I wanted to tell her to stop, but I couldn't find the strength to force the words out of my own mouth. There was a fury in

Ayre's eyes that reminded me of another Mountain Fae's rage, and that fae hadn't been condemned to a life of slavery for a crime so heinous even he thought he deserved it. The last thing I wanted to do was get between this fae and her quarry, but thankfully, another fae was more than happy to do that for me.

"Stop that, right now!"

Ayre froze, broom handle held high and face stuck in a snarl, the second before her makeshift weapon finally struck its target. The catlike creature writhed up onto its feet from where it had become pinned to its back and leapt up, not into Elvie's outstretched arms, but into my reluctant ones.

I only caught it out of instinct, and not a moment too soon. I spotted the sight of long claws retracting back into the creature's paws the second before they'd sunk into me instead.

Elvie stuck out her lip in a pout from where she still stood in the doorway.

"Ah, he likes you."

There was a slight sourness in her voice that she explained a moment later, by adding for my benefit, and mine alone, "Catsugas are loyal. Fiercely loyal. Now that he's picked you, I doubt he'll let any of us touch him."

"Not without first taking those claws out the rest of the way," Ayre added, bitterly, though her bitterness came from something more like hate than envy. Where Elvie was fixated on the thick, luxurious coat of fur that was tickling the underside of my chin now, the servant was far more interested in the massive padded paws still struggling for purchase on a lap nearly too small for his hunched form.

Elvie let out a sigh. "He's just a kitten too. You're so lucky. I always wished one would pick me."

"Yeah, if luck is keeping a pet around who's more than capable of ripping out your throat now, let alone when it's full grown." Ayre looked over the pile of fur and claws between my arms with contempt. "In my court, we wore their pelts as a sign of bravery."

"Yeah, well, here we don't kill off the lesser fae for sport," Elvie snapped at her as she finally peeled her jealous gaze away from me to glare at Ayre. "Surely, there's something better for you to do than sit here harassing our first guest in a literal century?"

Ayre's lips pressed into a thin line, but she didn't argue. I watched the door a second too long after she was gone, long enough for Elvie to give me a small nudge on my shoulder to draw my attention away.

"What's the matter with you?" she asked. "Don't tell me you're scared of your servant."

Your servant. Those were words I never imagined I'd hear, never even in my wildest dreams.

The thought wasn't enough to keep a small shudder from wracking my shoulders. The Catsuga in my lap stiffened, eyes turning up to peer back into mine.

"Should I not be?" I glanced once more at the door, hands curling a little tighter into the soft fur enveloping my thighs. "What'd she do to end up here?"

"There are fates far worse than … "

"Than death?" I asked, repeating what her grandmother and great-uncle had been all too happy to already impress on me before her. "Eternal servitude seems pretty up there to me."

"Yes, well, it's not so bad when the reason you're sentenced to it is because of all the deaths you caused."

My stomach twisted. "So Ayre …"

"Is a murderess."

My blood ran cold. As if sensing this, the Catsuga in my lap leaned closer, head nuzzling up into my chest.

"How can she … should I …" I found my words unable to form a coherent sentence until finally my spinning thoughts settled on something it could get out. "Seren promised me I was safe."

"And you are." Elvie started to reach for me, as if to comfort me, but the Catsuga in my lap stiffened again and let out a deathly snarl. I felt the claws in his paws start to come out, but they thankfully withdrew when Elvie did, and before they had the chance to pierce through the sheer fabric bunched between us. "More now than ever," Elvie added, taking her turn to narrow her eyes at the creature in my lap.

"You're going to have to give it a name, now."

"A name?"

The two of us looked down at the Catsuga, eyeing it as carefully as it was eyeing us now. The more I stared, the more its silver coat reminded me of the conjunction that first night.

"How about Moon?"

It was such a simple name that I nearly blushed saying it out loud, but the Catsuga immediately let out a purr of pleasure and nuzzled his head up against my chest in a clear sign of approval. That, or he'd just gotten very lucky with the timing of this little display of affection.

"Ugh," Elvie said, jumping up from the bed to shake her head. "You've already bonded now, too? Come on. That was supposed to be me."

She said it with enough good spirit that I knew she only was halfway to becoming worryingly jealous. She moved about the room, opening the windows one by one as Moon and I exchanged a few more deep gazes that were almost unsettling in their intensity.

However, as much as this creature and I were supposed to have "bonded" as Elvie claimed, the moment she stepped back from the windows to examine her handiwork, the Catsuga suddenly leapt from my lap and went straight out the nearest one.

We both sat in shock for a moment, before Elvie added, likely to make sure that I wasn't imagining the graceful creature splattered on one of the courtyards below, "Don't worry, I'm sure he's fine. See, there?"

She pointed toward a narrow ledge wrapping around the outside of the tower. My gaze followed her pointing finger just in time to see the flicker of Moon's tail whipping around the corner. Just beyond, a flash of silver moved between the open archways of one of the palace's many outer corridors. I didn't have time to see who it belonged to, but from the muttered swear that dropped from Elvie's lips, *she* did.

"What is it?" I asked, panic lacing the edge of my voice. I didn't want to know what it was that would make a fae like Elvie swear, where having a murderess under her nose hadn't so much as made her flinch.

She shook her head, a small breath sucking in between her teeth.

"I think Tarrack had the same idea as me, coming here."

Together, we watched as the figure appeared in another archway, moving ever closer.

"Why are you here, actually?" I asked, finally. "Are you here to spy on me for Itris?"

"Spy on you? Not quite, though you could say I'm here because of her." She stopped and bowed her a head in embarrassment. "I chose to escape my grandmother's wrath to come find you instead," she admitted. "She had a bit of an incident with her glamour this morning. I don't think anyone wants to be anywhere near her."

"I think if avoiding angering her is your point, coming here was the wrong idea."

"Actually," she said, turning back to me with a strange glow sparking in her eyes. "I think you might be right. Tarrack might have had the same idea as me coming here, but now I have an even better one."

"And that is?" I asked, already wondering if I even wanted to know what this *better* idea was.

"If Tarrack is here, it means the Seer's chambers are empty."

10
DELPHINE

Tarrack's lab was nothing like my fears had once made me imagine. Rather than implements for cutting and examining, the Seer's chambers were filled with various vessels meant for what I can only guess was some kind of scrying. It wasn't just pools of that dark water I'd started to grow used to, it was other things too—mirrors, crystals, shiny bits of metal—basically anything that could conjure up some form of reflection.

It was also the only room I'd been in yet without some sort of window up into the sky.

I'd grown so accustomed to the open sky that the minute the door shut behind us, a creeping sense of claustrophobia snuck in. There was no way to tell if we were above ground or deep beneath the surface of the mountain, since I'd come to learn that the doorways in this palace weren't guaranteed to take you to the room on the other side. If I had to bet on it; however, I'd put all my meager earnings from the Otto estate into this once being a cave.

The vaulted ceilings had been either carved from stone or masterfully made to look as if they were shaped from one solid piece. The chamber was really several round chambers connected through these massive-vaulted archways lit by hanging orbs that circled slowly overhead like stars of their own. The moving lights caused dark shadows to fall across the wall in their wake, flickering with the ridges of the architecture while they themselves gave off a steady, almost eerily blue-tinged light.

The orbs seemed to be aware of us, always circling slightly away as we passed the various pools and instruments placed methodically across the room. Elvie watched me out of the corner of her eye, a slight smile turning up the outer corner of her lip the way it did every time she caught me gawping in wonder at something she'd long since come to view as ordinary.

Not that I could ever imagine actually viewing this room, or anything else in the realm of Elysia, as something so simple as *ordinary*.

Not when the more time I spent here, the more steeped in glamour this place seemed to be. I wondered briefly, head craned back as one of the orbs darted past us a little quicker at our approach, if this was what it had once been like in Avarath. If that place too had nearly quaked with magic just daring to be pulled forth … or if it wasn't the new realm at all.

Maybe it was always there, in Avarath, too, just out of reach. Maybe it was me that had changed, me that could now feel it.

"Here we are."

Elvie finally came to a stop in front of one of the plainer vessels. It reminded me of a bird bath, the water dark enough that even standing right above it I could barely make out the shape of my own face in the reflection.

"And here is?"

The fae's eyes sparkled again, even in the dark, the same way they had when she first announced her plan to take me here. "The distance scrying pool."

"Distance?"

"Enough to see into Avarath, and if we're lucky, beyond."

My heart nearly stopped at her words. "Are you saying … are you saying you can see into Alderia?"

Her lips curled up into a proper smile that time, a small nod shaking her head with an excitement of her own. "Now that you're here, maybe."

It was all I could do to blink back the hot tears burning at the back of my eyes.

Alderia. The thought of glimpsing it, however briefly and however darkly in the pool in front of me, made my head swim and my heart sing.

"Can you … can you see anyone in particular?"

"Do you want to see anyone in particular?" Elvie asked, arching an eyebrow.

"My brother." The words tumbled out of my mouth before she'd finished speaking herself. My eyes dropped down from hers to the pool as my breath stilled in my chest, his name coming out like a near silent whisper as I wondered what it would be like to see him again. "Sol."

The back of my throat felt thick, and it was everything I could do to keep the tears and choked sob from spilling out of me too.

"Brother? Oh, well, you can have mine. Isn't there someone else you'd rather see?" That raised eyebrow twitched. "An old friend. A boyfriend, maybe?"

"No," I said, a little too quickly, a little too close to snapping at her. "There's no one else."

No one else that mattered, anyway.

Though she looked a little disappointed, Elvie nodded and began lining up a set of stones across the smooth edge of the vessel. They were more stones and crystals, all in a range of silver to black tones. She moved them carefully, with precision and calculation, each one placed in an exact order. Her brow furrowed slightly at the task, lips moving in silent concentration.

At last, she instructed me to stand across from her, her foot striking out to nudge mine into the correct position before she set herself on the opposite side.

"Keep an ear out, will you? I sometimes get a little distracted when I'm trying to concentrate too hard, and it'd be better for both of us if we're out of here before Tarrak gets back."

Elvie's voice had dropped to a whisper, and she cast a hasty glance over her shoulder.

I followed her glance, that nervous pit returning to my stomach the way it had so often these days. "What'll happen if he catches us?"

Elvie waved her hand far too dismissively for the worried shadow that had crossed her face a moment earlier. She took a deep breath, eyes returning to focus on the perfectly still pool of water between us. Nothing happened right away. I wasn't sure if it was supposed to yet, and I was too afraid to ask. At least *one* fae here didn't insist on trying to trick me in exchange for basic information, and I wasn't about to go and ruin that by coming across as overeager.

Even if I was. I was so overeager that it was all I could do to keep my hands from shaking.

"Tarrak's line is much better at this, but I've been practicing."

"Isn't Seren the Seeker, though? Your uncle? He's not in your line?"

"A lot of Starlight Fae use portals for their magic, but we're all good at using it differently. Or not at all. It can get kind of … stale …" she stopped long enough to wrinkle up her nose before continuing, "so I decided a long time ago that I wanted to at least be able to see Avarath, even if I was never going to be able to go there."

Her words made me pause for a second. "Your brother said you'd been?"

Her voice dropped conspiratorially. "And you're not about to go telling him the truth now, are you?"

She straightened up before I could answer, then laid her hands out across the outer edges of the vessel and motioned for me to lay my hands on hers.

The moment I did, I expected some cataclysmic jolt to race through my body, or for the world around us to begin to crumble as it had the last time one of these fae had used their magic for me. Instead, however, nothing happened. Not at first.

The stillness and silence stretched on long enough that I'd begun to doubt the magic had worked, but just when I was ready to give up hope and tug my hands back from where they'd grown too warm against Elvie's, something began to glimmer inside the pool.

It stared deep within, tiny pinpricks of light racing and dancing and intertwining with one another. The moment Elvie saw it, her hands tightened around mine, and the threads inside began to weave together. At first it was nothing more than gold and silver light, shifting in unrecognizable shapes. But slowly, ever so slowly, they began to form into something more. Sunshine. Waving trees. A figure.

A face.

And not just any face, Sol's face.

The surface of the water was so still that it was like looking straight through a window with my brother on the other side. It was so real, so lifelike, I was certain if I could only reach out and into the water, I could touch him.

I was also certain, however, that what I was feeling was

brought on by the overwhelming nature of the spell, and knew without having to be warned that if I released Elvie's tight grip on my hand for even a second, I'd lose Sol again.

So, I gripped Elvie ever tighter, until I was surprised she didn't flinch back from the way my fingers tried to crush hers between them.

I couldn't see much more than Sol's face. Every so often he would move, lift his hand to brush back curls that had grown altogether too long from his face and a nightshirt that had grown altogether too short in the span of a single summer. Less than that, just a few weeks.

I'd seen it then, that last day at the cottage before Caldamir tricked Lord Otto into giving me up. Tricked me into trusting him.

I'd known Sol was on the cusp of adulthood, the last of his boyish years fading with each passing second. I just hadn't realized quite how true that was. It was like I'd gotten the last true glimpse of him as a boy. Now, already, he'd started to transform before my eyes.

I could see him. See the face I'd thought I'd lost forever. See that he was safe, that he was oblivious to the dangers that lurked so much closer than any of us could ever have imagined.

I could see that he was happy, even.

It was everything I'd hoped for my brother when I left him, and everything I'd feared would be taken from him ever since I learned I'd been tricked.

Why then did the sight of him make my heart break?

11
DELPHINE

THE LOOK OF EXCITEMENT ON ELVIE'S FACE FADED THE MOMENT SHE met my eyes.

"Oh no, did I do something wrong? Was that not your brother?"

Her hands suddenly reached for mine again, but she moved too quickly, knocking into several of the carefully placed stones laid out across the top of the pool. One of them slipped beneath the surface of the water before she could reach it, and she let out a snarl of a swear.

I absentmindedly reached to help her fish it out, my mind still staring almost without seeing anything in front of me, but she caught my wrist before my hand could so much as break the now rippling surface of the water.

"It's lost," Elvie said, with an air of finality to her voice. "Better not to lose you too."

We both stared down into the pool together for a long, long moment. Though Elvie had joked about me being welcome to take her own brother, I knew that was all it was, a joke. The same heartbreak I felt was mirrored on her face, and I wondered if she too was thinking about what it would be like to only be able to see her twin in small glimpses like this.

"Is there any way to speak to him?" I asked, finally.

"Not with Tarrack's kind of magic."

"But Seren spoke with me."

Elvie tilted her head to the side. "The Seeker's magic. Much more complex. But I would do it … if it didn't turn you inside out instead." She mimed her chest expanding and then folding in on itself, as if I needed any more images to join the already haunted ones invading my unwitting thoughts. "Even I can't manage it, yet."

THE BACK of my throat was thicker than it was before. The words that made it out sounded choked and broken, nearly as choked and broken as my heart felt squeezed between the confining ribs of my chest.

"I didn't think it would hurt so much to see him," I breathed, finally. "Alderia. Home. I'd given it up once, but now … now I'm not so sure."

Elvie nodded her head slightly, as if she was trying to understand, but there was something she was biting back. She was clearly debating whether or not to say what she was thinking, but it wasn't long before the more curious side of her won out.

I didn't care. I'd welcome anything that might distract me from the deep spiral my thoughts were determined to pull me into.

"So, the brother—however annoying they might be—I understand. Alderia, not so much."

"What do you mean?"

Elvie took a careful breath, head tilting to the side again. "I haven't heard much good about the human realm. Humans are simple and cruel. I mean, they sent you here, didn't they?" She shook her head, eyes pinching together followed by the way she scrunched her nose up when she was thinking. "I wouldn't be so keen to go back to a place that had sold me out so easily."

"What do you have in Alderia that you're so desperate to get back to? Is there even a life waiting for you?"

I opened my mouth, ready to snap out at her for real this time, but the words once again stalled on my tongue—though for an entirely different reason. That reason being that … she was right.

What *was* I so eager to go back to Alderia for? Certainly not Lord Otto and my begrudging work at the estate, even if it might be greatly improved now that the head of the servants had mysteriously ended up in a bloody grave the same night that fae prince was welcomed under that roof.

Certainly not for Leofwin, my once-lover who now made my skin crawl to think of him. He'd been handsome enough for a servant boy, but compared to even the most hideous of fae, I didn't think I'd be able to ever look at him that way again … and that was even if I ever cared to forgive him for his disgusting cowardice, or the fact that he was all too happy to betray me too when the time came.

Even my friend, my one true friend, Ascilla, would she even be happy to see me? She'd always been kind, but I'd seen the way our friendship made her life difficult. Not as difficult as mine, I knew, but enough that she had to suffer right there alongside me.

I hadn't seen her in the scrying pool, but I had a feeling if I did, that I would see a life much like the one I'd glimpsed of my brother's. Like Sol's, her life had likely gotten better now that I'd left.

But still, I wasn't ready to face the thought of *not* going back. Of *choosing* not to go back.

"I have to go back, for Sol. I can't leave him there. It's dangerous."

"You think it's dangerous for him there, in Alderia? Is he bullied like you were?"

"No," I said, still breathless. "But …"

"And he's not fae?"

Her words made me stop altogether then. I shook my head a couple times, mouth working before I spluttered out, "Of course not. He's my half-brother, born of my father. The fae came from my mother."

Though I'd never had the luck to meet her, I'd heard stories about her my whole life. She'd looked like me, so much like me, but where my white hair marked me as some kind of faerie beast, hers marked her as a beauty—simply for the fact that she hadn't been born with the pitch-black eyes to match.

Erin nodded her head again, her own expression telling me that she was carefully reading the shifts in mine.

"Now, doesn't that mean you're the one in danger?"

"What?"

"If you leave Elysia, and go back there, won't Calda—what and the other princes, won't they just come get you again? And then if your brother is lucky enough not to be killed in the second encounter, you surely will be … and then he'll just end up enslaved."

"But … but won't Caldamir and the other princes just come here to get me? Seren was able to do it easily enough."

Saying the Mountain Court ruler's name aloud was enough to make hatred rear its ugly head.

Elvie let out a scoff. "The realms touched for a second. They're not connected anymore. Besides, without magic, there's no way the princes would be able to get you here. As long as the realms are separated, you're safe here. And as long as you're safe here …"

My head turned to peer once more at the long since stilled pool of water. "Then Sol is safe, too."

Elvie nodded along with me, and as much as she tried to keep her face composed, a small amount of delight managed to slip its way out.

"I'm smart sometimes, for only being a hundred and twelve." There was so much pride on her face, I couldn't bring myself to argue.

It wasn't just the pride though, it was because she was right.

My thoughts, once muddled and turned over, cleared until I was finally able to see the clear line before me, and most importantly, where it led.

I knew what I had to do.

It was what I had to do, all along. It was why I went with Caldamir, and it was why I left Caldamir.

I had to protect my brother, even if that meant protecting him from me.

Elvie stood beside me, beaming, unaware of the cracks that were spiraling out and taking root inside me. We'd done what we came here to do. I'd gotten what I so desperately wanted.

And now, after everything, I knew what I had to do. It was the same thing I'd been trying to do all along, but I'd needed another reminder.

Seeing my brother's face, Sol's face, was just that.

Knowing all this, seeing what I had, it did nothing to ease the heavy weight that had come to rest over my shoulders and head. Elvie had started moving between the pools, her excited chatter turning into background noise that seemed to grow louder and louder until I couldn't take it anymore.

"I have to go," I said, suddenly, cutting her off in the middle of an anecdote about some crystal or other with mind-reading properties.

She stuttered to a halt, guilt flooding her face as she took me in. "Of course. How stupid of me. I should have realized ... do you know the way back?"

I nodded my head, even though I knew it was a lie.

I knew I'd be lost on my way back, but I didn't care.

All I knew was that I needed to be alone, and I needed to be alone now.

Still, for a long moment, I stood just inside the open doors before I left the Seer's chamber, my head craned up to look at the intricate iron work spiraling across their frames. Gems glittered darkly from where they'd been inlaid all across the surface, not just in the doors, but in the walls too, in the ground, the very stones beneath my feet. They raced through the stone in veins of cut diamond, singing underfoot with each step.

When I first arrived here, I thought it was an echo, but I was wrong. It was something more.

It lived and breathed through every surface of this place, and the longer I was here, the less it sounded like noise, and the more it sounded like music. The song it played?

Daggers. Knives. Sharp and pointed, driving further and further up between my ribs toward my already shattered heart.

12
DELPHINE

How many times would I have to give Sol up?

I'd no sooner pressed my back to the closed door of my room, eyes slipping shut as a hand reached up to undo the choking laces at my throat, when I heard a hissing sort of screech announcing I was not as alone in my room as I thought. My whole body stiffened, pushing forward off the door and into a wide-footed stance, in case fighting or fleeing was required—though I hoped fleeing would be the option, since I wasn't sure I could fetch my fae dagger out from under the mattress in time.

A second hissing sound drew me whirling to face my would-be attacker, only to catch the silver and white Catsuga pressed up into an angry corner of the room.

"Oh, it's just you Moon," I sighed, shoulders slumping in relief. No sooner had I begun to fall back toward the press of the door when a second, all too recognizable voice announced my mistake.

There *was* an intruder in my room, and it wasn't the cat.

Waylan the demon stepped out of a shadow I hadn't so much as noticed and looked down the considerable length of his nose at the cat-like creature hissing at him again in its corner. "You actually named that godawful creature?"

My jaw physically dropped at the sight of him, arms frozen at my sides as my mind short circuited and temporarily went blank. The moment I regained movement in my arms and legs, I flew across the room to throw my arms around the wrinkly old demon. He was cold and ever so slightly slimy to the touch, but I didn't care.

He was quite possibly one of the only beings who'd been genuinely kind to me since I arrived in Avarath, so my heart practically sang to see him now, despite the fact that he was a highly dangerous being just as likely to skin someone into a new hat as he was anything else.

I'd need the hat, of course, because by the time he was finished, I'd probably be bald from all the aggressive hair brushing.

Waylan stiffened at my touch and remained that way until I'd disentangled my own clammy arms and legs from his significantly wirier ones. The only part of him that remained anywhere near my person by the time I'd finished extricating myself from his sorry excuse for arms and legs was his hand, hovering altogether too close to the knot at the back of my head.

"I promise, I'll brush it out," I whimpered, eyes already fearfully scanning the tops of the dressers for anything that might be within reach.

There was doubt in his eyes, a look that somehow made me want to reach out and hug him all over again. I held back this time as I took him in, the joy at seeing a familiar, friendly face starting to wane as the reality of him being here began to sink in.

"How did you get here?"

"I hardly think that's the question you should be asking,"

Waylan said, head slightly bowing. The knowing look in his eye told me all I needed to know.

His demon magic. Of course. He'd told me it operated separately from the glamour of the faerie realms.

My momentary joy quickly turned into suspicion. It took all my concentration not to glance nervously back at the door, though I was sure Waylan noticed the way my feet subtly shifted me back toward it, just in case. Not that I could escape the demon if he really wanted to catch me. I'd only seen small glimpses of his magic, but I didn't know the particulars of it to know *that* much.

"What are you doing here? Does Armene know you're here? Do the other princes?"

"No," he says, but his voice comes out a little too slow, too calculating.

"Then why are you here?" I asked again, restating the question he all too carefully chose not to answer the first time. "Are you here to fetch me back?"

"No," he answered again, too, and I cursed myself for impatiently asking him another question that could be answered so simply. Waylan was never one for wasted words, but for once, I wished he was more like Elvie—eager to share the thoughts running behind those narrowed, calculating eyes.

"If he didn't send you, then what are you doing here?" I straightened myself up, knowing full well it did nothing to make my slight figure any more intimidating. "I'm protected here, you know. You can't do anything to me."

"Would you believe me if I said I was simply checking on a dear friend?"

Something seized inside my chest, even though I knew it wasn't true, or perhaps *because* I knew it. Of course, I doubted there was anything Seren or any other Starlight Fae could do to stop Waylan if he was really here with malintent.

Now I *did* risk a wary look toward the door, worried that Ayre might choose this moment to slip inside. I hadn't gotten used to the erratic servant's routine yet. Meals appeared somewhat regularly, but I wasn't sure if that was her doing or some other serial killer the court had wandering around with a thin silver chain in lieu of shackles. Either Ayre would be thrilled to see a demon carrying news of the princes of Avarath, or she'd be furious—and I wasn't sure which reaction I was worried about more.

Whatever Waylan's reasons for being here, he seemed in no rush to share them. Keeping one wary eye on Moon, who'd now slunk back to sit on the edge of the bed closest to me, he started pacing around the outer corners of the room, his head swiveling sharply side to side as he took everything in. He took particular interest in the bath, still sitting abandoned and empty now, in the middle of the floor. It looked out of place here, a relic of a time that had long since been forgotten. Everything else was all silver and white and gemstone. It made the brass, however shiny, somehow appear dull.

"You left Avarath in quite the uproar," Waylan said, at long last. He'd come to settle at the window, eyes darting between the crossing rooftops and the dark sky above. I noticed that he didn't move too close to the sill, but rather hung back, clinging to whatever shadows he needed to keep from being spotted.

Which meant he didn't want to be seen.

I said nothing, hoping my silence would force him to continue.

"The Mountain Court will never be the same. The people might forgive Caldamir and the princes for what they tried to do, but monarchs … they're the ones that don't forget those that betray them."

My thoughts immediately went to Caldamir's guard, Tallulah, and my heart took on a new ache.

I couldn't see her face in those last moments in Avarath, but I could imagine the way what she'd done there in the end must have pulled at her very soul. I'd seen the way she pined for her prince, seen the fealty she swore to him with every ounce of her body and mind. Twice she'd defied him.

Twice she'd saved me.

I hated to imagine what fate she'd faced once I was gone, once her betrayal had struck her prince the way Waylan's words promised. Though, I had a feeling as I watched him, it wasn't *her* betrayal he was considering. It wasn't another fae that darkened his brow, causing the closest thing to indecision to flicker across the demon's face that I'd ever seen. It was an eerily human emotion on that stretched skin of his, and I didn't like it.

"The princes are more obsessed with finding you now, than ever," he admitted, finally turning his back to the window to face me again. "It's strange, what a small glimmer of hope can do to fae once it's ripped away. It'll only be a matter of time before they find a way to you."

A small hollow feeling settled in the pit of my stomach, because I knew he was right. Elvie and Seren and all the other fae here could promise I was safe, that there was no way to get here from Avarath, but that wasn't true, was it? Seren had come for me. He'd stepped between the realms.

And then, standing right before me, was living proof yet again.

"You'll have to take Armene and the princes here if he asks you," I said, quietly piecing together his warning.

Much to my surprise, however, a sly smile tugged at the

outer corners of Waylan's mouth. "There are limits to what the prince is allowed to demand of me."

"And this isn't one of them?"

That smile grew wider. "I have no love for the fae. The last thing I intend to do is help them to their own benefit where I'm not required."

Waylan had never made his lack of love for the fae courts a secret, which was why his next question took me off guard more than anything else. His tone changed, eyes softened, and voice dropped to something a notch less raspy than the one that usually whistled out past his wizened vocal cords.

"The Starlight Court, they're treating you well?"

The question hit me like a slap, making me sputter. "Well enough," I answered, finally, when he treated me to the same silence that had finally prompted the loosening of his tongue. "I'm not a prisoner, if that's what you're asking."

He nodded, and I swore for a moment that I saw something close to relief in his eyes. His reason for visiting satisfied, the demon didn't linger.

"Protect yourself, Delphine of the Starlight Court," Waylan said in the moments before he disappeared, blinking out of existence as if he'd never been in Elysia in the first place. "The rulers of this realm can only protect you so well as they can protect themselves, and like Avarath, time has made them grow lazy. Fae have the bad habit of thinking they're invincible, and more often than not, it's their downfall."

In the moments that followed Waylan's warning, a selfish hope bloomed inside me.

If Waylan had said was true, then it might only be a matter of time before my staying away from Sol wouldn't be helpful. In fact, I might *need* to be able to get back to Sol. Waylan had come to warn me, sure, but rather than make me fear, he'd made me hope.

He'd made a good point, and I don't think he even realized it, but I did, and now that I saw it, I couldn't *unsee* it.

If he could get here, to Elysia, then maybe it was only a matter of time until the fae of Avarath did, too.

Here, I wasn't the only Starlight Fae, and that meant I was no longer the only fae who could undo the spell that kept their king—and their glamour—asleep.

It was a selfish thing to even think, because it meant my world—Alderia—was in more danger than ever.

More than that, it meant that I, somehow, was once again in the position to have to save it.

If the fae found their way to Elysia, then the human realm would need to be warned.

And I would need to be prepared.

13
DELPHINE

I KNEW WHAT I HAD TO DO.

It had to be done.

There was no other way.

It was a long stretch, I knew, worrying that the fae would somehow make it here to Elysia and free me to return home, but I couldn't bring myself to stop thinking about it. There was more than one thing that Waylan was right about. Hope, however small, was a strong thing. Even the fear of it being ripped from me next wasn't enough to stop the seed of it from taking root.

I was careful not to act rashly. I was all too aware of the fact that it was only just before Waylan paid me a visit that I'd come to the conclusion that I *couldn't* go back to Alderia. For days I tried to talk myself out of it. I spent my time locked away in my room, alternating between looking for Moon and looking out for Ayre each time she delivered me a meal or came to draw me another freezing bath.

Elvie kept me company as much as she could, but she had her own lessons to attend, and I kept getting the impression that Itris was trying to keep her too busy to visit me. She never said as much directly, but she didn't need to. Alder visited once too, but he was too shy to say anything, and instead took on the role of lookout, careful to redirect Tarrack any time he looked like he might be on the way to try and whisk me away from my rooms.

I could have used the time to explore the palace, sure, but I was far too preoccupied with my own thoughts. Soon the days passed into a week, a full week in Elysia, and still the thoughts plagued my every waking and sleeping moment. I finally had to admit even to myself that there was no denying it any longer.

I had to make a deal with Seren.

Even if I came to regret it, I wouldn't be able to move on until I did what I'd known I was going to do from the moment Waylan showed up in my room.

Elvie had been right that day in the Seer's chambers, there was nothing left in Alderia for me. There was nothing that should have driven me to desire, even for a moment, to go back. Nothing but my brother. Nothing but Sol.

But for someone who'd had so little to cling to all of her life, that was enough. Enough to make me do something that made every muscle in my body scream at me to stop. Enough to make me do something very, very stupid.

If it weren't for Waylan and his warning, I'd never have reconsidered the deal that Seren offered.

The last thing I wanted was an audience to what I was about to do, so I finally took my chances with the maze of passages that made up the Starlight palace. It wasn't long before I began to doubt my choice not to ask Ayre to call for Elvie, or ask the servant to bring me to the Seeker's tower herself, but by the time the thoughts were flitting through my mind, I was already so well and truly lost that there was no point but to continue soldiering on.

There was no way to tell how long it actually took me to

find the tower, not that any time had actually passed … since apparently no time passed here. I'd yet to wrap my head around the concept, and I sincerely hoped I never had to take the time to understand it. That was why I was here, after all, my hand pausing only for a second before it knocked on the door that I was at least fifteen percent certain led to Seren's workspace.

The knock echoed through the crystal garden until it faded to silence.

I hesitated, fist still raised before I knocked again. What would I do if Seren wasn't here? I hadn't considered the alternative. He hadn't visited me since the last time he sent me away. For all I knew, he wasn't even here, in Elysia. I didn't know how the fae worked.

He'd made sure of that when he refused to tell me anything more until I agreed to make a deal with him. A tactic that, unfortunately, worked in the end … because here I was. Ready, at last, to sign over the last bit of my soul that was mine.

I glanced up once overhead and tried to read the shifting stars, but it was impossible. It could be the middle of the afternoon or the middle of the night, and I'd have no way of knowing. So far, I'd relied on the delivery of regular meals to my door to keep track of time, but the nerves twisting my belly were enough to confuse even the sensation of hunger—or lack thereof —from helping me decide what time of day it was.

The second time my hand moved down to rap on the door, it met air as it swung inward. A warm hand caught my wrist on instinct the second before it collided with flesh instead of wood. Seren stood before me, eyes glassy for a moment, before he blinked them into focus and looked down at me.

"I wondered if it was you."

"What, does no one else knock?" I asked. "I would have

asked if you smelled me, but I'm freshly bathed, thank you very much."

Seren's face looked like it didn't register my words. "No, no one enters. It could break my concentration."

"Though," he added, "I would have known from your scent. Scents are like fingerprints. They're unique."

"You think my scent is unique?"

"Your scent is …" His hand turned mine over for a moment, the inside of my wrist drawing dangerously close to his lips. He drew in a deep breath, taking in my scent with fluttering eyelids before he finally let go of me. "Intoxicating."

He left me standing, speechless and mouth dry, in the doorway as he turned back toward the tower.

"Forgive me if I seem like I'm not here. It takes me a while to readjust to the realm when I've been travelling. Not that I need to tell *you* that."

"Your sister …"

"Ah yes, well my sister is another matter entirely," he said, waving his hand dismissively. He moved his shoulders like he was working an overused muscle, rocking back first one, and then the other as he tilted his head from side to side. "She should be viewed as the exception, not the rule."

"I'll keep that in mind," I muttered, finally following after him. My footsteps were timid, my eyes darting over to the edges of the room that spilled over into the sky, no barrier between the two.

Seren moved to the waterfall, one hand lifting up toward it where it hovered just above the surface of the flowing water. A soft light glowed within, and a moment later, the water began to slow until it was only a drip, and then nothing at all. Silence enveloped the tower without the soft trickle of water. Seren kept moving, his footsteps slow and heavy, until he came to a stop mere inches away from the open ledge. He was bathed in bright starlight there, so close to that place where the floor met empty sky.

The silken neck of his robe slipped down over his shoulder as he tilted his head again, exposing perfect porcelain skin that glowed beneath the unearthly light.

I discovered then where all the moisture that had been sucked from my mouth went, and felt myself subtly crossing my thighs beneath my skirts as if it could do anything about the growing ache there.

I willed myself not to forget why I'd come here, but I found my legs unwilling to bring me closer to where Seren stood, the shake in my knees not entirely from the height. I had to do something, say *something*, however. I couldn't just stand there staring forever, no matter how good the view was.

"You said you were travelling, but you're not wet."

"Were you wet when I pulled you through the pool into Elysia?"

"No ..."

"That's right. Like I said, I don't like my concentration to be broken. Luckily I can handle a little knock on the door better than I can my sister's arm jerking me back."

A silence spread between us as I searched my mind for something else to say, only to cringe when I found it.

"It's a nice tower you have here."

Seren stiffened, finally turning back to me so that I could see the suspicion drawing across his face. "You're being polite," he said, bluntly. "What do you want?"

"Can't a girl be polite without wanting something in return?"

"You're not a girl, you're fae," he said. "And I've never known you to be polite, so why else would you have a sudden change of heart? Unless ..."

He stopped, suddenly, as understanding replaced his suspicion. "You're here to make a deal."

Never before had I felt the weight of words land so heavily on my shoulders.

I wanted to shrink back, to deny it, but I couldn't … because he was right.

I didn't have to answer for him to see on my face that he was right.

I expected Seren to be smug, righteous, something. Whatever he was feeling, however, he managed to keep to himself.

Instead of stepping up to claim his prize, he remained frozen where he stood. "You know what I said last time."

"What, that you're my enemy? This doesn't have to change that."

Seren's head tilted forward, and his tone changed as something dark flitted across his face.

"No … Delphine," he said, enough condescension dripping into his voice that it made anger flare in me before I even heard what he said. "My offer changed. I'm not going to just make a deal with you now. Not unless you beg."

"I … what?"

Horror drenched me as thoroughly as if I'd stepped between the waterfall I now wished would break this awful silence.

"You heard me. If you want to make a deal with me now, you're going to have to beg me for it."

The condescension had been replaced with a tone so very matter of fact, and yet somehow, that was worse.

I'd never begged for anything in my life. Not even *for* my life, not once in the many times it had nearly been taken from me.

I had half a mind to turn on my heel and storm out, to forget about this whole thing once and for all. I would, too, if it was just for me. For my life.

But it wasn't.

Sure, there was no guarantee that I would need to get back to Alderia, no guarantee that going back would be an option. As it was, I was still the greatest threat to Sol's safety.

But Waylan's warning wouldn't be forgotten. I needed the option open, I needed to be able to choose to go back if I needed to. I might not be able to save Alderia, might not be able to save Sol, but I could at least offer them a warning.

For Sol. I could do it for Sol.

If I was going to do this, if I was going to beg a fae for the very thing that I'd promised myself I'd never do again, I wasn't going to grovel. If I was going to beg, I was going to do it with dignity.

I ignored the screaming muscles in my legs, the nagging voice in my head, and forced my legs to carry me slowly forward until I stood directly before Seren. I kept my eyes fixed to his, gaze never wavering, and neither did his. My knees wanted to shake, but I held them steady as I began to lower myself down, moving slow and controlled, until first my left knee and then my right rested on the cool gemstone-lined ground.

Seren towered over me as I kneeled, silent, blinking up at him waiting expectantly above me.

Still, he said nothing.

He was really going to make me do this.

I gritted my teeth and pulled my hands from where they'd begun absentmindedly clutching my skirts so that they pressed together in front of me instead, as if praying.

"Seren …"

"King Seren."

It was all I could do to keep the surprise from flickering across my face, but apparently my efforts weren't good enough. The fae saw through me, and the surprise he saw there made pleasure pull at the corners of his lips. He leaned forward, one hand reaching out to stroke the side of my face. His features were cast in shadow, but I didn't need to see the details of him to feel the danger seeping from the predator above me. I sat as still as I could as his hand traced the line of my jaw, stopping only so that his thumb could hook up to tease the bottom of my lip.

"That's right, dearest Delphine, you're no longer dealing with little princes."

His thumb pressed between my lips, and pried past my teeth, seeking for the heat of my tongue until I reluctantly offered it.

"Bite me."

I thought he was joking at first, but then his expression hardened. There was no mistaking the sharpness in his voice the second time.

"Bite me, now, Delphine, before I make you bleed instead."

I swallowed, hard, resisting the urge to bite his thumb off entirely as I did as he asked, my teeth pressing into his flesh until I felt the surface of the skin break. Only then was he satisfied enough to straighten up, pulling his thumb from my mouth before I so much as tasted a drop of iron. The pleasure on his face turned wicked as he brought his thumb back up to swipe slowly, methodically, across his own bottom lip.

Even with his face still cast in shadow, the red of blood was striking across his alabaster skin.

"I can taste you on my blood. Just like your scent," he whispered, fighting the urge to lick the blood from his lips, "intoxicating."

The sight of him was as mesmerizing as it was terrifying.

"Continue," he said, once again tilting his head down and dropping his voice dangerously low. "This time, like you mean it."

I bared my teeth at him. "You're a sadist."

"And you're begging to make a deal with a fae. Unless, of course, you're too scared to go on?"

I knew he was bating me, and I didn't care.

I rose to the challenge in his voice.

"King Seren," I said, voice dropped down low to match his. "I'm here, before you, *on my knees,* begging you to offer me the deal."

Seren cocked his head to the side, false innocence coating his tongue. "What deal?"

I gritted my teeth again. "The deal I turned down the first time."

"And the second time?"

I nearly bit my tongue off. "I turned it down then, too."

"Well, for a fae who's asking to make a deal with me that she's turned down not once, but twice, you're sitting awfully high on your knees."

Hot blood rushed into my cheeks, but I'd already gone this far. I couldn't give up now.

I lowered myself down further, until the backs of my thighs rested against my calves, but I still didn't look away from him.

Still, it wasn't enough.

"Lower."

My hands met the cold floor before me, my neck now bent up until it ached to look up at him.

"Lower."

I had no choice but to break the eye contact that had bound us together. The cold of the night enveloped me in an instant, making my throat start to close and more heat rush through my tingling body. My legs ached from where I crouched, knees stung, feet tingled where the blood had been cut off.

I pressed forward into my palms until my face was level with his calves, his feet, the floor.

Hot humiliation resurged inside me.

"King of the Starlight Court," I said, my voice muffled now against the fabric of his robes. "I beg you."

"Say my name again."

"King—"

"Just my name, this time. My first name."

I lifted my head then, just enough to catch his eye again as the humiliation broke inside me. "Please," I whispered, this time, in earnest. Tears had started to gather in the corner of my eyes, from humiliation, anger, rage, or fear … I didn't know. All I knew was that I couldn't take much more of this. "Please, Seren," I said, again. "Please make a deal with me."

In that moment, he broke too.

He yanked me to my feet and pulled me so close that our chests touched, so close that our whole bodies melded together. One hand wrapped around my waist, pulling me closer and closer until there was no space left between us. The other wrapped around my wrist tightened too, and though I knew I'd find bruises patterned there in the morning, I didn't pull away.

The pain that bloomed there ached, sure, but in a good way.

It was there, pressed against him, that I felt the true depths of his excitement. It sparkled in his eyes, raced along the pulse beneath his skin, hardened his growing length pressing against my stomach.

"I, King Seren of the Starlight Court, choose to make a deal with you, Delphine of the same court," he said, voice ringing out across the open tower. "You let me show you what it is to be Starlight Fae, and if the midsummer festival comes, and you wish to return to Alderia, I will take you."

He pressed our lips together then, so briefly that it wasn't really a kiss. It was just enough to seal the deal between us not just with magic, but with blood.

The moment I tasted the hot iron of it, I felt every vein in my body ignite.

I knew, from the spark in his eyes, that he did, too. The magic of the deal sealed his wound so that, unlike the one that bled between my breasts, his lip wasn't so much as scarred.

I half expected him to take me right there and then. The heat between us burned as bright as the stars outside. I didn't know if it was the magic of the deal sealing the bond between us, or if it was my fae instincts reacting to the touch of another fae, but it didn't matter.

Nothing else mattered.

That's why I didn't fight him when he started to move us together, eyes remaining locked with mine as we swept together toward a new doorway.

I wouldn't be able to refuse him. I couldn't. But instead of his bed, he'd taken me to the great hall.

And we were hardly alone.

Hundreds of eyes turned to look up at us. We'd emerged from a door behind a long table stretching so that the chairs, placed only along one side, faced a massive hall lined with more tables.

The faces looking back at us were expectant, sure, but I couldn't quite place what that expectation was.

"What are they looking at?" I hissed, trying—unsuccessfully—to wrench my arm free of where Seren still held it tight.

"You, of course," he said, before straightening up and jutting out his chin toward the gathered fae. His voice raised loud enough to carry to the very backs of the room and out through the open arches into the night.

"As promised, I introduce to you the lost member of our court. Delphine," he announced before turning to look into my eyes again, his next words spoken just for me. "Welcome home."

14
DELPHINE

This time, the words didn't sour in the pit of my stomach the way they did the first time Seren had tried to use them on me, and I knew why. This time, when he said it, I wasn't trapped in Elysia anymore. This time, I had a way home.

Really home, and it made all the difference.

I'd dined at two different courts since I'd been dragged into the faerie realms, but nothing could have prepared me for the Starlight Court. The space itself reminded me of a mix of Nyx and Caldamir's great halls. The long table at the head was like that of the Woodland Court, while the vaulted stone ceilings were more reminiscent of the Mountain Court.

What set this place aside was not the court itself, however. It was the fae.

Seren's announcement hadn't so much as turned into an echo when a cheer rose up to drown it out. The faces turned toward me showed no malice, no fear, no hatred, not even the sense of morbid curiosity that I'd found all too common in humans and fae alike.

When the fae of this court looked up at me, they didn't see a creature to be gawked at, or a means to mend their precious magic. When the fae of this court looked up at me, all they saw was fae.

One of their own.

If it weren't for the soft press of the king's hand on my lower back, I might never have been able to force my feet from where they were planted on the ground.

Seven seats lined one end of the head table facing the rest of the fae. Two of them were empty, and it was these two that Seren guided us over to.

Food and wine appeared magically before us the moment we sat down. I didn't reach for the wine at first, not until Seren saw me hesitating and waved his hand at the cup in front of me. A small, almost intangible silver light glowed like a whip from the end of his fingers. It stretched out to curl around the base of the glass, lifting it up and dragging it weightlessly through the air to hover directly at mouth level. My mouth watered at the scent, both sweet and bitter at the same time.

Faerie wine. I'd had a taste of it before, that last fateful night at Caldamir's court, and I knew how strong it could be. I wasn't sure I wanted to indulge tonight. I wanted my wits about me. The fae of this court, though they'd quickly fallen into conversation dimmed only by the clinking of glasses, could still prove to be a danger to me despite their earlier enthusiasm.

When I only glanced at Seren and didn't take it, he moved the glass impatiently closer until it actually brushed against my lips. I could practically *taste* the wine now.

"What are you so afraid of?" he asked, brow arching. "Think if you drink it, you'll be stuck in faerie?"

He lifted his own glass up to his mouth, using his hand instead of bothering with magic. He tipped the glass back to take the smallest of sips, washing away the last smear of blood blooming across his lips.

Heat flooded through me again, despite the ice that had frozen me earlier at the sight of our sudden audience. I'd already drunk fae wine, so if I was damned to stay in faerie forever because of it, another sip wouldn't be my undoing.

And I was going to need more than a single sip to keep my gaze from lingering too long on the fae who was now pulling his throne-like seat altogether too close to mine.

"That seat you're in now is usually reserved for the head of the seventh line, but the last of that line hasn't been seen since before the war," Seren explained, lips so close to mine that I could feel his breath rustle my hair. "Normally it remains empty, but I think tonight, we can make an exception."

I finally snatched the wine glass from where it hovered before me and tipped it back, allowing myself a much larger mouthful than Seren. It had a sharper taste than the wine of the Mountain Court, but it had much the same effect, immediately giving me enough liquid courage not to lean away from Seren.

"Head of the seventh line?" I asked. It wasn't the first time he'd mentioned something like it since I got here.

He nodded his head toward first the seats on our right, and then turned slightly to nod toward the seats stretching out on the other side. "We're the keepers of the greatest magic of Elysia, magic strong enough to break the fae who wields it. It allows us to protect the fae of our realm while still keeping the old magic, the magic that the other realms long since let be watered down, alive and flowing here."

I spotted Elvie sitting at the table directly in front of us as Seren spoke, with her brother and grandmother at her side. The two twins were both staring up at me, but Alder was sure to look away the moment our eyes locked. He was the first one to blush, the action meriting him a swift pinch from his grandmother without her so much as needing to follow his gaze to know what he'd been caught staring at.

Itris was, quite possibly, the only fae I could see who didn't look happy at the news of my joining the court, however temporary that might be. I thought it strange, especially given the fact that she might be one of the only fae here who actually knew how temporary that *could* be. Seren didn't strike me as the type to go around announcing that I planned on leaving as soon as I was allowed, which was, according to my latest count of days, just a little more than two months off.

Two months. I just had to make it two more months.

"You have nothing to say to that? I thought if nothing else, the magic would interest you."

"Magic, yes. The monarchy? Not so much," I answered, keeping my gaze forward at the small drama unfolding in front of me as I took another sip of my courage-inducing wine. "It sounds to me like you're telling me in a very roundabout way that you and the other kings of Elysia are keeping all the strongest magic for yourselves."

At the table in front of us, Elvie tried to mimic Seren's trick with the glass from earlier, but she ended up with a face full of red wine splashed across the front of her silvery gown. The color matched the flush of her cheeks until Itris, tutting, waved her own hand and the wine flowed like water onto the ground and dissipated in individual droplets scattered through the rivulets of the stones.

"You're lucky I'm in a generous mood, because if I ever hear you accuse me of something like that again, I won't be so forgiving."

I tore my eyes away from the table in surprise, but before I had the chance to read the expression on Seren's face, it was twisting into a smile at something in front of us.

Elvie had appeared before me, beaming. Her cheeks had retained their earlier flush, though now they were red from the wine and her eyes glassy.

"My grandmother wants to see you, uncle," she said, cocking her head back to motion at the scowling woman still seated at the table, now with one empty seat beside her. "I wouldn't keep her waiting. You know how she can be."

Seren let out a low growl. "Yes," he said, and I wondered if he was thinking about how she'd dragged him out of the traveling waterfall during my first visit to the tower when he agreed. "Yes, I do."

As soon as Seren had stood to attend to his sister, Elvie leaned across the table and dropped her voice so only I could hear her whisper.

"He likes you. Everyone can see it."

"Alder?"

I tried to crane my neck around her bent figure to catch sight of her twin brother, still surely blushing somewhere at the table where she'd left him, but Elvie was already shaking her head.

"No, not my brother. My uncle. Seren."

I nearly choked on my next sip of wine. "What? No."

It wasn't an entirely honest reaction. I'd felt the heat, the draw between the two of us.

Though, apparently, I wasn't the only one who'd felt it. If Elvie had seen it, then that meant others had, too. That thought made me want to choke a second time.

"Good thing too," Elvie continued. "I heard he didn't even like his wife that much."

I actually did choke then.

"His *wife?*" I asked, a tight hand gripping my heart as I gasped for the air that had nearly been stolen from me. I'd managed to swallow the wine I choked on, rather than ending up with a far less forgiving stain to add to the small pinpricks of blood dotting the bandages across my sternum from the unhealed fiend blade, but I wasn't sure I'd ever get back my breath. Not now.

"Yes," Elvie said, nodding obliviously to my panic, "before the war."

"Before ..."

It was Elvie's turn to swing her head round to look for the shape of her uncle in the crowd of fae. "She died in it, along with his whole family."

"The whole ..."

"The whole line was wiped out," Elvie said, a somberness seeping into her tone. "Everyone except for me, Alder, and my grandmother. Not that anyone acknowledges it. I've never gotten it ... just because time has stopped here, doesn't mean the past doesn't matter. I don't think the court ever truly let itself grieve. They like to just pretend that because time doesn't pass, that nothing ever has to change."

She stopped and shook her head, and I knew from my own swimming vision exactly why she felt the need to clear it. "But maybe I'm just too young to understand."

I hardly could agree with her, given the fact that her "too young" was already nearly a century older than I was.

Her momentary dark mood didn't last, however. We both saw the shift in the table as Seren got back up from his sister, their whispered conversation making the two of us exchange a tentative look between us.

"It's good for us to have you here, and I don't just mean for Seren," Elvie said. "We all needed this, we needed you." She beamed again, but this time, there was the tiniest bit of sadness behind her eyes. "I hope you choose to stay, Delphine. I'm not sure what I'd do if we lost another fae."

As quickly as that sadness appeared, however, it was blinked away into something wicked. "Even if she is a dirty half-human."

Elvie left me gawking as she bound away. *That little …*

"My niece bothering you?" Seren asked, settling back into his throne at my side. There was no pretending it was anything else. All the rest of the Starlight Fae sat on benches, while only the seven—or six—at the head sat at such ornately carved chairs. I wasn't so wine drunk that I considered myself one of them. Yet.

I shook my head. "No," I said, surprising myself with the truth in my words. "She's just being friendly."

Whoever would have thought … a friendly fae. I'd been *friendly* with fae, far *too* friendly with some, but never had I actually so much as imagined I'd have a real friend in one.

Maybe it wouldn't be so bad, learning what it was to be a Starlight Fae. It was a part of me, as much as I'd been trying to deny it. Seren had been right. My fae senses were calling to me, demanding to no longer be ignored.

Besides, it was a part of the deal. I would learn what it was to be a part of me, and in return, Seren would take me home—if I chose it. He'd been particular in his wording. There was no vague promise to take me away from this place. No indiscriminate date. I appreciated the fact that he wasn't trying to trick me, not in any way I could see yet. It was *his* job to show me what it was to be fae.

I didn't have to agree. I just had to let him try.

If ever there was a fair faerie deal, this one was the closest thing to it.

For the first time since crossing into faerie, I wondered if I might actually be safe—not just in the physical, someone-is-always-out-to-get-me way, but in a deeper sense. I could feel it echoing in my bones.

It seemed, however strong that feeling may have been, that I wouldn't be allowed to feel that way for long.

Not even, I discovered, through the end of dinner.

The minutes sitting beside Seren stretched on into hours. More courses were brought out. Musicians flitted between the outer corners of the room. Wine flowed. The cold white walls warmed with the heat of bodies and slurring conversation.

I was very close to losing myself in it, to falling into the same ease as the rest of the fae around me, when something the very opposite of *ease* stirred. It started as a ripple, the slightest disturbance somewhere outside the open archways of the great hall. If I'd had even one more sip of wine, I probably wouldn't have noticed, but as it was, I'd been careful to toe that line just beneath actually getting drunk.

None of the other fae seemed to have managed that, including Seren at my side, whose chair had slowly inched ever closer until it wasn't just the pale colored marble touching beneath the table. His knee had spent the better part of the last hour brushing against mine, and as much as my logical senses kept reminding me over and over of how I should be disgusted at his touch, I couldn't get myself to listen.

I wasn't able to pull myself away, however much I was convinced I wasn't actually drunk, until that unease stirred again. The second time it happened, it was more than a ripple I felt. Something sparked to life outside in the darkness, something too low to the ground to be a star, even a falling one.

I half rose from my seat to get a better look, only for Seren to immediately lean toward me to fill the gap. His hands roamed a little low on my back when he reached for me, the scent of wine dripping from his loosened tongue.

"Where do you think you're going? The night has barely begun."

I kept my eyes trained forward, my brow knitting further together as I searched for that momentary *whatever* I'd spotted in the darkness.

I was just about to give up and sit back down when I felt it again. This time, it wasn't just a ripple.

It was a shudder—and it was enough to make more fae start to get up from their seats, their heads snapping toward the same patch of darkness where I still stared.

I felt Seren's hand stiffen on my back the moment before he suddenly lunged to his feet.

"Prepare yourselves!" Seren's voice called out. He kicked the heavy throne out from behind me as if it was nothing, and then wove his hand in front of me in order to draw me back, half behind him.

He waved his arm, and I felt a cold soberness pass over me. The other fae around us did the same, and the mirth of the hall died as quickly as it had begun.

The magic washed through my veins, clearing my head and sharpening my movements.

I didn't have time to ask what he was doing before I felt the fae all around me brace themselves. A moment later, with the third and final ripple that was all too much like the collision of realms I'd lived through once, I found another great hall dinner interrupted by the arrival of some all-too-unwelcome visitors.

A tear opened before us, just outside the doors to the great hall, lingering in that narrow space between the ground and sky. It was only visible for a moment, its jagged edges fading just as quickly as five figures appeared in its place.

The moment their feet stepped foot on Elysian soil, four out of five of the dark figures rushed forward, out of the darkness and into the light.

The first was a fae with hair black as night and honeyed skin. The second, with ebony skin and gold rings in his hair and stacked on every finger to match the gold in his eyes. The third so beautiful with his auburn locks and full lips, looked as if he floated rather than ran across the gemstone corridor.

The fourth, of course, was a fae whose features were washed out by the blind fury stretching across his features.

The last figure remained behind, silhouetted in hard angles against the darkness, but there was no mistaking who he was … *what* he was.

Waylan had come back. And this time, he'd not come alone.

The demon had broken his promise.

He'd brought the princes of Avarath with him.

They came prepared for a fight, eyes and swords flashing, but they seemed to have forgotten one very important thing, or perhaps they hadn't considered it in the first place. Swords, however well wielded, were nothing compared to magic.

The braced Starlight Fae didn't allow the princes to take so much as three steps inside before their weapons were torn from their hands. Caldamir was the last to let go, his wrist straightening at an awkward angle until he was finally forced to part with his sword as it was pulled away by long lines of blue light.

The moment they were unarmed, another ripple broke through the air and guards swarmed from the dark at their backs. They were the first guards I'd seen yet in Elysia, summoned by the motion of his outstretched hands, using Seren's portal magic.

It happened so quickly that by the time the four princes were captured, my own silver skirts were still settling around my ankles from when Seren had pushed me behind him. They struggled against their captors, but more blue lights shot out and wrapped like cuffs around their wrists and ankles.

Caldamir's face twisted in a snarl as he realized they were beaten before they'd really even begun.

"Unhand us! We are princes of Avarath, and we will *not* be treated this way."

Seren pushed forward through the crowd, and I noted how even the Starlight Fae in the hall shrank back, leaving a space for him to pass through, unhindered. Standing there, apart from us all, he practically shone with that same light of the stars not so far up above. He drew himself up, practically growing before my very eyes.

There was no fear in him.

No intimidation.

Only contempt, and it leached into each syllable of the words of his reply.

"Princes? How cute. In this court we have kings."

15
DELPHINE

RESTRAINTS LOOKED GOOD ON THEM.

Nyx.

Tethys.

Armene.

And, of course, Caldamir.

The four princes of Avarath stood before me, before the whole of the Starlight Court they had once sworn was long gone.

I wished with all my might that I was drunk, that I was so intoxicated that this was some kind of terrible hallucination instead of reality.

Not because I was afraid, not even because I hated them, but because I didn't.

Because they'd made both my deepest fear and greatest desire come true in an instant.

I didn't hate all the princes, but I did still hate one.

Anger was all I felt when I looked at Caldamir, so much of it that one glance at him forced my gaze to skitter away, as if I was *unable* to truly look at him. I didn't want to see there what

I'd seen before. I didn't want to see the rage that outmatched even mine, or worse—the disappointment that I'd survived.

But looking at the others, at Nyx, Armene, and Tethys, that came with its own set of complications. It wasn't rage or disappointment that marred their faces in my memory.

I was ashamed to admit that the tiniest ache of longing sprung up within me when I looked over their faces. Though longing for what ... to punch them in each of their stunned faces, or to reach out and plant a kiss on their lips, what was what I wasn't entirely sure of.

That, at least, I could blame on the wine, however little of it remained swirling in me after Seren had wiped its effects away.

The rest of the kings of Elysia stepped forward as more guards swarmed forward to take a more secure grip on the princes. Nyx fidgeted nervously, his head twisting back as if to keep a close eye on the condition of his nails as his hands were bound with more glowing ropes of magic. Armene's head hung, eyes focused on the floor in front of him, as if he was ashamed of having been beaten. Tethys stood, hip cocked and tongue visible where it was pressed into his cheek from between his parted lips. Annoyance flashed across his face as his shoulders were jerked back a bit too aggressively for his liking, but he said nothing. To him, this whole situation looked like nothing more than a minor inconvenience.

When the soldiers came to Caldamir, he was not so quick to accept another round of ropes wrapped around his wrists. He was prepared for them. The moment the next soldier approached him, the Mountain Prince lashed out, head flying forward to bash the head of his attacker. Only, like before, Caldamir had once again underestimated what it was to be a faerie court that still had magic.

His head didn't collide with the solder, it collided with a thin film of light shielding him. So, while he cried out in pain and lost his footing for a moment, the soldier approaching him didn't so much as flinch. He took advantage of the prince's unsteady footing and wrapped the next cord of binding light around his arms—twice, for good measure.

Caldamir pulled against it, fought it, but it was no use.

By the time he'd managed to straighten back up, it was clear there was no way to be free. Not without magic. The brute force the Mountain Court had learned to rely on would not be enough here. Then, and only then, was when I was able to look back at his face.

I saw the moment that Caldamir realized he was well and truly beaten, saw the last of the struggle go out of him, and that, at least, was undeniably satisfying. His broad shoulders slumped despite himself, and no matter how he tried to jut his chin out and hold his head high, he couldn't hide the way the muscle twitched in his clenched jaw.

It was a good look on him, too.

It wasn't until the guards started marching the princes out of the hall that I felt the first seed of worry—and even then, it was only because of the flash of the emblem I saw stitched into the silver fabric of their uniforms. A flame inside a circle. I'd see it too many times before.

They were whisked through one doorway by these guards in their accursed uniforms while Seren and the other kings started marching toward another, this one placed on the opposite side of the hall. Any thoughts of finishing dinner had been forgotten. Abandoned plates and jugs of wine sat glittering dully under the lights. The polite conversation had turned to anxious chatter and scattering feet, the fae moving in waves toward the many arching exits.

For one split second, I stood between the princes and the

kings, my head whipping from one side to the other as I tried to decide which way to go. I caught Tethys' eye for a moment, and then the slight, callous smile that pulled up the corner of his mouth. Beside him, Armene nudged him back into line, and they were swept away with the rest of the guards.

I had no choice now. I didn't want to be left alone with the soldiers bearing the emblem of the last fae who tried to murder me ... well, the last fae before the princes tried the same thing. At least the princes had the decency to warn me ahead of time, so I could prepare. I'd prefer that over being snatched in the dark in the midst of a hoard of fiends.

I had to run to catch up with the noble figures, tripping over my skirts more than once to make sure I made it through the doorway alongside the last of them. I'd just begun to get used to the palace's corridors, and I knew that the same archway they took now might not take me to the same place if I reached it a moment too late.

Even then, I had to shoulder myself through their whispering, towering forms to reach the one at their head. I was out of breath by the time I reached Seren's side.

"What'll happen to them?"

He didn't so much as turn his head to look at me. His face was pointed staunchly forward, eyes narrowed and his own jaw set. His mind was focused on something far before us, something only he could see. I hated to interrupt him, but I was also focused on something.

"But the guards. Their emblem." I mimed a circle patch across my left breast, and at least I was glad to see, drew the slightest, shortest flicker of his gaze. "I've seen it before. I don't trust them."

"Well, you can trust them here. You have nothing to worry

about from our guards. The princes, on the other hand, would be wise not to underestimate them."

"But, Seren, surely—"

Seren came to a sudden stop, eyes closing. "I told you, they'll be dealt with."

There was no harshness in his voice, but there was no mistaking the finality. When his eyes fluttered open again, Seren turned to seek out another king behind us in the entourage that had followed him in.

"Tarrak, will you escort Delphine back to her rooms?"

The sound of his name made the muscles in my back seize up.

Tarrak? The same fae that everyone had been warning me about ever since I got here?

The Seer hurried up to my side the moment Seren beckoned to him. He might be a king too of this realm, but it was clearly apparent who the other rulers looked to in times of crisis. And right now, what with princes from a faerie realm that was not supposed to be able to travel to this one out for the blood of one of their court, was a fairly big crisis. Outside of myself entirely, it would be a crisis.

These were the fae that were desperate to undo the magic the Starlight Court had died for so long ago. These were the fae willing to make all the loss, the death, the missing fae that haunted the empty halls of this court be for nothing.

"I can't concentrate if I'm worried about your safety. We have to decide what to do next."

It was an invitation not extended to me.

The rest of the kings swept forward, leaving me biting the inside of my cheek in annoyance as Tarrack shuffled ever too close beside me. I felt, rather than saw, the way he leaned in to get a whiff of my scent. I decided not to ask him about it, because I was sure of one thing, and that was that I didn't want to know why.

The halls were strangely empty once the kings had left us behind. It was only then that I looked for Waylan, but he was long gone. I cursed myself for letting myself lose sight of him in the scuffle that ensued with the Prince's attack.

Damn.

If I hadn't seen him there, in the shadows, I would have thought the princes found another way here, somehow. Part of me still couldn't, still *wouldn't* believe it. I'd just seen him, just been promised—though not in so many words—that Waylan wouldn't be the one to do this.

He was supposed to be my friend, or if not my friend, then at least not my enemy. I thought that was understood.

I guess I thought wrong.

It was my turn for my shoulders to slump. When they did, Tarrack pulled me a little closer to him.

I expected Tarrack to take advantage of my guard dropping to try to chat my ear off or lure me off to the Seer's chambers and reveal a secret poking and prodding lab he had hidden away there after all, but instead, he just let out a small, short sigh.

"So, off to the prison, then?"

"What?"

My response came out too short, no time to hide the shock in its tone.

Tarrack had fixed me with a blank, nearly disinterested look. "Yes," he said, "I was assuming you didn't want to go to your rooms and hide. You'd rather see where the guard is taking your princes."

"They're not *my* princes."

"So, you don't want to see them?"

I gritted my teeth. "Just take me."

For all the warnings I'd been given about Tarrack, he did exactly what he promised.

He did it in what I believed was a far more roundabout way than necessary that allowed him plenty of time to ask prying questions about how it was to grow up in the human realm, but we did, eventually, end up walking through a doorway that lead into what could only be described as the Starlight palace's equivalent of a dungeon.

It was the only place where gems didn't line the walls and pattern the floors. I hadn't realized the energy that they carried with them, not until it was missing. Like the starless Seer's chambers, it was a kind of nakedness, the feeling of something missing that I couldn't quite put my finger on.

The hallway leading down toward several cell blocks wasn't exactly drab, but without the stones and that inner light they carried in them, it felt like it was.

It had taken us long enough to follow the princes to their prisons that they had long since been separated and the guards that accompanied them scattered across the front of their enclosures. I didn't think that calling them cells was quite right, not when they were hardly prison boxes separated from the hall with thick iron bars. Thin cut crystal was set into the walls in lieu of bars. Inside the frosted glass, the rooms were bare enough. A bed, a desk, a glowing orb of light. A small area was blocked off in the back of each cell, and I guessed that was where the chamber pots were.

I briefly wondered if the princes had been treated to the same magic pots that removed the waste before it even touched the bottom of the pots, or if they had to deal with ordinary ones. *Ordinary.* It wasn't too long ago that I faulted Elvie for taking the magic of the court for granted, but somehow, I'd already fallen into that same trap. My nose wrinkled at the thought of having to go back to using the dirty pots.

It was the only place in the palace where, I noticed, there was nothing shiny enough for someone to use as a scrying mirror. Much of the Starlight Magic relied on these sorts of objects and portals. Even the water in the princes' cells was provided in a small trickle carving its way along one of the walls, too narrow to catch even a glitter of light's reflection. There was an indignity to it, but given the travelling I'd seen these fae do using puddles of water, I understood.

It was a strange sensation, seeing the princes locked away. Seeing them guarded changed the way they stood, the way they acted, the very way they looked. It did something strange to each one of their essences, pulled out something deep and personal out of each of them.

Armene knelt as if in prayer, ignoring everything around him.

Tethys stood, pacing, his face a plain mask without emotion, as if he remained completely indifferent to the current state of his imprisonment.

Nyx had taken to sitting on the ground, his legs spread out in front of him, and his hands clawing at the hard ground. He was mesmerized by something, not lost in thought staring at the floor the way Armene was.

And then there was Caldamir.

My footsteps stopped short the moment I saw him.

He sat, back pressed against the wall and one leg outstretched in front of him. A large bruise had begun to blossom across the front of his forehead, and one of his eyes had burst a blood vessel from his failed attack, marking the white of his eye a scarlet red. He didn't look at me. Tarrack had guided me along the shadows of the opposite wall so that, so far, no one had noticed our presence, not even the guards.

I kept a wary eye on the fae wearing those cryptic symbols that had been following me ever since Alderia. Seren might say I had nothing to worry about, but he'd also said I was safe here … and how long had it taken for Caldamir to come for me?

While the guards stood, clustered and whispering together, Caldamir just sat, staring forward. Whatever thoughts turned inside his head he kept hidden from me or any of the guards who might still be watching him. The only sign of movement from him was the slow, methodical drop of pebbles from his hand. The steady sound was like a timer keeping track of the seconds that never actually passed here.

I started searching out where Tarrack had wandered off to, ready to leave this haunting image of the princes in their prisons behind when apparently, I was finally spotted.

"Delphine …"

Caldamir's voice sounded too quiet. Too soft.

It immediately infuriated me.

"No," I hissed as I turned on my heel to face him again. "I have nothing to say to you."

He cocked his head to the side with a sigh, like he'd expected this, like he'd prepared himself for having to deal with a petulant child who wouldn't want to play.

"Delph, do you have any idea what you've done? Do you have any idea what you've destroyed?"

Somehow, of all the things I expected him to say, that I imagined he might say, *this* was not it. It *should* have been what I expected. I should have known this was exactly what he thought. He hadn't exactly tried to hide those thoughts from his face when I left.

"I'm glad I did," I hissed at him. "I'd do it again. I'd do it a thousand times."

It was as if he didn't register a word of what I said.

"You have to get me out of here. Do you have any idea what will happen if it's found out that all *four* princes of the realm are gone?"

No, it was more than him not paying attention. He was completely delusional.

It made me feel slightly better when I replied, lips curling back, "Frankly, Caldamir, you should have thought of that before you tried to murder me."

"It was a necessary sacrifice."

"You still think so?" I spat back at him.

His face didn't betray any hint of emotion when he responded, without a single moment of hesitation, "I stand by what I chose."

A sickening silence stretched between us, a silence that would have continued to grow until one of us chose to break the loathsome connection of our gaze, if we weren't—rather gratefully—interrupted.

"I'm surprised to find you here, though, I suppose I shouldn't be."

Seren and the remaining four kings had arrived to check on their captives. While the rest of them fanned out, their voices dropping low and serious as they moved to survey their prisoners, he came to stand beside me.

"And why is that?" I asked, finally tearing myself away from the cut crystal. My breath still remained in an angry haze where my lips had nearly pressed to the barrier.

"Because you're never doing what I expect you to, let alone what you're supposed to do." "Speaking of which … "

He finally spotted what he was looking for in the crowd.

"Tarrack, I thought I told you to bring her to her rooms?"

"She wanted to come here," was all Tarrack said in response. He made no apology, and though Seren's face twisted slightly in annoyance, he didn't demand one. He couldn't, I suppose, not at least from another king.

"Well then, I'll ask another … "

Seren hadn't so much as finished what he was saying when I saw Tarrack's face fall. I should have been grateful for the excuse to have another fae lead me back, given all I'd been warned of Tarrack—and despite the number of times those same fae that had warned me had then tried to assure me he meant no harm.

Instead, I found myself blurting out something that surprised even me.

"No," I said, hastily. "Tarrack is fine. He was just telling me it was time to leave."

He had, of course, been completely ignoring me ever since we arrived, but that didn't matter. No one else had been paying us enough attention with the four fae princes here to distract them, or if they did, none of them dared disagree.

I wondered if I was going to grow to regret this decision, but the last thing I was going to do was look weak in front of Calda—

Seren.

The last thing I was going to do was look weak in front of *Seren.*

I didn't care what the Mountain Prince thought of me. Not in the slightest.

Looking at his face didn't remind me of the time when I'd seen something other than hatred there. It didn't make me think of the way he was the first fae to draw out my nature, the first to pull me to him with an irresistible lure. It certainly didn't bring back the memory of his hot breath on my skin, lips so close to mine I could still remember the way the air tasted between us.

Not one bit.

Prince Caldamir was nothing to me. He never had been. He never would be.

I was certain of that. Or, at the very least, certain that I *should* be certain of that.

Tarrack was soon back at my side, arm looped through mine as he started to nudge us back toward the exit together. Before we could leave, however, Seren caught me by my other arm, gently this time. He ducked his head to whisper in my ear, his voice kept low enough for no one else to hear.

"Are you alright?"

The question made a lump rise in the back of my throat, and though I managed to keep my face composed, I allowed myself one small shake of my head.

"No," I admitted, "but I will be."

"The real reason I was surprised to see you here is because I didn't expect you to want to see them. I thought, after all they did, that you'd hate them."

I cast one, small look over my shoulder at Caldamir. He was watching the two of us too intently, trying to read what was passing between us. It only made me pull my shoulders back further, and I made sure to answer while Caldamir could read my lips.

"I do hate them."

I waited until I saw something like hurt flicker across the Mountain Prince's face before I turned away. I was finished with him. I needed him to know that.

And that was what I told Seren, too.

Seren nodded, but he didn't look entirely convinced. "I can only protect you from physical harm. I can't protect you from anything else. If you keep coming back here, I can't promise you they won't find other ways to get to you."

"Then I won't let them," I said. "I won't be back. If they ask, be sure to tell them that, would you?"

I looked forward then, tightening my grip on Tarrack's arm on my other side. "I know who the real enemy is here."

16
DELPHINE

THIS TIME, TARRACK'S FOOTSTEPS CARRIED US WITH A SENSE OF purpose that wasn't there before. He'd fallen into a strange silence—strange only for him, because it wasn't silent at all, it was just reduced to what anyone else would consider an appropriate level of casual conversation.

Even that I was barely able to listen to. My mind was elsewhere, trapped in that cell with the prince and the gall that he'd had to say the things to me that he did.

I'd wonder where he got the audacity ... but I already knew. It had something to do with the absolute entitlement of his kind coupled with the royal blood he'd been so unfortunate to be born with.

Tarrack and my footsteps shuddered to a halt so quickly that I thought we must have taken some kind of shortcut back to my tower room. That, however, was quickly proven wrong when I looked up and was finally jarred from the thoughts that had been consuming me—and apparently blinding me too, because there was no other way to explain how I'd missed the figure now barring our path.

It was Itris, her feet planted wide, hands on hips, and her chest puffed up so full with breath that her intimidating figure nearly appeared to double in size. Seren's sister held one hand out in front of her, her pointed finger as powerful as a wielded sword.

"You."

She fixed me with a glare that made me wish that Tarrack *had* taken me to his chambers to probe and cut me open when I first thought he would, if only to save me from this terrifying other fae's wrath.

"This is your doing. I warned Seren, but he wouldn't listen," she said, voice practically quivering with the effort it was taking to keep herself in check. "We had peace here before you."

"Everything is fine, Itris," Tarrack said, surprising both Itris and me when he stepped forward slightly in my defense. I didn't miss the slight quaking in his hand as he tried to stand tall, but he was nothing compared to Itris' imposing figure. "We kings have everything in hand."

"You kings? Typical." She let out a sound that could shake mountains. "Is that what you're calling it now? Fine?"

"The princes have been apprehended," Tarrack said, as if any of us needed reminding. We'd all been there, we'd all seen it firsthand. "They won't cause any further trouble."

"How can you be so sure?" Itris asked, nostrils flaring in anger. "Do you even know what they came for? Further still, do you know *how* they got here in the first place?"

That was the first time that it struck me—had no one else seen the fifth figure? Had Waylan really gotten away unnoticed?

A horrible ache settled in my stomach. If the demon was still free, then Itris had every right to be as concerned as she was. With Waylan's magic free, and with his newfound delight in pleasing the princes he'd claimed to have no desire to before, we were all in danger.

Misreading the sudden shake in my own hands, Tarrack managed to make his still long enough to tighten them around mine as he defended me once more. "They came for Delphine, I think that much is certain. And however they got here, well, Seren is sure to find out soon."

"Well, if he doesn't, I hope he's ready to use the rest of the court's arsenal."

Arsenal. The word made me shudder a second time. I'd only seen small glimpses of the Starlight Fae's powers, and already I wasn't sure I wanted to know what kind of magic a court of fae kings used like weapons.

"You know Seren will do everything correctly," Tarrack answered, without really answering. "It may have been some time since the court was in session, but I promise you, we judges have not forgotten how to rule these realms."

Though Tarrack's words did little to cull the rage still causing Itris to suck vigorously at the inside of her cheeks, it seemed she still knew enough of where she stood to guess she'd get no further with either of us tonight. Or really, with Tarrack, since I had no doubt that if I'd been caught here alone, this interrogation would have only just begun.

"I have my eye on you, girl," she hissed at me. "I won't let this court crumble for one half-fae. Something more is going on here, and I'm going to find out what it is before it's too late."

"What do you think she meant by that?" I asked once I was sure from the faded footsteps that Itris was out of earshot.

"Think nothing of it," Tarrack said, patting my hand to try to reassure me. "Itris has always had a temper. She resists change more than the rest of us, and that's saying something in a court that literally never changes."

His still shaking hand did little for the stutter of my heart, however.

I knew that Itris had it out for me from the beginning, but this was something more. She'd at least been willing to surrender to her brother's desire to welcome me to the court before, but I had my doubts she would continue to do that now.

Worse, however, was that I didn't blame her. She was right. My coming here *had* ruined everything. It had disturbed a peace that had reigned here for god-knows how many human years, a century here, at least. It was a hard-fought peace, too, from what I'd heard, and my heart ached to think that I'd brought it to an end.

Whoever would have thought that my heart would come to ache for the fate of a faerie realm?

Tarrack and I returned to our journey through the corridors, if at a slightly faster pace this time. I wasn't the only one who kept checking over my shoulder to make sure we weren't about to be accosted by someone more terrifying than Itris—if that was even possible. I wondered who Tarrack was looking for, but I knew who *I* was. His was fae. Mine was demonic.

Itris' confrontation had served some purpose aside from rattling me, at least. I knew that the court here didn't know how the princes had gotten out of Avarath yet.

I could tell them myself, I *should* tell them, but I found myself hesitating.

Waylan had visited me before and I'd not mentioned it to anyone. I doubted I could bring up the fact that I knew how the princes had gotten here now without admitting to that little detail, too, and I didn't like to think what Itris would say to me then.

Despite our shared concern, we managed to make it back to

my tower room without so much as a shadow—fae or otherwise —crossing our path.

We both did nothing to mask the collective sigh of relief we shared.

"I've been meaning to ask, back there, when you were talking to Itris, what did you mean by the judges?"

It wasn't the first time I'd heard the term used. Ayre had used it, once, but I'd been a little preoccupied with what it was that had gotten her sentenced than who it was that had actually done the sentencing.

"Oh, has no one told you? We're not only kings here, in our realm. We're the judges of all fae. Or, we were, once. It's been a long time since we've been called to order."

I gritted my teeth. "No one's told me much of anything before tonight," I admitted. "Seren was supposed to start now that I've struck the deal, but the princes sort of interrupted."

"A deal? How interesting?" Not for the first time, the sparkle in Tarrack's eyes was a little disturbing. I knew he was itching to know every detail of what this new deal entailed, but he surprised me once again when—rather than demanding to know more—he instead reached into a deep pocket of his robe and produced something for me instead.

It was a map.

"I've been trying to deliver this to you all week," he said, "but every time I came to your rooms, you were either gone or Alder seemed to be hanging about, needing assistance for one thing or another. Never thought that boy was interested in scrying before, and honestly after the week I've had with him, I sincerely hope he's lost whatever interest that was. He's absolutely not cut out for it, but I don't have the heart to tell him."

His words trailed off for a second, ending in a strangled

syllable before he said, suddenly, "Oh no, have I done something wrong?"

I wasn't aware of the tears welling in the corners of my eyes until then.

I blinked them away, dismissing them with a wave of my hand. "No, no, I'm just tired," I lied, too embarrassed to admit how much the gesture meant to me. Tarrack looked a little confused, but he didn't pry more as he handed over the rolled-up bundle of scrolls. At first glance they were a little difficult to read, but that was until I realized it was because the map wasn't just parchment—it was enchanted. The passages that seemed to shift before my eyes *were* shifting, their labels moving as the doors and stairwells changed to point toward new rooms and hallways every minute.

It was a wonder I ever found Seren and his tower without it. It would be even easier to get lost in this palace than I thought, and easier still to never be able to find your way back.

I looked up to Tarrack with so much gratitude he shifted a little awkwardly where he stood.

"As much as I'd like to continue our chat, and trust me, I'd like that *very* much, I'd better be going. Itris may be a bully, but she brought up some good points. Seren may be willing to listen to me where he won't listen to her."

A new small ache pulled at my insides at his words, and I found it hard not to look at the fae with pity.

I somehow doubted that Seren would be willing to give Tarrack consideration he wouldn't even offer his sister, but I had a feeling the Seer already knew that from the way he took a moment to steel up his nerves again. It was brave of him, really. I would have given up long ago.

He was a better fae than I could ever hope to be.

17
DELPHINE

AYRE WAITED FOR ME IN THE TOWER ROOM, AND FOR ONCE, I WAS glad to see the murderous fae. I was far too exhausted to properly undo the laces of this latest gown on my own and had just figured I'd spend the night permanently disfiguring the silk by sleeping in it if I'd had to try. Not that I'd be able to get any sleep. Something about the fabric here, I'd still been unable to fall asleep beneath it. I'd taken to curling up with Moon, the Catsuga, who'd thankfully formed the habit of showing up on my windowsill so long as I left it open before going to bed.

I only had to lift my arms and motion to the laces running down the backs of my sleeves and either side of my bodice before Ayre dropped whatever it was she was doing with my water jug to help me start undoing the ties that bound me inside my soft silver prison.

Her fingers moved awkwardly tonight, struggling enough with the laces that I wondered if she'd been indulging in the faerie wine too before our newest guests decided to join us. Maybe she hadn't been so lucky to be touched with the same anti-hangover spell that I had been. I knew I was tired enough with it.

Soon, at least, I was shrugging off the sleeves and waiting only for Ayre to finish undoing the laces that would allow the rest of the dress to be slipped over the top of my head. I was already half dreaming, my mind firmly imagining how it would feel to finally rest upon the pile of pillows scattered haphazardly across the top of my bed, when I caught her casting a furtive glance toward the door.

"Who was that with you now?"

I yawned so wide that I felt muscles pop in the back of my jaw. "Tarrack, of all people."

She let out a small grunt of disapproval, and I found annoyance rising up in me.

"You know, he's really not so bad."

She made another one of those grunts, and though I felt my brow furrow, I was too tired to argue. It wasn't exactly a secret what the other fae here thought of their Seer king, so I doubted anything I had to say would change centuries of past judgement, however wrong that judgement might be.

And there were probably many, many centuries of that judgement to try to overturn.

Though fae didn't show age the same way that humans did, there was something about Tarrack that told me he was positively ancient. If I had to guess, I'd guess he was one of the oldest fae here, the oldest fae I'd met, yet. I could be wrong, it could just be that he was the most *tired* or perhaps the closest to going insane that I'd met yet.

I could see how Tarrack might get on my nerves if I was stuck with him for as long as the other fae here had been, but there was a strange innocence to him too. He hardly deserved the contempt the others treated him with. I felt guilty for falling into their same assumptions when this whole time he was trying to help, and not just with words. He'd pinpointed exactly what I needed most and done what he could to help me, perhaps more than any of the other fae in Elysia.

The second I was free from my silks, I dropped my chemise and practically threw myself onto the bed.

For a moment, I thought Ayre's eyes flickered away from my naked body with discomfort, but I must have imagined it. She'd seen me in my natural state at least a dozen times now, and never once had she ever so much as seemed to acknowledge it. I was just another body, and one probably not nearly as remarkable as a full fae's body at that.

Despite the ache to be alone and process everything that had occurred tonight, from the deal I'd finally made with Seren to Waylan and the princes showing up here with me in Elysia, there was something comforting about the fae's presence now that she'd gone back to poking and prodding the fire at the foot of my bed.

I rolled over on the mattress, my back turning to Ayre, right in time for the door to creak open—revealing Ayre again, this time, barging in with an armload of fresh linens from the hall.

"Sorry," she grumbled in that reluctant way of hers. "The whole palace is in an uproar. You wouldn't believe how hard it was to get up here—"

She hadn't made it two steps inside before she froze, her unfinished words dying on her lips.

It took me a few bleary, sleepy moments of blinking up at the fae standing slack-jawed in the door before I began to piece everything together.

The anxious worrying about the fire. The unfamiliarity with the laces of my dress. The discomfort at my nudity.

If Ayre was there, in front of me … then who … *who was the person who had just undressed me?*

I'd never felt exhaustion leave my body so quickly. I leapt up to my knees on the bed just as the fake Ayre sprung too. She moved so quickly that I didn't actually see her, not until she was standing directly behind the real Ayre—the door now firmly shut behind her. Her hands reached up to cover the real Ayre's eyes, and a second later, before I could so much as scramble to the edge of my bed or think about drawing a sheet up to protect my modesty, the fae dropped down to the floor, unconscious.

I opened my mouth to scream, but another creature did that for me.

Moon let out an earsplitting yowl and leapt from where he'd appeared—as usual, and not a moment too late—in the window. He flew across the room, claws extended, and latched onto the chest of the false Ayre. The two of them fell in a tumbling mess that allowed me a moment to ignore my first two instincts and do the only thing that might actually help me. I fished the fiend-bladed dagger from beneath the mattress and wielded it out in front of me.

The blade caught the yellow firelight and cast it at the two creatures tumbling on the floor in front of me.

And *creatures* they both were, because no longer was it a double of Ayre wrestling with the Catsuga on the floor—and losing, I might add.

It was a demon.

"Waylan!" The moment his name was out of my lips, the knife sagged in my hand.

The demon shot me a look from between the slash of claws, growling, "Would you be so kind as to call off your demon, or are you going to let your damned pet rip me to shreds?"

A giggle caught in the back of my throat at *his* calling Moon a demon, but I managed to stuff it back. I clapped my hands together and knelt down, urging the Catsuga to release his target.

It took several minutes of coaxing before Moon finally agreed to unlatch himself from the demon, and even then, he only retreated so far as to wind his way around my ankles, his eyes fixed determinedly on his pray—just in case.

The Catsuga's coat was a bit ruffled, but Waylan was by far the worse one for wear. Several long gashes had sprouted across his forearms, to say nothing of the scratches that had nearly taken out his left eye. It was one of these scratches that Waylan took a crisp, white handkerchief from his pocket to dab at.

Between the two of them, it was clear who had been winning that fight.

I cast one grateful look down at Moon and made a mental note to shower him with praise the moment Waylan was gone. Elvie was right when she said I was lucky he chose me. I might not ever find myself actually have to use the fiend dagger so long as I had this creature by my side.

"So?" I asked, while Waylan continued to pout and pat at his scratches. "What are you doing breaking into my rooms and impersonating servants? I assume *she's* going to be fine, because if you killed Ayre, we might as well end this conversation here and now, because whatever it is you came to say, I don't want to hear it."

Waylan finally spared a glance over at the still form of the real Ayre sprawled face-down on the floor.

"She'll awaken as soon as I leave, with no memory of this happening."

"Awfully convenient," I said, crossing my arms across my chest. I kept the dagger in view, turning it over between my fingers so that it kept catching that firelight. "Especially convenient for a kidnapper. I assume that's why you're here? To take me now?"

"Take you? No?" Waylan suddenly forgot his wounds and straightened to face me. "I'm here to offer my most sincere apologies."

"Apologies?"

"For betraying you," he said, dipping his head for a second. "I know I told you I had no intention of bringing the princes here, but I was given an offer I couldn't refuse."

"And what could a demon not possibly refuse?"

"My freedom."

The words hung between us, long and loud as the silence they filled.

"Well, you're very lucky, because that might be the only thing you could possibly say that would allow me to forgive you."

Shock crossed the demon's face as I tossed the dagger onto the bed and fell back down beside it.

"You'd forgive me so easily? How?"

I shrugged. "I would have given you up too, for far less," I admitted. "Being released from eternal servitude, well ... " I glanced over at the unconscious form of the servant on the floor again. "No one can fault you for that, not even me."

Waylan was dumbstruck for a minute, and I took the opportunity to pull some of the sheets up over my most sensitive bits —only to stop at the last second. I might be all too willing to forgive the now free demon for his betrayal, but that didn't mean he no longer deserved to squirm.

When I fixed the demon with my gaze again, he'd finally managed to compose himself.

"So, what now?" I asked. "Now that you have your freedom, I'm guessing you no longer plan on serving the princes?"

"To be honest, Delph … " he said, trailing off a bit, his words uncertain for quite possibly the first time, "I'm not sure."

"There is *one* thing I know for certain," he said, bowing his head again. "If ever you should have need of me, you need only call on me, and I will come."

"You don't owe me this," I said, though I did sit up slightly at the words. A favor owed by a demon like Waylan could be a useful thing. "I didn't free you."

"No," he said, swallowing. "But you were my friend, and I betrayed you. I'm offering you this in hopes that it can, at least, keep us from becoming enemies."

His words made tears gather at the inner corners of my eyes. Twice now, in one night, I'd been offered valuable gifts from those I least expected to give them.

"But … but I'm fae. You hate fae."

"Half fae," he corrected me, a sparkle in his eye the closest thing I was going to get to a smile from the lizardly demon. It was the second time I'd been reminded of that today, but this time it wasn't actually meant as an insult. He took the sight of me in again, and this time he didn't even flinch at the sight of my curves on display. "You know, really, I'm surprised you aren't angry."

"I should be," I admitted, falling back on my bed as the exhaustion once again started to creep in now that the adrenaline had faded. "But instead, I almost feel like I have to thank you."

I saw him stiffen out of the corner of my eye.

"Whatever for?"

I let out a guilty sigh. "Because of you, and your betrayal, I get to go home."

18
DELPHINE

In the shock of everything unfolding, I hadn't realized it before, but here it was.

The impossible had happened.

The fae of Avarath had found their way to Elysia, to the Starlight Court.

All the human world was doomed, sure, but at least I got my little selfish wish. Thanks to Waylan and the princes he'd carried here, I would get to see Sol again.

I'd taken a gamble on a fae deal, and for once, it seemed to have paid off.

My mood was greatly improved by the time that strange, brighter starlight signaled morning. True to Waylan's word, Ayre had awoken as soon as the demon left me again and remembered nothing of him. She assumed she'd knocked her head on the doorway on her way in and had left me with clean sheets, only a few muttered curses, and a bump on her head as a souvenir of the attack.

A new somberness had fallen over the palace with the arrival of the princes. It led most of the fae court to keep to the shadows, their heads bent in quiet whispers—but I didn't care. It was all the same to me, if not better, because it meant that I could explore the palace now without interruption.

And this time, I had a map.

I knew within the first few turns through the palace corridors that even with a map like the one Tarrack gave me it would take days—if not weeks—to explore the entirety of it. Even then, that was only if I didn't stop and linger too long at the many curious and curiouser things marked across the magic papers. The Starlight Palace was in and of itself a small functioning city within a city. The sheer size of it alone was breathtaking, to say nothing of how oddly empty it seemed the further I explored. It reminded me of what Elvie had told me of Seren's line, and how the whole thing had been wiped out during the fae war.

It made sense, then, that the palace seemed to have been built for so many fae. There once must have *been* many. What walked the halls now, well, it wasn't truly the Starlight Court. It was what was left it.

Of course, a map of the Starlight Court wouldn't be complete without its most distinguishing feature—*the pools.* There were pools after pools, too many to count, but since one thing the map failed to determine was whether or not these pools were the 'lost to the ether for all eternity' variety or not, I just made special note to avoid them as much as possible.

Avoiding the pools, however, turned out to be the least of my worries—not when the real problem was something that could simply wander into me as easily as I could wander into it.

And by it, I meant *him.*

I didn't recognize him at first. Admittedly, I was paying more attention to the map I had my face buried in than I did the actual palace I was trying to navigate. I'd found that if I wasn't careful, it was easy to take a wrong turn, even with the map, so I'd taken to barely looking up from it. There was a particularly suspicious looking pool marked in one of the courtyards near this part of the palace, so I was trying hard to make sure I didn't take an accidental turn and step right into it. Though, admittedly, it probably would have been a lot easier to avoid that if I was paying any attention to where my feet were actually carrying me.

Just as it would have been easier to avoid Avarath's Prince of the Sea, too.

I should have heard the way my last footsteps were muffled, I should have seen the figure planted in the middle of the room as he loomed ever closer. But I didn't, and that was my fault.

Even after I collided with the figure too like a marble pillar in both stature and firmness, it took a moment for me to recognize him. It wasn't until the strong, dark arms appeared from beneath the swirl of silver silk to steady me that I felt the first flutter of my beating heart.

His hands tightened around my upper arms with a familiarity that both warmed me and sent a shiver down my spine at the same time.

It took me too long to force my chin up to check what I already knew was there. My body worked against me, wanting to refuse me. It wanted to keep staring straight ahead into the strong chest before me at arm's length.

I was afraid of what I would see when I looked up, but despite all that fear, nothing could prepare me for what I found —not in the familiar full lips, golden eyes, or square jaw–but in myself.

I thought I had to be imagining things at first, but there was no imagining this. The best memory conjured in my mind might have been able to make up the shape of the fae clutching me in his arms, but nothing could conjure up the way I felt when the scent of him washed over me. It clung to him even here, so very far from his court. Salt and sea air mixed with a sweet, pine-like pitch.

It was a scent that had clung to me once, too.

It made me forget everything else, if only for a moment. All I felt, there in his arms once again, was the rush of him beside me. And then he spoke in that honeyed, salt-broken voice of his, and it was all I could do to keep from melting into him entirely.

"I was starting to wonder if you were avoiding me, Delphie."

It was Tethys, alright. Solid. Undeniable. Real.

So very, very *real.*

Not even a single day had passed since his arrival here, and already one of the princes that had tried to murder me was walking free, casting the glitter of his gold rings across Elysia's palace halls.

I remained frozen to the spot, neither my feet nor my voice willing to move for fear of what they might do.

Worry drew Tethys' thick brows closer together, his head dipping to look at me better. It was almost too much to have him here, so close to me.

"Are you alright, Delphie?"

There it was, again. That, at least, finally allowed my tongue to loosen.

"Why are you calling me that?"

"Delphie? It's the name I came up for you while you were gone."

"Were you really so lonely? I wasn't gone very long, and that isn't very original."

I regretted the question instantly.

The white of Tethys' perfect teeth flashed in the dark. "I told you, *Delphine*. Being apart from you—for any amount of time—you have no idea. You drive me mad."

I looked up into the smoldering prince's eyes and, at long last, finally broke free of his spell—just as I broke free from his grip on my arms. Or at least I tried to, but his hands were like iron and refused to budge.

"And you're about to drive *me* mad if you don't let go of me."

He let me go with a shrug that was supposed to make me think he didn't care, but I caught the slightest flicker of disappointment in the way he bit at the corner of his lip.

I took a couple steps back from him, just to be safe—as much from myself as from him. The air between us was cold and empty, too empty. Now that I had a chance to get ahold of where I was and just *what* was happening, I turned around in a full circle, seeking out the arched halls for some sign of one of the fire sigil-bearing guards. There wasn't so much as a single one in sight.

Tethys was watching me, shoulders slumped back and hands in the pockets of the borrowed robes that didn't suit him. The shape of it obscured the exquisite cut of his muscles. He was all hard edges, but the Elysian gowns were all soft lines. They didn't complement each other, instead making Tethys appear swamped beneath the fabric. I could imagine silks like these wouldn't last very long near the harsh sea air. They would mold and tear too quickly, to speak nothing of how they would cling to the skin in the damp air.

Not that I'd mind the way it might look clinging to Tethys. I certainly hadn't minded the way it looked on Seren.

I had to forcefully shake my head to cast the images from my mind. There was so much wrong with every picture that just sprung up there. I couldn't believe that I had to remind myself that one of them was my enemy and the other—also my enemy still—could turn out to be my grandfather or uncle or something close enough to it that the very reminder made bile rise at the back of my throat. Both were excellent enough reasons to stop lusting over the way silk would cling to their bodies, if only the brain between my legs would agree with the brain in my head.

It would be best for myself, best for everyone, if I were to leave both the fae to their own devices—but Tethys' appearance meant a visit to the other was in order. Seren needed to know Tethys, if not *all* the princes had escaped.

It wasn't until then, when several calming lungfuls of air had joined the physical space between us, that I realized the true danger of the situation I was in.

Tethys was out.

He had escaped, somehow, right? That was the only explanation I could think of for why he was standing out here in the palace halls. This had to be a trick, an attempt to lure me somewhere so that he and the other princes could take me away.

Tethys saw the shift in my features and something mischievous tugged at his own. It annoyed me. I wanted to smack it off … or kiss it off. If I was being honest with myself, which I probably shouldn't be, I couldn't really decide which I desired more.

"Off to give Caldamir hell again?" he asked, all too knowing.

"You saw me down there, then?" I narrowed my eyes at him. "I didn't see you."

Tethys feigned mock offence as only he could, one hand clutched to his chest as the other made a dramatic arc out toward the empty hallway. "I did have a hard time not faulting you for not visiting me. After all, I came all this way to see you, and you didn't so much as say hello."

"Yes, well, you'll have to forgive me for that," I said with a half snort, half snarl. "But you're wrong. I'm not off to see your oh-so-devoted leader, Caldamir. I have no intention of going back to the dungeon. I was trying to avoid you, you know."

He nodded slightly, allowing that pouting lip to stick out again. "You wound me again."

"Speaking of which," I continued, completely ignoring his further dramatics. "What the *hell* are you doing out here? Should I be screaming for the guards?"

"No. You should be screaming for me." Tethys lowered his head and looked down at me through hooded lids. "I can still remember the sound of it. Can't you?"

Of course, I could remember it.

Damp earth. Clear sky. Trees reaching overhead. The taste of sweat and crystal water from the pool. The rough, woodland fabric tangled between my legs. And him.

Tethys. I was tangled in him, too.

A sharp breath brought me back to my senses, and once again, I stepped back from the fae as if more empty space between us could ever keep us apart.

"I'm not going to the dungeons because I need to see Seren, first. There's no way he knows you're out and about already, just wandering the realm."

"Actually ... " Tethys said, cocking his head to the side with that sheepish grin making a reoccurrence. He lifted up his left wrist and gave it a shake until the thin metal bracelet encircling it caught the light.

It took me a second, but then I realized what it was. I'd seen it before, of course, on Ayre's wrist.

"The closest thing to a shackle here, in Elysia," he said with something close to a wistful sigh. "So long as I behave, I can roam free. No magic. No problems."

I pursed my lips together, still unconvinced that this was in any way a good idea. "And do you?"

"Do I what?"

"Do you plan to behave?" I asked, setting my jaw and letting my brows raise high enough to show what I truly thought.

Tethys laughed, and once again, the sound of it wanted to turn me inside out.

"That all depends on you," he said. "I'll behave if you do."

19
DELPHINE

I KNEW SEREN DIDN'T LIKE TO BE DISTURBED UNDER EVEN THE BEST of circumstances. These were far from best circumstances, but I'd been left with no other choice.

I knew I was lucky to find him in his tower room and not one of the many meeting, welcome, or war rooms scattered like pieces of a complicated puzzle throughout the Elysian palace. I was not so lucky, however, to find him alone.

The sound of his name died before it fully made it out of my mouth when I saw the circle of kings gathered around him—all eyes turned to me the moment I'd flung the door to the Seeker's tower open wide. I immediately regretted my choice, if not for the unwelcome stares I was gathering from more than one of their faces, but for the fact that a little tact might have let me eavesdrop on what would have surely been a very good conversation to drop eves on.

My only small consolation, one that allowed me to take a deep breath and continue further into the room—if with a little more care this time—was that Itris was not here to witness my blunder.

"Seren … I was wondering if I might have a word?"

It was obvious from the rest of the kings' faces what they thought of my interruption, but Seren graciously whispered his apologies and started to leave the circle that had gathered around the spilling waterfall portal in the middle of the room.

He hadn't so much as met my eye again before he was stopped, however.

"Seren, we really must continue these discussions. They can't wait. I know you were excited about bringing a fae back, we all were … we all *are* … there are just some things that—"

Seren held up a hand to stop him. "Of course, Catrian. This will only take a minute, and then I give you my word that you will have my undivided attention for as long as you need to finish discussing … what was it, again?"

The second fae king, Catrian, pressed his lips together. "The distribution of resources, should an emergency arise."

"Ah, yes, that's what it was."

Seren ignored the sour look on King Catrian's face and instead swept forward toward me, motioning for me to follow him out through the archways onto the open terrace surrounding the tower. The only fae who looked genuinely happy to see me was Tarrack. While the rest of the kings mirrored Catrian to some extent, a smile creased the Seer's face as he craned his neck to follow our retreating silhouettes, and I made a mental note to thank him again for the map. I had no doubt I wouldn't have been able to find the tower room today again if I didn't have it.

Seren and walked side by side toward the dizzying tower border, not quite close enough to let our hands brush as we walked, but still close enough that I couldn't ignore the electricity that crackled between us.

I'd never let myself come this close to the edge before, and I honestly wished I hadn't. The drop was so fierce and sharp that I couldn't see where the bottom of the tower actually led, not without leaning out over the empty edge of it—something I was never, *ever* going to do. I was already sure I'd faint from the fear of it and fall to my death if I tried.

Standing this close to it, with that warm, lifelike wind, was already enough to make my breath catch unsteadily and my head start to swim. As if sensing this, Seren shifted his feet so that he was angled slightly between me and the edge.

"Has something changed?" He dipped his head to look me in the eye, searching for something, and he kept his voice low too, so we wouldn't be as likely to be overheard. "You said you were alright last night. I would have walked you back to your room yourself if I thought you weren't."

"I was fine last night," I insisted. Despite our whispered words, I glanced over once at the gathered circle of kings. Something had changed in them from the first time we met. I couldn't really blame them, just as I'd never been able to blame Itris for how outwardly she distrusted me. It still made me uneasy to feel the way their gaze flitted over to us now, more out of concern and suspicion than it ever had before.

I shuddered to think what would have happened had Seren been the one to accompany me to my room. Would he have noticed Ayre was off right away? I'd yet to tell anyone about the demon's role in all of this, and for now, I'd like to keep it that way.

Besides, that wasn't why I was here, now.

Already the kings were shifting restlessly, so I got to the point.

"I ran into one of the princes *outside* the dungeon. He claimed he was allowed to roam free so long as he wore one of those, I don't really know what they're called, an anti-magic bracelet. Are you aware of this?"

"Of course, I am," Seren said. "As prisoners, they can't exactly be allowed access to the glamour, but as royalty ... we can hardly force them to live like animals trapped in a cell for eternity."

"And is that wise?"

Seren's eyebrow shot up at that. "Of course, it isn't *wise,* Delphine. If we were making the wise decision here, all four of those princes would already be standing trial for their crimes. But as the judges of the realms, we have rules that must be adhered to ... principles that must be upheld ... even when it's obvious to anyone that it isn't necessarily *wise.*"

I chewed on the inside of my cheek, not ready to accept what he was saying. He wasn't wrong, of course, but it also didn't sit quite ... right.

"I just think that a little time in a cell is a safer bet than letting them walk free," I said, after a moment's consideration. "Haven't they caused enough trouble without magic so far?"

"Yes, well, we have rules on how long a fae can be forced to remain in captivity like that. It's inhumane to make them wait that way for trial."

"Well, how long could it take?"

"Well, since we're one judge short and there's been no sign of an heir to take the throne ... it could be forever before we open the court again. And I mean that, of course, in the most literal sense."

"Oh."

When he said they couldn't be left like animals trapped in cells for an eternity, he actually meant *an eternity.*

"Our guard might be a little out of practical practice, but I can assure you they're more than adequately trained to keep a few grounded princes in line," he said, with a glance over at the shifting circle still waiting on him, on us. His hands reached out to rest reassuringly on my upper arms. "Nothing will become of you here. Just as I promised you before, you're *safe*."

Instead of reassuring me, of course, he made another wave of heat wrack my body.

From the way his head tipped forward, long silver hair falling to hide the flush that colored his face when his eyes dropped, for a moment, from my eyes to my lips, I knew he felt it too. His grip tightened a bit and he pulled me to him an almost imperceptible amount.

Almost.

The motion was enough to make my throat tighten and need draw more heat to the space between my thighs.

Both our breaths grew shorter, lips parted, and chests heaved. I was grateful for the skirts that hid my own signs of desire, especially when Seren's did little to hide his own body's response. His thumbs, still bracing either of my arms, traced a half moon across the exposed skin above the drape of my dress' sleeves.

"We have another problem, don't we," he said, this time, barely above a breath. "One that has nothing to do with princes or prisoners."

I nodded, forcing my lips to press together as I tried to steady my breath. The last thing I wanted was for the many pairs of eyes watching us to catch on to the heat that had dripped into our whispered words.

"Tell me why you're not eager to act on it," Seren asked, the bluntness catching me off guard. "I feel it too, almost as strong as I've felt you trying to resist it."

I bit my lip, willing myself to pull away, but finding myself unable to even as I admitted the reason.

"I can't be with you," I said, slowly, carefully, each word forced out between lips that wanted nothing more than to be pressing to his. "Not like this. Not until I know, for sure, that I'm not from the Seeker line."

"Well, there's a way we can figure that out," Seren said. A determined look flashed across his features, as if he was finally deciding something. "It was about time you started learning some magic. Tomorrow, we learn what you're capable of."

My heart—and something else, that something between my legs—practically throbbed at his words.

"You mean, we could know as soon as tomorrow?"

That need inside me reared its increasingly stubborn head and tried to whisper thoughts in my ear that made me want to shudder.

Tomorrow already felt too far away.

As if reading my reaction, Seren pulled me even closer still. I could feel the heat of his breath on my face, taste the sweet scent of him on my tongue. The tease of the last time our lips met was almost enough for me to fall prey to the devilish voice in my head telling me to forget the fact we might share blood, but only *almost*.

A slight smile pulled at the outer corner of Seren's lips, as if he was reading my very thoughts. "What's one more day when I've already waited an eternity?"

20
DELPHINE

One day.

I could handle one more day.

But, of course, it wasn't so simple as that.

It wasn't Seren that showed up at my door shortly after I'd chosen to take my breakfast alone in my room with only Moon for company. It was Tarrack.

"Seren sends his apologies," he said, the moment he saw my face start to fall. "The kings can't wait today. You know how they can be, human or fae, they're all the same."

I narrowed my eyes up at him. "Aren't you a king too? Shouldn't you be there, with them?"

Tarrack looked taken aback for a moment, as if he hadn't considered the idea. After a moment of careful thought, however, he only shrugged.

"I suppose I'm just lucky, then," he said, with a sheepish smile. "I get to spend the day with a beauty like you while all the rest of them have to keep on staring at each other's ugly mugs."

I forgot to pretend I'd never been to the Seer's chambers, but either Tarrack didn't notice or wasn't at all surprised when I already seemed to know my way around the joining circular rooms.

"Seren wants me to see if you have a particular affinity for Seeing, though to be honest, I'm not sure why," Tarrack said, muttering half to himself as he led the two of us between the many instruments I'd already seen—and some I swore had only appeared in the few days that had passed since Elvie and I were here last.

"Most fae start with smaller magics," Tarrack continued. "Still can't figure out why he was so insistent we jump straight to this, but I suppose that's the thing with Seren."

"And what is that?"

"Once that king sets his mind to something, he gets it. There's no stopping him. Sometimes, it's like he forgets he's not the sole ruler of Elysia."

"Ah, but," he stuttered, glancing sheepishly at me and then back at the small bowl of crystals we'd stopped over, "I'd prefer that not to leave this room, what I just said. Sometimes I let my tongue get away with me. I have the greatest respect for Seren and I'd hate—"

Tarrack had started rambling and would have likely continued to until we both crumbled to dust if I didn't reach out a hand to rest, ever so gently and just as briefly, on top of one of his own.

His face was flushed when he looked up to meet my eyes, the words slowly turning to mumbles that disappeared entirely.

"Don't worry," I said, "your secret is safe with me."

I gave him a wink to reassure him that I knew it was hardly a "secret" even, and that blush in his cheeks only grew deeper. His hands went a little unsteady, fingertips shaking as he went back to setting and resetting the crystals in the glass.

"Suppose there's nothing to do but try then, eh? Are you ready?"

I paused, taking a moment to really take in what Tarrack had set out before us.

"We're starting with something simple. It's harder to see when scrying than it is to hear."

"These crystals will help hone the glamour. A skilled Seer can hear even the tiniest of sounds, let alone the voices of other fae—the flap of a butterfly's wings, the beat of a rodent's heart, the whisper of wind between two blades of grass. Today we're aiming for something a little simpler."

The bowl of crystals was carved into the wall on one side, so the two of us had to stand close, almost shoulder to shoulder, in order to both face it. The cold stone wall was odd to face, so instead I fixed my gaze on the crystals overflowing from the bowl. They were clear white and cut in a variety of lengths, some as long as my forearm and others so small they could better be described as pebbles.

Where Elvie had found and lined up crystals like these along the edge of the bowl, Tarrack just laid his hands out across the top of these clustered inside. I started reaching for him automatically, but he shook his head and so I froze instead.

His eyes closed slowly, and almost the moment the lids fluttered shut, I felt it. It was like a prickling in the air, carried in by warm tendrils of wind that seemed to move of their own accord. Then I heard it, next. It started out as a whisper, something soft and sharp at the same time. At first, I thought they were fae voices, or human, but something about it sounded wrong.

"Stars," Tarrack added to the whispers. "What you're hearing are the *stars.*"

I'd heard glimpses of them before—in the gems that lined the walls, in the whisper of the silk that made up the gowns and robes of the court, heard them in the very echo of my footsteps. I'd heard them, yes, but never like this.

Tarrack drew my attention and then motioned upward. I followed his gaze until I saw the orbs of light that moved around the rooms, lighting them with that eerie, shifting, uneasy glow, had once again begin to move. They floated closer to us, converging in the space above our heads first, and then began to turn and tilt around each other. They formed their own kind of constellation, catching and reflecting the song in the crystals until it flowed all around us.

Not just around us, it flowed *through* us.

That spark that had lit in me my first days here joined in. It was like that energy inside me was reaching out for the song, for the stars, longing to join it—and that longing, once it had felt what it wanted, lingered long after Tarrack stepped away from the crystals and their song too quickly faded.

"Now, you try," Tarrack said, nodding down to the bowl that felt so much emptier now than it did before. "The vessel is primed, so it shouldn't be too hard to draw magic from it. You won't be in danger of overexerting it, or yourself."

I took Tarrack's position, doing my best to mimic the exact way that he held his hands … and then I froze. What was next? Was I really supposed to feel some sort of magical tug, some instinct that would show me how to draw the sound of the stars into a clump of pretty rocks that had been dumped into a bowl?

Back in Alderia, I would have thought this was some kind of joke. A prank meant to make a fool of me.

Even though I knew this wasn't, I still felt anxious energy more than I felt anything else.

I'd supposed that magic came with being fae, but I'd never thought much of it. In Avarath, when they first introduced me to this side of myself, I wasn't ready to accept it. I still wasn't ready, even though I'd now had no choice *but* to accept it.

It still didn't mean that any of it felt real, and it still certainly didn't mean I'd expected to be able to wield the same glamour the human realm had been fearing for centuries. It was the very thing that we feared about the fae, not the fae themselves. Without magic, they were just long-living, tall, pointy-eared bastards that liked to think themselves better than us.

Better than humans, I supposed.

I wasn't one of them anymore. Not really. Just like I wasn't really fae.

It was strange, this, stuck between two worlds. I'd been stuck here all my life without knowing it, but knowing it didn't necessarily make it any better. And it *certainly* didn't make it any easier.

Tarrack shot me a pointed look and then took a deep breath I was meant to mimic, so I did. I didn't do well enough the first time, since apparently multiple, small, terrified breaths didn't add up quite the same way. Eventually, though, after a few repeated attempts and several long, counted exhales, I was finally matching the rhythm of his almost painfully slow breathing.

Nothing happened for a long time.

When I did start to feel something, it wasn't a magic tingle or some kind of racing sensation, it was just a lingering sort of nausea that started to twist the bottom of my stomach. My feet shifted uncomfortably where they were planted on the floor. A cold sweat broke out across my brow.

It grew more and more difficult to maintain those slow, careful breaths. The nausea grew in my stomach, boiling over until it raked at the back of my throat and made me feel as if I was choking.

All I wanted was to let go of the vessel and gasp for air, but I held on, forced the illness down, and tried to concentrate solely on the crystals in front of me. But the harder I focused, the sicker I became. Those cold drops of sweat began to run down the sides of my face. The hair clung to the back of my neck. Hot and cold chills flashed in alternating currents through my body.

I thought I was going to be sick, really sick—and then, only then, did it happen.

The moment I let go, prepared to double over and be sick all over the beautiful crystal floors, I finally felt *it*.

I felt the glamour.

It erupted through me in a surge like nothing I'd ever felt before. It was like fire in my bones. Like ice in my veins. Like starlight searing across my skin.

It shot through me in an instant, but in that single instant, it left me feeling more alive than I ever had before.

The burst of glamour had found its target, driving through me into the crystals.

Instead of being filled with whispers, however, a loud keening sound split the air. It grew louder and sharper until I wanted to cover my ears, but I reflectively clutched Tarrack's hands harder. The moment I did, the bowl of crystals in front of us exploded. Shards of crystal flew like glass around us, my hands finally letting go of Tarrack in time for the both of us to duck down to our knees, narrowing avoiding the rain of crystal from ripping either of us to shreds.

We remained there, crouched in the silence that slowly swallowed us, until the crystal dust finally began to settle.

"So much for not overexerting it," I said, voice flat.

I expected disappointment to show on Tarrack's face when our eyes met, but all I saw was an excited sparkle there.

"Was that your first time doing magic?"

I looked up at him, breathless, barely able to nod—let alone form words.

"Don't worry, you'll get a hang of it, eventually. All Starlight Fae have the ability to wield our glamour, but only the magic from your specific line will come naturally."

Seren swept in right as that long-expected disappointment finally did begin to overtake Tarrack's features.

"Ah, I'm guessing Delphine doesn't show much of a proclivity for Seeing?"

Tarrack let out a low sigh and shook his head.

"Well then, at least you can take Tarrack to your bed now if you wish."

My face grew red with the heat of embarrassment—and fury. "Shut up," I hissed at him, my gaze shifting sideways to see Tarrack's reaction to his crass comment. Thankfully, he seemed too engrossed with trying to clean up the mess I'd made of his lab to be paying us any attention. "Unless you *want* me to find a reason to fuck another fae, of course, then go ahead … be my guest, keep on going."

The way Seren cocked his head to the side, a smug smile pulling at the corner of his mouth, only served to make my fury burn brighter.

"Oh, I don't care about that," he said, slow and measured. "I think we both know you could make your way through half the palace, and that would do nothing to change the way you burn for me."

21
DELPHINE

SEREN'S WORDS LEFT ME SEETHING.

Not just his words, just … just *him.* Seren made me seethe, inside and out.

Combined with that overwhelming rush of magic, *magic* of all things, I needed a release. I needed something to soothe the ever-tightening muscles of my body, or else one day soon I was going to tighten up as hard as a marble statue and be stuck that way forever.

I was tired of shivering cold baths that never seemed to really get me clean. I needed to scrub all this off of me, out of me, and there was only one place that was going to happen.

A trail of warming, steamy air grew thicker through the hallways leading up to the bathhouse. After the last two weeks of freezing baths, the rise in temperature was enough to make the knot of tension that had been building inside me sing at the very idea of coming undone.

The baths themselves were dark and shadowed, the steam thick enough to provide modesty from any prying eyes more than a couple feet away. Still, I stopped just inside the doorway to listen for signs of anyone else who'd had the same idea of making an afternoon visit. There was some splashing and a few low-murmured voices coming from one of the pools at the far end of the room, but because of the way the baths were divided, I thought it should be easy enough to avoid them.

I could try coming back later, of course, if I wanted the baths truly to myself, but the call of the hot water wouldn't let me. Two weeks of freezing baths was enough to make me practically start ripping the clothes from my body the moment I found a small, empty pool as far as I could from the stir of voices.

The going was slow without a servant—or even the unskilled hands of a demon—to help me. Thankfully, I'd chosen a dress with fewer laces today, so it only took me a few minutes before the silver silk finally loosened enough for me to tug it carefully from my shoulders. It draped neatly over a hook set beside the pool, the steam already working to loosen the creases in the fabric the same way I hoped it would soon start to loosen the creases of *me*.

My dreams of relaxation were shattered before I could even start to remove the last thin layer of my chemise, however—when the voices floating over to me through the thick steam suddenly made me pause. They were hushed enough that I couldn't make out the words themselves, but something about the sound of them refused to be drowned out.

These were mixed baths, but the fact that the voices were male wasn't what bothered me.

It was that they were all too familiar.

I checked first that there weren't any other signs of fae in the nearby baths that I might disturb before I pulled my chemise a little tighter against my body and started picking my way slowly across the damp stone. The voices grew louder with each step that brought me closer, but it wasn't until I was able to see the dark shapes of their silhouettes too that I finally, fully recognized them.

Or, that was what I told myself, anyway. I think I knew exactly who they were, I just needed to see it with my own eyes to believe it. There was no mistaking the shape of them, though.

I hadn't been long in Avarath, but in the time I was there, I'd grown all too familiar with the shape of the Sea and Sand Courts' princes from the waist up. One of them I'd grown quite familiar with from the waist *down* as well, but the third figure in the bath made any thoughts of that kind dissipate even before I recognized his voice as well.

It was Alder. He sat on the edge of the baths, gratefully still covered by a towel wrapped around his waist. With wide eyes and an eager—if a little nervous—grin, looked like he'd stumbled across the two princes and become all-too-willingly entrapped by them.

"So, you really have no magic then? Like, none at all?" he was asking, responding to something Tethys had murmured.

"Why else would we have been so quick to give it up?" Armene asked, lifting up his hand so that the silver cuff around his wrist glinted in the dark.

"If you want another piece of advice, an actually *useful* piece of advice," Tethys began, sitting forward as if he was about to share a secret. Secret or not, he never got to share it. The very least I could do was save Elvie's twin from making the mistake of listening to these two fae for one second longer than he had to —for his own good.

"Yeah, no," I cut in, making all three of them jump—but none so much as Alder. His hands snapped up to cover his lap, only to find his forgotten towel there with a sigh of relief. It did nothing to stop his face from growing as red as it always did when I was around, however. I could see that here, even in the dim light.

"You shouldn't be here, listening to these fools, Alder," I said. "You're better than that. Besides ... does your grandmother know you're here? Somehow, I doubt she'd be very happy to hear you were talking to these two."

The very mention of Itris made the boy's face pale.

He shot the two princes a worried look before scurrying off, the towel pulled tight around his waist, even as he forgot to grab whatever clothes he probably brought with him.

"I had no idea you were here, Delphie," Tethys said once the boy was gone, shifting in the dark water so that his back was no longer facing me.

"Stop calling me that."

"Is that what you really want?" Tethys asked, head cocking to the side. "I only call you that because you remind me of the selkie fae that used to play in the sea at my palace. A lot of the court thought they were a nuisance, but I always thought they were beautiful."

It was my turn for heat to flush my skin.

"That wasn't very nice of you, sending the boy away," Tethys said, sticking his lip out in a pout. "We were just trying to give him some advice."

"Yeah, sure," I snorted. "Terrible advice that was guaranteed to get him into trouble."

"Of course," Tethys said. "Otherwise, what would be the point?"

Armene glared at him then, but the Sea Prince ignored him.

"Though, more to the point," Tethys continued, eyes raking over the shape of my body beneath the ever-clinging fabric of my chemise, "is whether or not we can get you into trouble, too."

I half expected Armene to argue, to try to save me from the other prince with some attempt at chivalry, but then he too moved to face me, naked above the dark water—and, presumably, below. He tilted his head up to look at me though his own hooded eyes.

"I didn't come here for trouble," I said, but the two princes each gave me a skeptical look.

"Then please, Delphine," Armene said, leaning forward slightly to peer up at me from the bath, "enlighten us why you *did* come here?"

"Unless, of course, you yourself don't know," Tethys practically purred beside him. "Then we'll be more than happy to give you a reason."

I leaned forward too, lips parting in preparation to tell them off—when I stopped.

Tethys had moved closer, the gold in his swept-up locks winking at me with the same mischief that glittered in his eyes. His own lips parted and I found mine softening to match his, a breathy sigh replacing the venom I'd been ready to spew.

"I believe in fate, Delphie, you know why?" He drew up a little from the dark water so that his modesty was barely covered by its rippling surface. Here amid the shadows and steam, every one of his muscles shone and glittered too. Water and sweat beaded across his skin, racing in lines down the hard line of his abs until the disappearing stream of water left my eyes lingering too long at the parts of him I *couldn't* see.

"Why is that?" I asked, indulging him. It was easier than fighting him, and right now as the hot air enveloped me further, pressing the already sheer chemise to my skin, I was finding myself too tired to fight anymore.

"Because you and I, we've always bonded over water, haven't we?" he said, that mischief pulling at his smile now. "Fate draws us together like this. First, at the pool, and now …" He trailed off, eyes never breaking from mine as he cupped a handful of the dark water and brought it up to watch the steam rise between us. "Lady fate has done it again."

The water slowly began to trickle from between his fingers. Hot droplets of it spilled onto my knees and splashed up to speckle my gown with translucent glimpses of flesh. I hadn't even realized I'd come to sit on the edge of the bath, but here I was.

I nodded towards the many gold rings encasing Tethys' fingers. "Careful now, or you'll lose one of those this time."

"No need to worry about that," Armene said, his broad form slipping closer too. He rose up out of the bath further than Tethys until the full, already hard length of him rose from the water too. "I offer my hands in service, unless you prefer the kinds of ... service ... I provided last time."

Heat pooled between my thighs, making me grateful for the water that had already halfway soaked me there. One prince I might have been able to deny, but two?

And here, so close, and with that burning need inside me begging not to be ignored ... I only had to slip my knees out from under myself and into the hot water of the bath.

So that's exactly what I did.

The moment hot water enveloped me, so too did the princes. I sank into the water as they rose to meet me. My hands skimmed across the hot planes of Armene's chest, heated from the bathwater until steam rose from each one of his tanned muscles. Behind me, Tethys slipped his hands around my ribcage and pulled himself to me. His excitement pressed hard into my back and his hands, so large they could wrap halfway around me, grazed the bottom of my breasts until my hardened nipples showed through the sheer chemise.

While Tethys' hot breath mingled on my back, Armene ducked his head to kiss a second line of heat across the base of my jaw. He started beneath my ear, trailing the kisses until he was brushing close to my lips, but then he stopped to dive beneath. He knelt in the water so that his head came level with my breasts. He pressed his lips to the sodden fabric, sucking on first my left nipple and then my right, teeth nibbling ever so gently through the fabric until my breaths had grown too ragged.

Both princes fumbled for the edges of the chemise until together, they tugged it off of me, leaving it to tangle between my thighs in the bathwater. Armene walked us backwards until his legs hit the submerged seat and he sat down, pulling me on top of his lap. He latched onto my bare breast now and began to suckle, one hand looping under my ass to steady me and the other slipping down below the surface of the water to stroke himself.

Behind me, Tethys pressed himself over me, one knee lifted to rest on the bench so he could angle his length between my thighs. I felt the hardness of him slide across my slit, gently at first, and then growing harder and pushing a little deeper up into the folds of me with each thrust. One hand dug into the softness of my thigh while the other wrapped around to knead the breast that Armene wasn't currently teasing with his tongue.

Armene let out a moan that followed mine, the hand wrapped around his shaft working harder. He tilted his member up then, so it too pressed at the apex of my thighs, sliding the tip between my legs in rhythm with Tethys, but neither one of them ever quite daring press inside.

I let out a groan, half out of pleasure, and half from frustration. I couldn't take his anymore. Every inch of my body demanded more, and I couldn't wait one more second to take it.

My fingers dug into Armene's shoulders and I started to spread my thighs to settle down onto him, but strong hands caught me around the waist, and Armene's slow shake of the head froze me in place.

"Not like this," he whispered, though the throbbing cock between my thighs protested otherwise. His lips quivered, and that appendage pressed against me harder. I could tell it was taking all of his willpower to resist, and I wondered if he'd still be able to resist if he knew how much of my own willpower it was taking for me not to coax him over the edge with me.

The growl of frustration died in my throat when Tethys leaned in, his lips grazing my earlobe so that a shudder raced through my body.

"I bet our Sand Prince has other ways for you to please him," he purred, his lips pressing to the skin of my neck to bite the soft flesh there. Tethys wrapped his hand in mine and, with his member still pressed firm and swollen between my thighs, he guided my hand down beneath the surface of the water.

He didn't let go right away. His hand guided mine from the tip of Armene's member down to the shaft, our shared slow strokes mimicking the way Tethys' own need pulsed harder against mine.

Armene's hips bucked forward slightly and he threw his head back, eyes soon following suit as they rolled to peer up into the dark ceiling. A deep, guttural moan slipped from his lips as he twitched beneath our hands, each stroke moving in time with the rocking of Tethys' own hips. He was pressing so hard into me now that it was a small miracle the wasn't yet inside me.

A shudder wracked Armene's body. "Ugh, yes, *good girl,* Delphine," he groaned again, almost choking on the words. "Yes, just like that."

I was nearly choking too, desperate for the same release that teased Armene now so close to the edge. Right when I thought he'd finally cross over that edge, when all three of our breaths had grown ragged and Tethys was starting to press inside me at last, suddenly Tethys was pulling away—and tugging me along with him.

"Not like this," he growled, his hands rough and strong. "Armene might think he wants a good girl, but we'll see what he wants after I show you how to be his slut."

The baths rang with the rattle of the bench Tethys pulled to the edge of the bath. He dragged me up next, turned me over onto my back, and—careful to steady me so I didn't fall off—instructed me to tilt my head upside down over the edge.

It was a precarious position. I had nothing to hold on to, nothing to keep myself from slipping except for the hands digging into my thighs like they depended on me as much as I did them.

"Tethys—"

The prince standing over me licked his lips. "Oh, how I like it when you say my name. But now do as I say, Delphie, and I promise you'll like what we're about to do. You're going to like it very much … because you might be Armene's *good girl*, but I'm a little more partial to a whore."

He tugged me into him a little harder so that my thighs were spread on either side of his hips. His considerable length lay across me, pressing hard into my stomach where it reached almost up to my navel. The sight of it made more heat pool between my thighs and my mouth water. A second steaming form rose up from the bath behind me and gently took my head in either of his hands.

I let my head be guided back then, tipped back until my mouth hung open and Armene pressed the tip of himself inside—just as Tethys did the same between my thighs. Only where Armene progressed slowly, letting me wrap my lips around his member to suck and tease him, Tethys was only able to manage a few short strokes before he let out a frustrated groan of his own and gave in, plunging all of himself in at once.

I let out a soft cry—or would have, if the moment my throat widened Armene wasn't filling it too. My body wrapped around them both, choking—this time with pleasure. One of the prince's hands found the sensitive place between my thighs and stroked me too, in time with them until I felt myself close to an apex of pleasure. My eyes watered and I choked for breath now too, but when Armene tried to pull back in worry, I reached up and grabbed him by the hips, pulling him back into me.

His next thrust was the one that pushed him over the edge, his heat spilling into my belly with each guttural groan that rattled through the Sand Prince's chest. The moment his climax finished, he drew out of me and knelt to help lift my head, trailing kisses from my jaw to my lips as I caught my breath.

Not that Tethys was going to let me do much of that.

As soon as I gasped in my first deep breath, Tethys shifted his hands to grip my hips tighter. He pushed into me harder, faster, thrusting until that barely regained breath was tearing out of me in a scream of pleasure. Armene's hand clamped over my sticky mouth, muffling the sound as each wave drew the uncontrollable whimpers from my lips.

There was no one to quiet Tethys' moan when he climaxed too, his final strokes trailing off with the last waves of my own.

Tethys collapsed onto the bench beside me, one hand curling over to rest protectively across my rising chest. Armene planted more soft kisses, murmuring words into my hair that nearly sent me into another frenzy—and would have, if the finally satiated desire in me didn't give me the clear-headedness to slip into the dark water of the bath instead, searching out the soaked chemise I lost in its depths at some point.

This here, with them, it was a foolish thing to do, but I didn't regret it. No, so long as I didn't let my heart get involved in these moments that followed, then there would be nothing *to* regret. These were still the princes of Avarath, the same princes that had betrayed me.

Used me.

And now, at least, I'd gotten to use them, too.

I'd forgotten what it was like to give in to this need—or maybe, it was really that I'd never been able to give in like this before. It was all I could do keep the princes from seeing the way my knees shook, though despite my efforts, I didn't think I was very successful.

Not if the glint in Tethys' eye was any indicator.

"You can knock the smug look off your face," I said as I pulled the soaked strands of my hair from where it had tangled around my shoulders and twisted the knots up into a loose, dripping bun at my neck. "And you too, Armene," I added, twisting to shoot the Sand Prince an equally scathing look. "This hasn't changed anything."

The princes apparently had no intention of leaving the baths, and since I had no intention of remaining in their presence, I decided that would have to do in the way of bathing for now. I wasn't exactly *clean,* but at least some of that tension that had built to a maddening peak had been satisfied.

It was that thought that made me pause, just for a second, at the edge of the bath before I slipped into the steam to gather my things. I tilted my head to the side until I could make out Tethys and Armene's dark shadows sitting waist-deep in the hot water.

Nothing had to change, but that didn't mean I regretted what we'd just done either. If anything, what I felt was the opposite.

"My room. The West tower. The night after tomorrow."

22

DELPHINE

THE GLOW HADN'T EVEN HAD TIME TO FADE FROM MY CHEEKS BEFORE another fae found a way to wipe it off of me. It was, of course, the fae who'd seemed most determined to do that from the very beginning.

It would have been one thing if she was waiting for me at the top of the stairs outside the tower room I'd grown a little too fond of the last couple weeks. It was another thing entirely to turn the first corner out of the bathhouse and nearly run straight into a second towering fae in the span of one day—this one somehow more menacing than the first, even though the first was literally a prisoner.

Itris had been waiting for me. There was no doubt about it.

I didn't have to look at her face to know what I'd find there, but since I knew I'd have to eventually, I forced my chin up to meet her haughty, disapproving gaze.

"I see you've been keeping busy now that the princes have come for you."

"How would you—"

She cut me off before I'd fully had the chance to understand what she was really accusing me of.

"Next time you wish to keep a tryst a secret, better to pick a place with less … enthusiastic … acoustics."

Heat, this time not from anger, flooded my already red cheeks.

I opened my mouth, ready to spout apologies, but the words strangled themselves in my throat.

What exactly was it I was about to apologize for?

I didn't ask to be brought here. I didn't bring the princes here … and I certainly wasn't the one to then let them free. Instead of apologies, I felt anger as the embarrassment drained from my cheeks as quickly as it flooded there.

"If you have a problem with me, maybe you should take it up with your brother?"

Itris was visibly taken aback. I guessed it wasn't often that she was spoken to like that. She might not be one of the kings, but she certainly liked to behave like she was.

"The last thing I'm going to bother him with right now is something so trivial as what his plaything likes to get up to in his absence." Her lips curled back at that, before she added, "Thanks, also, to you."

If it was any other fae that said it, I would have been surprised. But ever since I arrived here in Elysia, Itris was the only fae who didn't immediately try to make me feel welcome. The fact that she stood here now, spouting the accusations that she did, didn't shock me so much as it further enraged me.

I moved closer, every inching step making me more and more aware of just how much larger this female was compared to me. She might have been willowy, but there was a strength that had always emanated from her—one that still seemed to grow larger each time we met.

"You somehow keep forgetting that I never asked to be here," I hissed. "In fact, if I had my way, I wouldn't be here now. But once again, the problem returns to where I've already told you to look."

I leaned back and straightened my shoulders despite the fact that I knew my dress was hardly in a state for me to be looking half as confident as I was.

"Please, if you do see Seren, tell him I'm looking for him. I think I'm ready for the next test. In case he hasn't told you, I'm going to find out what line I come from here. You know, since I'm one of you."

I didn't think she knew what I meant by my message, what I *really* meant, but in the off chance that she actually brought the message to her brother, all that mattered was that he *would*. I got more than a slight sense of satisfaction to know that.

"Well let's hope that whatever line you're descended from, it's not from ours."

"Oh, finally, something we can agree on."

Itris' eyes narrowed for a moment.

"Oh, and to that thing you said before … " Itris trailed off just long enough to let her gaze move over me all too slowly, too scathingly. She leaned in closer then, just before she stormed off and left me trembling in her wake. "You're not one of us. You never will be. You be careful, Delphine, you keep this up … and before you know it, you'll be down in the prison with the princes they had the good sense to keep locked up."

I KNEW I'd promised not to go back there, but after what Itris said, I found it impossible to stay away from the prison. There were a hundred other places to explore within the palace boundaries, a hundred other passages to get lost in, and yet each one—no matter which way I took—always seemed to lead me back to the place where the gemstones started to disappear from the otherwise glittering walls.

I'd just assumed that Nyx and Caldamir were walking free along with the other two princes, but that I just hadn't yet had the misfortune to run into them. Caldamir I could understand. He *should* remain locked away, out of sight, where if he couldn't exactly be made to pay for his crimes against me, he might at least be forced to think on them.

Nyx ... Nyx was a different matter.

Itris had tried to warn me, threaten me, even, but it wasn't me I was worried about.

I was only able to stay away for a day. By the time Elysia's equivalent of an afternoon had moons moving across the outer corners of the sky, I had once again found myself at the head of that stairway that grew ever darker with each step.

One thing had changed from the last time I was here, however. For the first time, guards stood sentry over something in the palace. Seren had assured me they were his guards, and that they wouldn't hurt me, but the fire-circle sigil branding their armor still made my heart beat faster at the sight. If it weren't for Itris' warning still burning in my ears, I would have turned on my heel at the first sight of them.

I might as well have, it turned out, because they didn't ignore me as they had in the past. No, the minute I stepped up and started toward the curving staircase, two sets of lances suddenly shot out to block my path.

My body froze, every muscle in it screaming for me to do what my instincts had instructed me to earlier. I had to force myself to stand still, and further yet, to keep my voice from breaking when I took a half step back to face the two fae guards standing sentry.

"Are we not allowed to visit the prisoners anymore?"

The two guards in front of me wavered just long enough to exchange a wordless, fleeting expression with one another.

"*You're* not allowed to visit the prisoners."

There was no nicety attached to the end of their words, but why would there be? Still, the way they'd spoken to me seemed odd and abrasive here, in Elysia, *almost* as odd and abrasive as their actual words.

"I'm ... I'm not allowed to visit the prisoners? Me, specifically?" I asked, after a second of silence stretched into two.

Once again, there was that short exchange before both of them nodded. Their gaze had returned to staring straight ahead, heads held high, arms still extended to the side to form a giant cross blocking my path to the stairs.

I took another step back from the two guards and noted the way they each took a small, barely audible breath of relief. At least whoever had trained this version of the demons that had haunted me so long hadn't instilled that same utter hatred of me I'd come to expect.

I decided to push my luck for more answers. "Is this Itris' doing?"

They had no response to that, though, just kept staring straight ahead. It didn't matter, anyway, not when I knew my answer. Of course, this was Itris' doing.

She was trying to get to me, trying to bend me to her will like so many other fae before her. Unluckily for her, I'd long since abandoned the practice of lying down and taking what was forced upon me. Also, unluckily for her, I had a map—a very good one—and unless I was mistaken, it looked like there was more than one way into the prison.

23
DELPHINE

THERE WERE SOME WAYS IN WHICH ITRIS WAS RIGHT, AND WAYLAN too. I thought, as I found the secret entrance to the back unguarded as I'd suspected, that if those two ever had the misfortune of actually meeting, they might find that there were a great many of things they actually agreed on.

One, for sure, was that the Starlight Court had gotten lazy.

It really had been too long since this court had guests, let alone prisoners, because not only was the secret passageway unguarded, it wasn't even *secret.* It was simply a second staircase, narrower and darker than the first, but hardly filled with cobwebs and rats. From the scuffed floor that wound both above and below the back entrance to the row of cells, it was still a well-used servant's staircase.

I was worried that once I'd found the back door, I might have a hard time finding Nyx without getting spotted first, but the moment I stepped through the door, his was the first cell I saw.

It was impossible not to.

The entire inside of the cell had been transformed in a matter of days. Where before, I assumed it'd been as empty as the cell where I'd seen Caldamir, it was now a small block of lush forest. Trees sprouted from the ground, their roots twisting and curling across the stone floor in a woven mesh of wood and fiber supporting not only their trunks and branches, but vines with large, dew-beaded leaves that pressed up against the glass. Grass and flowers sprung from between the mesh of roots and moss patterned any of the wall that might otherwise have shown through the trees.

The growth was so dense that it wasn't until I took several, cautious steps forward, that I was actually able to spot the Woodland fae.

What I saw when I did … it broke my heart.

The prince sat sprawled across the ground, his legs spread out before him. The roots of the trees had moved to provide space for him to sit on the soft heather that sprouted up between his knees instead of the hard roots carpeting the cell where he'd grown them. His face was tilted downward, transfixed in a near intoxicated state to something writhing between his outstretched hands.

In order to see what it was, I had to move forward again, but I hesitated. Another step would put me in line of sight of the main staircase at the end of the hall, and if the guards *were* to wander down to do rounds, I'd be the first thing they'd see.

My fear of being found out was eclipsed, however, by the intensity of Nyx's gaze. I had to see what it was that could hold his attention like that.

So, I took a step forward, one step, and leaned toward the wide crystal wall to see it.

It was a flower unlike any I'd ever seen before, faerie or elsewhere. With every masterful movement of one of Nyx's fingers, new petals sprung forward from the middle, layer after layer in shades of sunset. The magic he did was like weaving, each twitch and turn of his hands causing some part of the plant to grow exactly as he directed. The way it grew, it almost looked alive, *really* alive.

I understood the Woodland prince's fascination with it, because it was an enchantment in and of itself. I could have stared forever, but I barely got one glance at it before Nyx finally saw me. A twinge of sadness tugged at my heart when I saw the flower shrivel the moment his concentration broke, its stem browning, petals furling and eventually falling in soft, sad smudges to the ground.

For Nyx, however, it was as if the flower that had been his whole world suddenly didn't exist at all. He leapt to his feet, green eyes lighting up as he recognized me. In a second, the branches and vines of his cell reached out and swept him up off his feet. They carried him like great, leafy wings until he hovered just on the other side of the glass.

He pressed his palms to the crystal and leaned forward so close that his breath fogged against it.

"Delph, oh, Delph, I was starting to think that you were never going to forgive me."

Of course, I hadn't come down here to forgive the fae prince for betraying me, but I found myself unable to tell him, not directly, at least. Not when his face was practically shining, the delight in his smile more intoxicating than any wine. A few more moments like this, and I'd be drunk on it.

On him. On Nyx.

Nyx hadn't taken the Starlight Court's robes. Instead, he'd fashioned clothes in earthy tones, fabric woven from strands of the same forest he'd grown around him. He'd made for himself something like a toga, with flowered bands gathering the fabric together at his waist, then splitting to allow a more than generous glimpse of his leg and upper thigh.

I had to admit, I agreed with his sense of fashion. It would be a shame to cover up a single inch more of his fae body than was absolutely necessary—and he certainly hadn't. His modesty was so barely covered that it was all I could do to keep from staring.

Not that Nyx minded. He noted my wandering eyes and only smiled wider.

I'd forgotten what it was like to see the Woodland prince in his natural state. I'd gotten a brief glimpse of it my first day in Avarath, seen what fae royalty could do with even the slightest glimmer of the magic that had long abandoned them.

If I thought it was impossible to resist him before ...

I was suddenly glad of the wall between us, and not for the sake of my own protection.

This was a fae that didn't need magic to put a spell on me, but he *did* have magic, and that was the only thought that kept my head on even remotely straight. Magic was dangerous, even when the fae wielding it was ... well ... Nyx.

I forced my eyes from Nyx to rove the forested inside of his cell before allowing them to flicker back to the prince. "I thought you couldn't do magic."

Nyx lifted up his hand to turn the once soft, sun-touched skin over in the pale light. It hadn't taken long for the golden color to fade, leaving a slight, sickly pale in its place. The color still somehow suited him, of course, since I was fairly certain there was no color that wouldn't suit the overwhelmingly beautiful *Nyx* of all fae, but it did make something small choke up in the back of my throat.

"I couldn't take the bracelet," he said, after a long, forlorn look at his own naked arm.

I glanced once more around him, and nodded, once. I'd seen the way losing the glamour had affected him the most. Seen the way his heart broke at his dying forest. Now he'd gotten a taste of what it was to have it again, even if it was from inside a cell.

"I understand," I said, after a moment. "I don't think I could give this up, either."

For a second, Nyx seemed confused. He tilted his head, a slight furrow creasing his brow that filled me for that moment with the near overwhelming desire to plant soft kisses on the wrinkled skin until it smoothed.

Finally, realization dawned on him and Nyx started shaking his head.

"Oh, this?" He gestured once to the overgrown enclosure around him. Even as his hands waved over the grass and flowers, the stems seemed to reach out toward him, trying to stretch a little bit closer. "Oh, it wasn't because of this. I haven't had magic like this in so long, I've grown used to it."

"Why then?"

He looked back at me with a sigh that parted his lips, drawing my gaze toward them for far too long.

"I've never been able to pull off silver."

"Wait … wait, what? Silver?" I was finally pulled from his spell as I asked, again, "Silver, the metal … are you allergic to it or something?"

"Worse," Nyx said, his head slowly swinging from side to side. "I've never been able to wear it."

I didn't know what to say to that, but Nyx was more than happy to elaborate for me.

"It washes me out. Looks horrible against my skin." he continued, that sadness in his eyes deepening to something like sorrow. "I have my principles, you know. I have to stick to them when times get tough, or else, who would I even be? How would I look my people—let alone myself—in the eye?"

If it was anyone else other than Nyx, I'd think he'd gone crazy.

But this *was* Nyx. This was the fae I'd seen break up with a tree and claim to regularly fall asleep in puddles. If he was any less gorgeous, I'd be far more concerned for him.

As it was, I was already concerned enough.

"But Nyx … aren't you lonely?" I asked, slowly, trying to make sure I didn't sound nearly as condescending as I felt. Had this fae actually turned down freedom because the bracelet wasn't *his color?*

Nyx, whether to his benefit or not, seemed to remain completely oblivious to this.

"Why would I be lonely?" He gestured to the greenery that tightened around his wrists and waist as he said it. "I have plenty of friends here."

I bit my tongue to stop myself from saying any one of the thousand things I had to say to *that.*

And so, apparently, did someone else.

"Can you two cut the bullshit?" Caldamir's voice carried down the corridor in a way that made me flinch. I glanced at the doorway to the main stairs, trying to train my ears for the sound of footsteps—though I knew I wouldn't hear them until it was too late. I was lucky that we hadn't been caught already, but the Mountain Prince didn't seem at all concerned with the way he raised his voice again to make sure I heard what he said next. "What are you really here for, Delph? You're not here to see Nyx."

"As far as you're concerned, I'm not here at all."

"That's where you're wrong," Caldamir said, finally leaning forward. "I have every right to be concerned about you."

He rested one arm on his bent knee. He too had refused the Starlight Court's robes, but he hadn't used his own magic to make himself clothes that suited him better. Before I could wonder why, the glitter of silver on his wrist answered that question for me.

If Caldamir had accepted the bracelet, why was he still locked up? Perhaps he'd refused the offer of freedom—that would be like him.

I could ask him, of course, but I didn't trust his answer. I didn't trust anything to do with the prince of the Mountain Court.

"I know you don't want to hear it, but I never expected things to end up like this," Caldamir said, something about his tone making me pause.

"What? You never expected me to end up alive?" I hissed back, keeping my voice as close to a whisper as I could. Beside me, I saw Nyx's face darken. His lips twisted down and one hand crossed over his stomach, as if to soothe a sudden stomach ache.

"No," Caldamir spat back. "I never expected myself to care."

Anger rose up in me, making me forget to keep my voice low.

"You don't get to say that," I spat. I stormed several paces back toward him, my hand raised to point right into his face—or as close to it as I could get through the crystal—when I froze.

It seemed I wasn't going to get the chance to give Caldamir a piece of my mind that was currently racing with a million angry thoughts.

Someone was coming down the stairs. And as the footsteps always seemed to echo here in the palace, they came far too late to do anything about it. I braced myself, knowing it was too late to turn and run, and deciding it was better to face whatever was coming for me than to be caught running like a coward.

Only it wasn't a guard who appeared in the door—it was Tarrack.

Finally, for once, luck was on my side.

Tarrack took one look at me and then grabbed me and pulled the both of us out the back door through which I'd arrived. He did it so quickly I had no time to say goodbye—not that I would have given Caldamir the courtesy, but I felt guilty for abandoning Nyx.

"You need to be more careful," Tarrack said, as soon as he'd tugged me far enough away to be sure we were out of earshot. Still, he made no motion to let me go. "The court grows more unsettled by the day."

"It'll be fine. I just had to check that Nyx was alright."

Tarrack shot me a look that was far more astute than his usually were. "Is that what you've been doing, then? Checking on the prisoner princes?"

I stopped dead in my tracks.

"All I'm saying is that in times like these, it's important you know whose side you're on," Tarrack said, once again with altogether too much care in his words. He was usually the one to blabber on, stumbling over his words as often as he accidentally blurted out secrets. "Rumors are only rumors until they can be used against you."

"Please, Tarrack," I said, closing my eyes for a second and pinching the top of my nose with my thumb and forefinger to stem the headache that was starting to blossom there. "Can you be plain with me? What are you trying to say?"

"I'm saying that you've angered the wrong fae," he said, as blunt as I'd ever heard him. "Itris knows when to keep secrets, but more than that, she knows when *not* to."

I groaned aloud.

One day. One day was all it took.

I looked Tarrack dead in the eye. "Does Seren know?"

His lips pressed together in a way that told me all I needed to know. Another groan, this one from an even deeper place, rumbled past my lips. Tarrack nudged us forward, and though all I wanted to do was find a nice dark corner to hide in embarrassment, I let the fae lead me back through the twisting maze of corridors.

I shouldn't have cared that Seren knew about me and the prince's … adventures … in the baths. He'd said he didn't care, or at least something close to it, but the last person I would have wanted him to hear it from was Itris, of all people. I could only imagine how she turned my magic into something sordid.

"You're lucky the guards were distracted down in the prison," Tarrack said, after a few minutes of unusual silence had passed between us. "Another minute or two and you would have been caught."

Caught.

The word made me scrunch my nose in distaste. "And what would have happened if I was *caught*?" I asked.

Tarrack didn't have an answer to that, and that was what concerned me most of all.

"Let's just hope we don't have to find out," he said, and on that I had to agree—even if I didn't agree with everything else. "Promise me you'll be more careful, Delphine."

"I promise—"

"And by that, I mean promise me you'll stop seeing the princes."

My words stuttered to a halt, and so did our feet once again. We'd made it all the way to my tower room. Tarrack turned me to face him, both hands holding me tight on the upper arms as he searched my face.

"Promise me, Delphine. I wouldn't be asking this of you if it wasn't important. The rest of the court might think I'm an old fool, but I like to think you know me better than that."

He was, of course, right.

Tarrack was no fool. I, on the other hand, was.

Not just a fool, a stubborn fool, too.

So, though it pained me more than I was ever going to be willing to admit, I lied to the fae who had just saved me.

"I promise, Tarrack," I said, with a heavy sigh. "I'll stay away from the princes."

24
DELPHINE

I, OF COURSE, HAD NO INTENTION OF ENDING THINGS WITH TETHYS and Armene.

I wouldn't end it for Itris, but I *couldn't* end it for Tarrack … because I couldn't even end it for *me*. Being with the princes had awakened that fae side of me even more than before.

I couldn't end it.

I would just have to be more … discreet.

There was no way for me to send the princes a message to be careful, so in my own anxiety, I nearly gave myself away. Elvie had come to my tower room to help me prepare for the next one of Seren's tests.

Seeker. Seer. Reader.

Those were the three Starlight lines I'd been personally introduced to, though I knew there were four more—at least. There was once a time that I'd thought there were only four kinds of fae and one faerie realm, but so far that had been proven false too, so I wasn't sure what to believe.

And Reader fae, well, they were the hardest to believe of all.

The kind of magic their line performed would be reduced to

party tricks and travelling caravans in the human realm, if they were lucky. If they were unlucky, they'd be branded with some kind of heresy, whether it be against kings or gods, and probably find themselves at the wrong end of an axe for it.

I couldn't help but think that if humans had any idea, any *real* idea what magic and glamour could do, this would be the last thing they'd actually be worried about. I'd seen magic rend realms. Compared to that, the magic of the Reader line was nothing.

And still, I seemed unable to perform it.

Readers were like Seers in that their magic was a magic of the mind instead of the physical. Where Seren's magic physically transported him—and other fae—from one place to another, this magic was more like Tarrack's. Where the Seer magic allowed fae to see and hear into places in the physical, the Reader magic allowed a glimpse into far more uncertain territory—the mind.

From what I'd gathered so far, Reader fae had quite varying abilities among them, more so than the other lines. Some were particularly skilled at reading the future. Some were better at telling when a fae lied. Some, further still, could draw out the truth without a fae knowing they were being coerced in the first place.

The most common ability, however, was a kind of divination using cards.

Seren had suggested this practice in favor of the others, since —like the pools that Itris had warned me off of—Readers, or the fae who tried to mimic them, were in danger of being lost in the minds they delved into.

I'd had a taste of magic, and however brief and strange, I was hungry for more.

Seren had told me that the overwhelm of emotions was me learning to be fae, but that wasn't the whole truth. Maybe if I'd been able to access my magic as a Reader, I would have been able to see it for what it really was—a warning.

I'd wrongly assumed that by embracing this side of myself, I'd be able to satisfy it … but that was the thing. Seren had promised to teach me what it was to be fae, and I was learning quickly.

Being fae meant that there was no such thing as being satisfied.

The more I took, the more I wanted.

The more I indulged, the more I desired.

The more I learned, the more I questioned.

I was beginning to see why this was what Seren required in exchange for the deal. He was certain that this side of me would win over, that once I fully understood the unending, unquenchable thirst of the fae, that I wouldn't have the strength to give it up.

That I wouldn't have the strength to go back.

If it weren't for the fact that I was still human, still bound to that realm despite the fae blood that ran through my veins, he'd be right.

Really, if it weren't for Sol, he'd be right.

But I was human. I had Sol to think about. So, sure, I would learn what it was to be Starlight Fae … but in the end, I'd go back. It had nothing to do with my strength, and everything to do with my weakness.

The concept of the Reader cards was simple enough. With training, nearly all Starlight Fae could use them to some degree, whether that be to divine a vague future or help with a decision—or so Elvie had told me when she first delivered the new set that Seren had drawn up for me. Only fae from the Reader line would be able to read them naturally, but even that presented a very particular problem.

Even if I drew a dozen decks of the cards with the kind of precision that could foretell an unshakable future, it wouldn't matter. Not when reading the magic of the cards wasn't the problem ... actually, literally *reading* them was.

I'd never really considered how lucky I was that the fae spoke the same language as humans ... until Elvie so patiently explained to me that it had more to do with the predatory nature of fae than it did any luck on my part. All fae learned the human languages alongside their own for one reason, and one alone.

For a human to be able to make a deal, they had to be able to understand it.

The fae language was a kind of glamour of its own, understood by any who heard it—just as they understood any language spoken in return. It was a hunter's instinct, bred into the very stuff that made them fae. Just as a wolf didn't have to stop and wonder how to catch a deer, so neither did a fae have to wonder how to trap a human.

If only the same applied to humans.

There was a similar kind of card trick performed at festivals in the human realm, but in the human realm, the cards had images and symbols that anyone could look at and make some kind of assumption, some basic reading. They were images of angels and demons and fae, of plague and famine and wealth.

But looking down at these cards, I couldn't make heads or tails of them. They were all fae images, fae folklore, fae warnings and omens. Even those that seemed obvious enough, images of skulls, of shades and spirits, fiends with glowing eyes, or depictions of black, empty chasms—they never meant what I expected them to. The cards that I thought were evil actually depicted the presence of strong guardians nearby. The cards that looked good, like something positive, actually depicted tricksters and liars out to steal the fae soul.

Elvie tried to show me where the elaborate borders around the cards actually spelled out the titles of the cards, but I couldn't so much as make out the letters that formed fae language, let alone try to read the words.

No matter how I pulled them, no matter the order in which I arranged them, I kept returning to the same problem.

I couldn't divine the cards because they meant nothing to me.

I'd tried to explain this to Elvie already, after our first practice session yesterday evening, but she refused to be deterred. I didn't know if Seren had set her up to this, or if she was genuinely convinced I was suddenly going to be zapped with the glamour needed to read the cards, or maybe even if she just needed something to keep her own mind occupied, but no matter how I tried to convince her to give up one me—she wouldn't.

Today, Elvie had even brought her own deck of cards to practice with, citing that maybe there was something wrong with mine. Though she was exceedingly patient in trying to explain to me over and over the best way to try to *feel* the intentions of the cards, I couldn't blame her when at long, long last, she too had finally had enough. After another unsuccessful afternoon, the determined look on Elvie's face was finally replaced with one of disgust as she threw down the last three cards in her hands with an excitable huff and demanded to know what it was that had me distracted.

"You've been sitting like that all afternoon!" she said, waving her hands in a frustrated arc at the way I was hunched over at the open window. I wasn't just hunched at the window, I was practically leaning out of it, half ready to fall to my own death, if I was being honest with myself.

"I know you don't think that you can read these cards, but you haven't really given them a try. And don't give me any more of that "fae language" crap you've been sticking to. You don't have to be able to read the cards for them to work. You just … you just have to actually draw them with intention."

She narrowed her eyes at me. "And don't try and tell me you've been doing that, either," she said, scolding. "We both know that's not true."

There was no point in arguing, since, of course, she was right.

I *was* distracted.

I'd barely paid any attention to the last half dozen sets of cards she'd laid out on the floor, and it had less to do with the fact that I was convinced I was never going to sense any meaning from them, and more to do with the fact that with each second that passed, two princes of Avarath were more and more likely to show up at my door.

I was watching the passages I could make out from my tower window, looking for a set of silver robes that might warn me that the princes had started their way up to my rooms. I couldn't bring myself to regret asking them to come, but I *did* wish I'd been more specific. I didn't want to have to explain to Elvie what two princes of Avarath were doing drooling at my door.

I felt a slight twinge of annoyance as Elvie got to her feet and crossed her arms, the deck of silver-trimmed cards forgotten where they were splayed out on the stone floor.

"So?" she asked, her tone only finally pulling me out of my half daze when I realized I still hadn't answered her the first time. "What is it?"

I snapped forward, one hand shooting out to steady myself against the window frame so I didn't fall out of it after all.

"Sorry," I mumbled, shaking my head several times to clear it —unsuccessfully. "I haven't been sleeping well."

It wasn't quite like the lie I'd told Tarrack, but that wasn't entirely true, either, and I immediately felt guilty for saying it.

For the first time since I'd arrived in the Starlight Court, I'd actually been able to sleep beneath the sheets of my bed last night—and I had a feeling it had more to do with the heat of the fae princes than the heat of the baths. My skin, my very senses were more awakened than they had been before, but where I'd found it overwhelming before, it had begun to feel more ... natural. Sure, in giving into them they'd become heightened, but it was like my body was finally able to get used to them. To embrace them, mold into them rather than rejecting them like some foreign entity.

"You know you don't have to do this, not right now," Elvie said, her sudden shift in tone taking me off guard. "There's no rush. No one would fault you for needing to take things slow. To process things, especially now."

"What are you talking about?"

"I'm talking about the fae who tried to murder you, and how they're here, in Elysia ... under this very roof," Elvie said. "Or hadn't you noticed?"

"Of course, I noticed," I snapped back, then immediately winced at my own words. "Sorry, *again*."

I let out a small sigh. "Maybe I am on edge."

I looked down at the cards, wishing beyond all hope that I felt even the slightest pull to any one of them. Sure, both Seren and Elvie had warned me that reading the cards could take time, but I'd suspected from the very beginning that these cards weren't for me, and that *might* have had something to do with the fact that I was no closer to being able to read them then I was at the very start.

Elvie softened again, the accusation in her eyes finally fading as she looked back down at the cards with a sigh of her own. "That would at least explain the cards, then." She cocked her head to the side with a puzzled expression. "I've been getting the strangest reading all day, and I just haven't been able to make it out."

I followed her gaze, and for what felt like the millionth time, I tried—really tried—to make any sense of the cards.

Again, nothing. Just ... nothing.

Still, that didn't stop the pit from forming in my stomach when I saw how Elvie looked at the cards. I might not be able to read them, but she could.

I felt my body shift half involuntarily beneath me. "What do they say?"

My voice sounded strained, even to myself, but Elvie didn't seem to notice this time. Her lips were moving wordlessly as she read over the cards again.

"I keep getting this same set. Not every time, but enough," she said, finally, pointing out three cards that to me looked like they were just beautifully decorated with more of that delicate silver line work. "I've never gotten these three together before, so I'm not exactly sure if I'm reading them right."

An apology flickered across her face when she looked up at me. "Seren really should have assigned you to work with another fae on this. You know it's practically guesswork for me too."

"Yeah, well, at least you can *read* the cards," I said, trying to pass off an uninterested shrug and failing. I should have let it drop, found a way to get Elvie to leave before an even more awkward situation inevitably arose, but I couldn't help myself. I was intrigued now. I chanced one last look over my shoulder at the passage down below, and seeing no sign of movement, nodded back toward the cards.

"So," I asked, breathless despite myself. "What is it?"

"It's an omen," Elvie said, eyes still scanning. Her frown deepened. "A harbinger? A warning?"

She took too long to answer, and I found myself slipping away from the window to crouch beside her on my knees. A shiver raced down my spine as I looked over the cards despite the fact that I still couldn't read a single one.

"Of what?"

Elvie finally looked back up at me then. "I keep trying to think of something else it could mean. I just keep coming up with the same thing."

"And that is?" I was growing impatient. I didn't like the look on her face.

Turns out, I didn't like what she was going to say, either.

"Of death."

A chill settled over the room at her words. I sat back, scooting away from the cards to put some distance between myself and them. Elvie wrinkled up her nose, suddenly unsure of herself. She glanced between me as I folded my arms across my chest and tightened them, and then back to the cards.

"I'm probably wrong … "

"Or probably not," I said, quietly.

Elvie didn't argue again. She was reading me. Testing me.

Then, at long last, she blurted out the question I was sure had been picking at her all day.

"Is it true, then? Have you taken the princes from Avarath into your bed?"

I shouldn't have been shocked by her question, but I was. I stumbled over my words, the jumbled, broken sounds giving me away as much as anything else.

"How could you—"

"I may be a fae child, but I'm much older than you. I know about these things. People in the palace talk. And let me tell you. People in the palace, they're *talking*."

That shut me up.

Elvie and I sat, staring at one another until I finally willed myself to break the silence.

"Yes," I admitted, since there was really no getting around the truth. Elvie could claim it was all court gossip all she wanted, but there was a good chance she'd heard it from the horses' mouth, Itris, herself. Or her twin. He might not have been there to accost me with his grandmother, but he was likely the reason she found me there in the first place.

Either way, I knew I'd be a fool—more of a fool than I'd already been—if I dared hint either of them was a liar.

Elvie nodded, and the disappointment that I saw in her face made me want to crawl beneath my silken sheets again and never come back out. It would be easy to do now that my skin didn't prickle uncomfortably at their touch.

She picked up the three cards and brandished them out to me as if they were my fault, somehow. "This is a warning, Delphine. You have to stop, or fae are going to get hurt."

"Elvie ... "

"No," she said, more forcefully than she'd ever been with me. She drew herself up where she sat, and for one moment, I saw the resemblance between her and her grandmother more keenly than ever. "I can't let you do this to yourself. This isn't an option, Delphine. Tell me that you know that?"

I pressed my lips together, but I couldn't help but nod in agreement.

"I do know."

The slightest bit of relief softened the furrow between her brows. Her posture relaxed, only for a moment, and only so that she could once more lean forward and point a finger in my face.

"Do you promise me?"

I wanted to tell her no, to lie to her even, but I couldn't do either.

Three warnings. Three cards.

Three times I'd been warned to stay away from the princes. Three cards I'd been given, all omens of impending death.

"Promise me, Delphine."

The second time, I nodded too. "I promise, Elvie. I'll make things right."

Just saying it made that heat, that fire that had been stoked to life in me for the last day and a half, die in me a little. Still, I knew it was right.

I knew *she* was right.

I didn't have to be a magic card reader to know not to ignore those cards. I'd seen Elvie work before. She could call herself a beginner, a novice at magic all that she liked … but she was powerful. If she was powerful enough to summon Sol so I could see him, then she was powerful enough to pull forward a warning that shouldn't be ignored.

No matter how much I might want to.

25
DELPHINE

I'D MEANT TO KEEP MY PROMISE TO ELVIE—TRULY—BUT IT SEEMED that fate had no intention of leaving things up to me. No sooner had I made my promise then there was a knock at the door.

Of course, *now* they come.

I swore, inwardly. I shouldn't have stepped away from the window. I should have kept my guard up, been more careful, figured out a way to warn the princes off earlier. Really, I should have heeded the first two warnings offered to me and ended things before I ever planned to let them go any further.

Now, it was too late.

Maybe if I just ignored it, they'd think they got the wrong room and go away. Elvie hadn't looked up from where she was gathering up her cards from the floor, so I pretended I hadn't heard the knock the first time.

The second time they knocked, Elvie paused and glanced over at the door, then at me, like maybe she was hearing things. I still pretended to have heard nothing, choosing instead to lean out the open window as if I was looking for Moon, since he usually found his way up to my tower around this time of day, anyway.

Come on, Tethys … Armene … just go away. I wished the silent prayer over and over as I leaned out the window, neck craning up to look for any movement up or down the tower staircase that might signal they'd moved on.

It was all for nothing, however. The third time they knocked, there was no ignoring it, not when Elvie finally shot me a concerned look.

"Aren't you going to get that?"

"It's probably just Ayre," I said, knowing my voice hardly sounded as dismissive as I'd have liked. "I don't need her tonight."

The concern on her face twisted into something more like pity. "Don't tell me you're still afraid of her? I can tell her to go if you—"

"No!" I practically shouted, jumping off the window and over to the door before she could finish getting up from the floor. "I'll handle it."

She was watching me too closely, however, so I feigned a glance back at the window I'd just left and asked her to go check if she saw Moon out there after all. The thought of the Catsuga that'd adopted me distracted her enough that I was able to pry the door open an inch in order to hiss at the two princes that were, unfortunately just as expected, waiting outside.

Their dark skin was striking against the backdrop of white walls and silver robes, but it was nothing compared to the heat the sparkled in their eyes. Armene's widened at the sight of me, disheveled as I was from spending the day cooped up in my tower window looking for them. He let out a small swear-whisper that made my throat go dry. Tethys, meanwhile, broke into one of his signature roguish grins.

"We were just starting to wonder if you'd changed your mind … " Tethys said, voice deep enough to rumble through me. "Can't tell you how disappointed we would have been to find out we didn't satisfy you as much as we thought."

"Not sure that would be possible," Armene said, catching my eye again. "Not when I'm sure we can still both hear the sound of her—"

"Stop!" I hissed, finally coming to my senses enough to try to pull the door shut further, but Tethys stopped me with the tip of his boot. He leaned his arm against the door, pressing his forehead to it and nearer to me.

"What's the matter, Delphie? Don't tell me you've suddenly gotten cold feet. You're the one who said this didn't have to change anything, or have you forgotten?"

Oh, how I hated these princes right now.

"Of course not," I hissed again. "It's just that—"

"Is Ayre still there?" Elvie called out, from behind me.

I let out an annoyed sort of sound in the back of my own throat and cast a look over my shoulder. Elvie had just finished pulling back from the window, her own disappointment written across her face when there was no Catsuga to be found. "Maybe you could ask her to look for Moon while she's making her rounds."

"No, I think that's—"

Elvie cut me off with an annoyed huff and a roll of her eyes. "You need to stop being afraid of Ayre. If you won't ask her, I will."

"I—"

It was too late.

I didn't have time to shoo the princes away before the fae girl had started shoving her way between me and the door. I refused to budge, but she refused to back down. She just ducked her head beneath my arm to peer out at the servant she thought she'd find.

"You can't be so timid with her. Ayre, Delphine was just … "

She trailed off, her eyes lifting up to mine before I had the chance to finish shutting the door enough to block out the sight of the princes still lingering on the other side. That smile of hers faltered, and I knew she'd seen them.

Shit.

I wasn't sure if I swore out loud or not this time, but it didn't matter.

There was a strange tone in Elvie's voice when her head snapped back to look at me.

"Delphine … "

"This isn't what it looks like," I said, too quickly. I tried to shut the door again, this time kicking out Tethys' blocking shoe, but Elvie shot out an arm and jammed the door open on her own.

Both princes nearly stumbled into the room as the support was taken out from under Tethys' arm. By the time they were straightening their robes again, Elvie's face had gone positively scarlet.

It wasn't the princes she was angry at, unfortunately.

She fully rounded on me. "You're a liar."

"That's hardly fair," I said, though the two princes still towering in the doorway did little to lend credibility to my words. "I didn't have time to send them away. You know that. You were here, with me, the whole time."

"Uh, huh," Elvie said. "So, what were you going to do, bed them one last time before you sent them away? Slip just a few more Starlight secrets into their ears between sweet nothings?"

Her words stung, even though I'd be lying to myself if the thought of having them one *last* time hadn't crossed my mind.

I must have paused long enough for Elvie to know it, too, because she made a disgusted sound in the back of her throat. "I can't believe I trusted you."

Meanwhile, Tethys and Armene had frozen in the doorway. They exchanged a glance between the two of them, unsure of whether or not they should intervene … or, I guessed, whether it might be more beneficial for them to make a silent escape.

"You can trust me," I said, anger rising up for the first time in place of the raging embarrassment. "What happened, anyway? Did Itris put you up to this?"

Elvie looked offended, *really* offended this time.

"You shouldn't talk about my grandmother like that, you know. I might complain about her, but she's my flesh and blood. We're family. We don't even know what you are yet."

Her head tilted back, eyes going hooded. "For all we know, you're not fae at all. Maybe you're the one tricking us? Tarrack said you drew out some glamour, sure, but he'd be easy enough to fool. I wouldn't put it by you. You're clearly desperate enough."

My mouth hung agape. Just a few weeks ago, hearing that wouldn't have meant anything to me. Now, however, it left burning tears to gather in the corner of my eyes.

"Take that back," I hissed. "You know that isn't true."

Elvie only straightened herself up again. She pulled up her sleeve and grasped at a silver tattoo imprinted on her skin there. I'd never seen it before, but it reminded me of the lines I'd once glimpsed scrawled across her uncle's back.

"That isn't for me to decide, for either of us to decide anymore."

Barely a moment passed after Elsie's hand touched the tattoo before a familiar, strange sensation stretched across the space between us. I knew Tethys and Armene felt it too, because I saw them stumble the split second before first the flutter of silk robes and then the thunder of boots stepping down from the open arches of the window echoed behind me.

For one second, the windows became portals pulled open by a Seeker fae—but this time Itris was the fae to step through it. And she wasn't alone. Four sigil-bearing guards were pulled through with her, and three of them wasted no time marching past me and Elvie to roughly grab the princes before they'd even registered what just happened.

The fourth guard stopped beside me, and I felt despair settle in the pit of my stomach when his arm reached out to wrap around mine.

I knew what happened next. I didn't have to wait for Itris to tell me.

ITRIS DIDN'T OFFER me the courtesy of transporting me privately via portal.

No, she marched me through the darkening palace halls like a prize she wanted the whole court to see. Tethys and Armene had been escorted separately, and I'd have been willing to bet that they were on their way back to the prison cells they'd only just been freed from.

She'd sent a semi-reluctant Elvie away, at least before we started along familiar paths. I knew where we were going long before we got there.

The Seeker's tower.

Only this time, even when Itris barged in as only she did, Seren wasn't there.

No one was.

It was empty.

Itris swore loud enough for the guard holding me to stiffen along with his grip, but I refused to make even a sound, despite the fact that he was half crushing my arm.

"Where is my insufferable brother? Of course, he's always here unless I actually need him."

Itris marched toward another door, with the guard half-dragging me along after her heels even though I would have been perfectly happy to keep up on my own. It was like he was purposefully making me stumble, forcing me to lean into him and his crushing grip more and more until the muscles beneath started to smart.

This time, when we passed through the door, it didn't take us to the great hall as it once did.

Seren's bedchambers were unlike any I'd ever seen. They had to have been located in another tower, taking up the entire top floor. It wasn't the walls here that were open to the sky, it was the ceiling. Cut crystal domed overhead, reflecting and catching the light of the night sky in a breathtaking display. It was as if each facet of crystal had been cut to perfectly catch a star as it moved across the sky, and when it did, it caught its light in a way that made the crystal glow like a prism, casting a million dancing lights across the marble floor.

There were no windows into this room, only doors. A hundred arches made up the curved walls, each one—I was sure—leading to another place in the palace. Or Elysia. Or another realm, for all I knew. Spaced at regular intervals around the room were seven fountains, each one gurgling with more of that black water. It trickled down the sides of the fountains in small, controlled rivulets that ran through cracks carved into the floor. The sound of it made the room itself sound alive, like whispers spoken too low to make out the words.

The only piece of furniture in the room was a massive

circular bed in the very middle. It was draped with fine silver silks and soft white furs and surrounded by a variety of copper-colored instruments trained toward the sky.

It was from this bed of silks that Seren arose. He took in his sister with a flash of annoyance, and I was secretly glad for it, because that meant he wasn't looking at me. It meant he didn't see the way the sight of him here, like this, affected me.

He was naked from the waist up, his robes replaced with silk pants that accentuated every single muscle and line of his body from where they draped low across the cut v of his abs. He was a male with *no* shame, and why should he, anyway … when what he was so willing to reveal was something he should most definitely be proud of.

It wasn't the first time I was grateful for the fact my own body couldn't betray the desire the sight of him alighted in me. Not anymore than the flush I felt rising to my cheeks did, anyway.

"What can you possibly need now, sister?" he asked, as much exhaustion in his voice as there was that special kind of annoyance reserved for siblings. It was a second later that he registered the guard that she'd brought alongside her, and then, a moment later still, me.

"What's this? What's going on?"

His annoyance had turned to something sharper. His posture straightened and his eyes scanned the doorway behind us, as if looking for more figures.

"Has something gone wrong?"

Itris motioned for the guard to pull me forward, and so he tugged me up to stand at her side. Seren stared at the guard's hand on me, eyes fixated on the place where his hand met my skin.

"She was caught conspiring with the princes Tethys of the Sea Court and Armene of the Sand Court.

"Conspiring?"

Itris pressed her lips together. "Conjugating, then."

It was only then that Seren's eyes lifted from his own near murderous glare at the hand holding me—a hand that had grown decidedly gentler in the last few seconds.

"And I should be concerned … why?"

"It's a danger to us all," Itris said. "Who knows what she's told them. Who knows who's side she's on."

"So, you marched her here, to me?"

Seren's voice was calm. Too calm.

Dangerously calm.

Either his sister hadn't noticed this yet, or she didn't care. The guard at my side, however, seemed to care very much. He was barely touching me now, his feet shifting uncomfortably beneath him.

"You could have just portaled her to me."

Itris huffed as if that was impossible. "And risked her jumping out somehow? Hardly?"

Seren let out a sigh of frustration. "And why would she do that?"

Itris didn't have an answer to that, and for the first time, I heard the confidence in her voice crack. "But you ordered the guards to keep her from the prison."

"Yes, I did," Seren said, still so dangerously calm. "For her own safety, not out of *suspicion*."

Itris still wasn't ready to admit defeat. She leaned closer, eyebrows raising, voice dropping—pleading, almost.

"We don't know what she's capable of, yet."

"That's hardly what you should be worrying about," Seren

said, his voice finally snapping. "It's not a matter of what Delphine is capable of. It's a matter of what *I'm* capable of."

It was then, finally, that Itris saw the true depths of the rage that had risen inside her brother. She visibly shrank before me, her lips parting as her eyes widened in first confusion, and then understanding—understanding of her own mistake.

The hand holding onto me was no longer holding me in place. The guard was, instead, steadying himself on me. He'd started shaking, heart beating so fast that I could practically feel it through my own skin, even before Seren turned his wrath on him.

"You."

Seren glared down at the fae that had dragged me halfway across the palace to stand before him. His eyes practically burned with white hot fury. I wasn't at the receiving end of it, and even still, I felt myself begin to quake.

"Lesser fae have killed for her. Don't think I'll let myself be outdone if you keep giving me reason."

"Seren!" Itris gasped, eyes widening further. "You can't threaten our own guards. Our own fae."

Seren whipped to face her. "I will threaten whomever I please," he snarled. "And I'll make good on those threats. You were right. The Starlight Court has grown complacent. Soft. It's time we changed that. It's time we remembered just how *ruthless* we can be."

He moved so quickly, he was a blur. His head dipped to press so close he was almost kissing the guard's stubbled cheek at my side.

"Now let her go before you're the first fae tonight to know what that *ruthless* truly means."

26
DELPHINE

I THOUGHT I SAW RAGE IN CALDAMIR'S EYES THAT DAY SEREN TOOK me away, but it was nothing compared to what burned inside this king now.

He was consumed by it, driven to the brink of blind madness.

The moment the guard stepped away from me, Seren took his place. He caught hold of me and pulled me hard to his side, every muscle in his body so tense that it might as well have been carved from the same stone as the palace. A dangerous energy raced over and through him until I could feel the glamour seeping into *me.*

Seren threw one arm up in a furious gesture and a massive wall of black water erupted up before us, drawn in long strands from the streams running in rivulets through the cracked floor. I had one moment to observe our reflection in the glassy surface. I was tiny compared to him, so insignificant beside the very embodiment of power beside me. The glamour had completely overtaken the fae at my side. Every inch of him had taken on an otherworldly glow—the glow of fire and starlight—before the glassy reflection shattered, revealing a throne room beyond.

Seven thrones encircled a small dais in the middle. A beam of light funneled through a channel cut into the tall, domed roof set the center of the circle aglow. As bright as it was, however, it cast the thrones themselves into a darker shadow, still.

Itris and the guard huddled back, their faces cast in this shadow of the high-backed chairs while Seren stormed to stand in the center of the circle of thrones with me at his side. He threw up his arm again, and this time the rush of magic opened not one portal, but five.

A second later, the other kings of Elysia began stumbling out of them—various expressions of alarm painted across their faces.

"What is it?"

"What's happened?"

"Seren, what's this all about?"

Only Tarrack was silent, his eyes alighting on me where the other kings looked to Seren.

He already knew.

The rest of the kings soon followed Tarrack's silence when they saw the fury still radiating off the fae that had summoned them. An odd silence fell and stretched on, where the five other kings of the realm looked increasingly unsure of what they should say, let alone what they were meant to do. I saw more than one of them pause, unable even to decide whether they should sit in their own thrones.

"Have I not proven myself enough?"

Seren's question finally rang out, dangerous and low.

"For five thousand years, I've served as this court's Seeker. I've sacrificed more than any of you could ever dream. You are the remnants of your lines wiped out. I am a relic. I alone stand before you unchanged and untested from the very beginning of time."

With each one of his words, Seren seemed almost to grow.

His presence filled the room, his voice echoing through every nook and cranny until there was no escape from it.

"Do you know what I've learned in all this *time*?"

Carrigan was the only king that looked like he was about to answer and then—wisely—thought better of it.

"You kings are as fickle as any other fae … and I've grown tired of it."

With a flick of Seren's wrist, the light pooling over us began to grow thicker. It gathered together in flecks of gold and silver, then bands that began to string together.

"We were made to be better than this, and yet here you are, squabbling and gossiping against your own kind as if you were mere princes of the other fae realms. We were made to be judges of fae, but in order to do that, we must be above them. We must be better than them."

The thing made of light had begun to take form as Seren continued. "And more than that, still, we must *judge.*"

Carrigan at last found his voice. "But without the seventh king—"

"There is no seventh king," Seren snarled, the glamour inside him glowing brighter, and all the rest of the kings shrank back. "There is never going to be a seventh king. There's only one way to maintain the balance of the old court, and that's by bringing in a new one. Too long have we held onto the old traditions that bound us. The old era is passed. It died with so many of our fae in the great war, and it's time we admit it. It's time for a new era to begin."

It wasn't until his words echoed into silence that I finally realized what it was that he'd made from the light. The light had woven tight, solidified into something very real and very tangible.

It was a throne—a throne that towered above all the rest,

made from and still shining with the very starlight from which it had been created.

That's when it dawned on me.

That's when I knew what I saw unfolding before me, the gravity of the moment I was witnessing.

I was witnessing the birth of a king—a true king. A *high* king.

When Seren first dragged me here, to Elysia, he was one of many. After tonight, the other kings might keep their titles, but there was no mistaking who truly ruled over them.

It was all I could do to keep from collapsing under the weight of the power rolling off of Seren as he finally let go of me to take his place on his new, glittering throne.

"Any who wish to challenge me, challenge me now, and I'll hear you. I do promise you, though," he said, his voice dropping low with more danger than promise, "wait to challenge me and you won't be met with such kindness again."

I expected at least Carrigan to contest him, but even he stayed silent.

It was Tarrack, at long last, who was the only king brave enough to step forward—and it wasn't to contest Seren's claim. It was to solidify it.

"All hail Seren, *high king* of Elysia."

He bowed low, the trailing sleeves of his robes sweeping out to either side. When he straightened back up, there was something glowing there, on his face, something like reverence. Awe, even.

It was a look that slowly spread between the kings, one by one, as they mimicked Tarrack. And who could blame them? I found myself bowing beneath the weight, my knees nearly buckling as the voices of the other kings sealed what Seren had set into motion.

"All hail the high king of the Starlight Fae."

One by one, the other kings of Elysia took their own thrones, small and insignificant in the shadows. Two were empty now, but one Seren filled as his first act as high ruler.

"Itris," he said, eyes snapping to land on his sister still in the shadows. "It's time you took your throne. Unless, of course, you no longer want to be Seeker."

Itris took his offer with grace. The only sign that she was surprised by the act was the slightest, grateful glance she shot towards her brother.

The remaining empty throne was sealed by Seren's second act.

"Tonight, I seal the Binder's throne. As long as it remains empty, this court remains balanced. Seven kings were meant to rule the courts of Elysia, and seven kings remain."

Seven kings, sure, but it was clear where the true power now lay.

Seren bowed his head, a deep breath rattling through his chest. "If we are to protect the realms from the high king of Avarath, then we must protect all Starlight Fae. We must remember that we are all one people. We were united once, against the evil that tried to spread across our lands. We must be united once again."

It was only then that Seren finally turned to me, finally fixed those glowing eyes on me.

"I promised you once that I would protect you. I never imagined I'd need to protect you from my own court. Then again … it wasn't *my* court, yet."

But it was now.

27
DELPHINE

POWER SUITED SEREN. STANDING THERE, BESIDE THE NEW HIGH KING, I felt my knees grow weak—and not just from that power.

If it weren't for the other kings seated around us, one more look like that from Seren would have been enough to end me. If he'd wanted to, he could have taken me then and there on the court floor, and I'd not have had the willpower to stop him.

Fortunately, I wasn't going to be forced to make a fool of myself, at least not in front of the entirety of Elysia's fae court. Seren had no desire to hold court. Not tonight. Not yet.

He dismissed his new court almost as soon as he'd sat at its head.

No, not when there was apparently something much more important that he needed to finish, first.

He tore us through a portal back to his bed chamber, ordering only Tarrack to follow. The other kings sat in silence, hardly daring to breathe. I imagined they had much to discuss themselves once we were gone—but I couldn't bring myself to care much. Not when it was currently taking all my effort just to remember how to do my own breathing at the new high king's side.

The moment we were through the door and the portal closed, Seren whirled on Tarrack.

"You must be wondering why I brought you back here."

Tarrack nodded as he took in the expression not just on Seren's face, but wracking through his entire body. That power still crackled within him from earlier, but it had shifted. It was no less intense, but it had a new sort of nervous energy to it.

"We're going to administer the Seeker test."

I froze right alongside Tarrack.

"Tonight?"

"Now."

Seren threw up an arm as he did before, and the water—gathered once more from the trickling fountains surrounding the tower room—once more rose at his command. "Unless, of course, you take issue with that, Delphine?"

Issue? The only issue I had was trying to keep my hands from trembling. They didn't tremble from fear, rather, but from *excitement*.

I'd been warned that this test was too dangerous, but that was the last thing I was worried about at the moment. The greater danger was ignoring the fact that every vein in my body was screaming for me to give into Seren, to give into that intoxicating draw of the newly ascended high king.

"I'm going to have you draw through an object. It's simple … usually a Seeker is truly tested by passing through themselves, but I'd rather not risk it tonight. I'm sure you won't mind."

"Risk what, exactly?" I asked. That nervous excitement was rolling off of him into me. I felt reckless, invincible. I wanted to demand to do the test proper. I would do this right or not at all.

"Risk being torn into a thousand tiny pieces."

Or maybe not. Maybe an easier, substitute test would do.

Seren instructed me to stand beside the portal with Tarrack at my side, then stalked across to stand at the furthest point in the room. He nodded back towards the glassy portal when he caught me watching him, instructing me again to keep my eyes fixed forward.

"You must concentrate. It's not just about bringing the object through in on piece, it's about not allowing yourself to be broken up in the process."

"I thought you said … "

"The risk is smaller," he said, his voice slowing a bit, "but there's always risks with magic. I'm going to have you try to pull an amulet through, something kept in the royal treasury. Unless, of course, you'd rather wait."

"No."

I was a little surprised by how sure I sounded, how sure I was.

More surprised, still, was when I turned my focus to that portal and what lay on the other side without hesitation, either.

At first, the portal was all dark glass. It was all swirling black water. I couldn't see anything other than my own reflection but slowly, and with no small amount of murmured guidance on Tarrack's part, the portal began to fade. The edges remained dark and sharp as cutting glass, but the center cleared, allowing me to see beyond.

I couldn't see the whole treasury, only the one, dark glittering amulet that Seren had instructed me to focus on. I didn't have to ask him if this was the amulet he meant. There was a draw to it like the draw I felt now to him. If it wasn't the amulet he wanted me to draw forth, then it was the amulet the glamour wanted for me.

Either way, it was going to be mine.

If I was a Seeker fae, of course.

I concentrated with every part of my body. I focused, drowning out every other voice, every thought, every noise and doubt. I drew on the power I'd felt before, instructed it to bend to my bidding.

And nothing happened.

Though I felt the magic alight in my veins, there was no shift in the portal, not so much as a glimmer of my being able to pull the amulet through. It sat, just out of reach until, at long last, even that began to fade. The portal darkened again to that cold, black, glittering glass until all I could see was myself peering back at me, exhausted, but still in one piece.

I'd failed another test of my glamour, and for the first time, I was glad of it.

And from the fierce look on Seren's face, I wasn't the only one.

He moved towards me, slowly, each footstep drawn and placed with purpose. He was a predator and I was the prey he stalked. His eyes remained fixed on mine, refusing to flicker away for so much as a second, even when his words were meant for the king still standing at the edge of the unchanged portal.

"Go," Seren said, still locking eyes with me. "You can leave us now, Tarrack."

Tarrack cast one glance between us, undoubtedly feeling the ever-tightening string that drew us together at last. He bowed once and turned to go, but Seren—still refusing to look away from me—spoke to him once more.

"You know, I'm surprised you didn't contest me. You had more right than any of the others."

A sly smile, much too conniving for usually oblivious Tarrack, creased the corner of the king's lips. "Oh, I've never desired to be high king. That's a burden I gladly let you bear."

The weight that hung heavy in the room after he left had nothing do with this new burden, but it certainly had everything to do with *desire.* It was as if the moment we were left alone the stars themselves burned a little brighter over our heads.

Seren crossed the room to stand before me in an instant. His chest rose and fell with feral breaths, each intake sharp and each release too short.

"Are you certain this is what you want? I'll warn you, I'm not one of the boys you've played with before. If you're to be with me, you have to be prepared to be *wholly* with me."

He could have warned me of anything in that moment, could have warned me that by joining with him I'd grow a second head or only be able to speak in riddles, and I wouldn't have turned him down. I would have willingly given him anything, *everything,* if it just meant an end to the heart-wrenching tightness that had built to a peak these last weeks.

"I'm certain," I said, barely daring to breathe the words.

Seren's jaw worked, his tongue running alone the inner edge of his teeth as he looked me over, taking in each curve and edge of me with careful scrutiny.

"Am I going to need a safe word?" I asked, half joking.

Half not.

"Safe word? I don't think so. You're safe with me, Delphine." He moved closer then, slowly, until I was leaning into him too. "Until, of course, you're not."

In an instant, Seren's hands were on my shoulders. He shoved me back, hard, so that I tumbled back into the middle of the silken bed.

"Spread your legs. I want to see you."

I did as he asked, but apparently I nudged my knees apart too slowly. Seren let out a grunt and fell onto the bed over me, shoving his hands up under my silken skirts to hitch them up over my hips. He drove one knee between my ankles and his face between my thighs, tugging me closer to the lights glowing overhead.

"Fuck, Delphine," he growled, rising with eyes burning brighter than ever before. "You're *beautiful.*"

He dove back in between my legs, only to stop before his lips so much as grazed me. I started to squirm, my hips shifting uncomfortably as he took me in so closely.

"None of that," he snarled, voice growing even deeper. "Your body is a temple and I intend to worship in it. Don't you dare disrespect my religion."

His hands slid up to dig into my thighs, pulling me ever closer, and this time rather than resisting, I melted into him. He let out a groan of pleasure when I did and, at long last, dove in to devour me.

His tongue swirled in and through every part of me, lips parted for soft kisses and less soft bites that made me gasp. "More of that," he growled into me, the rumbling of his voice sending another shudder through my core. He buried into me again, hands tugging himself deeper as he drew increasingly fevered whimpers from my lips.

"Louder."

I parted my own lips and let my head fall back to look at the dizzying stars above. My whimpers turned to moans, the sound of which echoed back from the crystals overhead and made Seren rumble deep between my thighs again.

It was as if he could sense the way each movement drew pleasure out of me, and how to coax it out just enough that I felt I was going to crash over the edge over and over—only to withdraw at the last second and fill me with a new kind of pleasure, a new kind of teasing pain. At last, I couldn't take it anymore. His lips sucked and his tongue swirled at that perfect apex of my thighs and I was there, I could feel it, every thought vanished from my body aside from the sweet release now so close.

Or not.

Seren drew back, hands moving to press atop my thighs as he rose to fix me with his dark glare. "Don't come yet."

I moaned, this time from *real* frustration. "I can't … I have … Seren …"

His own grunt matched mine. "You're really going to make me beg this time, aren't you?"

I parted my lips, trembling with the desire held like a taut wire ready to snap inside me, but Seren was already rising higher, looming over me, the front of his robe fallen open to reveal the beautiful, naked line of his chest.

"Fine. Please, Delphine, hold out for me," he whispered, taking my hand and guiding it down to the ties that barely contained the hard member already standing at attention beneath the silk of his breeches. He pressed my hand onto him, wrapping each one of my fingers around the shape of him one by one. He throbbed beneath my touch. "I want to feel you wrapped around me like this when you come."

"Well then," I breathed, legs already shaking, "what are you waiting for?"

An evil glint shone in his eye and suddenly, Seren's hands were on me in a fury, tearing at my silk dress until it came apart in silver strands between his fingers. One hand grabbed both of mine and pinned them up above my head, pressing them into the bed. The other tugged free the hard length of him from beneath the waistband of his pants and thrust it forward—just to the opening of me, but not actually inside.

No, he teased me there too, pressing just enough for me to

feel the heat of him while his head dipped to swirl circles around my nipples. He lapped and sucked and pressed until I wanted to scream. Every muscle of my body grew tight until even my arms strained for release. My shoulders ached, my nipples grew sore, and my thighs burned from where he pushed them apart.

"Do you feel it yet?" he asked, rising at last from the erect pink of my breasts. "Do you ache for me as I've so long ached for you?"

I let out a strangled sigh. "Yes, Seren. Yes, I do."

"Then say it."

He pushed the tip of his cock against me, but still not into me.

"I *ache* for you, Seren."

"And who am I?" he asked, hips poised just above me, every hard muscle of his abs flexed and ready to plunge into me at his command.

I let out a moan so loud it shook my body. "I ache for you, my king. Please, *please* don't make me wait any longer."

And he didn't.

Seren plunged the full length of himself into me—or what he could fit of it, anyway.

He moved with the same urgency I felt. He didn't wait for my body to accept him, he just made it accept him. Each thrust shook the bed, pressing my arms down deeper beneath his grasp, strained my shoulders more, nudged my thighs wider—but the pain of it only made the pleasure sharper when it finally spilled out of him and into me.

We rode an earth-shattering climax together, my body tightening around his as his filled mine. Heat flooded through every vein in my body, setting me alight. For a moment, I swore I glowed too, just as Seren had when he took his new throne.

Seren collapsed beside me and rolled onto his back, his chest still glistening with sweat as he stared up at the stars in equal parts ecstasy and dismay.

"Fuck, Delphine. You're going to ruin me."

28
SEREN

I COULDN'T REMEMBER THE LAST TIME I FELT THIS WAY. I WASN'T sure if I ever had.

Things got lost when you'd lived as long as I had. Some things, however, you'd think you'd remember. I didn't have a human memory, so prone to forgetting that I couldn't trust my own mind ... but when the morning stars shone down on Delphine, lighting the shape of her half covered in my silken sheets, I was sure that whatever I felt in that moment I'd never felt before.

I would have remembered if I had.

Surely, because what I felt ... I felt with every fiber of my being. Every bit of stardust that made me up sang at the memory of our slightest touch. It almost made me afraid to reach out and take hold of her now.

Almost.

Because that fear was nothing compared to the *need.*

Five hundred years since I'd been touched, and still nearly five thousand more ... and never had it felt like that. Felt like *her.*

Had I known that it would be like this, I would have snatched her from that pool the day she arrived in Avarath. I would have found a way to save her from the princes there and then. I never would have subjected her to that deal that made her suffer.

I would have protected her better.

And somehow, knowing that did nothing to make me feel less like the monster I was.

Because I'd known she was mine. I'd known she too was made of the same stardust that made me, that made my court—the very court that I now had an even greater duty to protect—and still knowing that, I'd tricked her, betrayed her as much as any of those princes I'd left her to. All of that, and she'd forgiven me—or, if not quite forgiven me yet, had given me a chance that I hardly deserved.

She'd taken my offer to learn what it was to be one of us, taken another deal meant to twist her to my own will. It was a second deal I wished I could take back, but a deal, once made, couldn't be broken. Not even by me.

Not even by a high king.

Neither of us could break the deal, sure, but that wasn't what I worried about now, as I finally reached out to brush away the hair that had stuck to the back of Delphine's neck. No, what I was more worried about now was that she would break *me.*

Delphine's half-human heart thrummed like a hummingbird compared to that of a fae. Each beat pressed against my fingers, racing in her sleep as I traced the line of her slender neck to her shoulder. Her exposed skin was cool to the touch, and I found my fingers searching for warmth instead. My hands slipped down her side, beneath the blankets to drag along the dip of her waist and only stopping when I found the softness of her hips.

It was then that she finally stirred, her body responding to my touch by drawing back up into me. This time it was her soft curves that pressed into me, a motion that elicited the very opposite reaction of *soft* from my own body.

Somehow, almost impossibly, her heart beat faster as it registered the way I pushed back into her. My hands dug deeper into the soft flesh of her side, pressing harder, pulling tighter, grinding my pelvis into the back of her separated from me only by the thinnest veil of silk.

I ached to feel her skin against mine, but I wasn't about to take her in her sleep—and just as I feared what she was going to do to me, I was afraid of what I might do to *her* the moment our bodies met again. I didn't fear I couldn't resist her.

I *knew* I couldn't.

I wanted nothing more than to rip the silk from between us, to steal the warmth that currently cocooned Delphine and replace it with my own. I'd once warned her that this feeling between us was nothing more than her fae instincts, but I'd been wrong. If it was instincts only, then why did it consume me too? Why, after millennia of being fae, did being with Delphine make me feel as if I'd never known what it was to be my own kind before now?

I grew harder still as Delphine's lips parted and the softest sigh escaped her lips. It was more like a moan, really, than a sigh. Her chest filled with the last deep breath of sleep and then released as her eyes finally fluttered open, blinking as the two dark pools of them took in the soft silver light of morning.

Then she turned over, lips letting out another sigh, and I was unable to keep myself apart from her any longer. I tore that sheet from between us, prepared to sate that overwhelming desire that was on the brink of driving me mad, when I froze. In that moment—everything changed.

Everything.

Because before my lips could press to the soft dip between her collarbones, my eyes trailed further down. Not to her breasts, the taste of which still lingered on my tongue unwilling to be forgotten, but to the scar between them.

The healed scar.

I didn't know how I didn't see it last night. I must have been more blinded than I thought. Her cut … the fact that it had healed … that could only mean one thing.

Time was passing in Elysia. For the first time in five hundred years, *time was passing.*

But … but that was impossible.

Impossible.

I sat up so quickly that the supports of the bed groaned beneath the sudden shift in my weight. So did Delphine, her eyelids finally shuttering open the rest of the way the moment before concern registered on her own face and she sat up, drawing the silk up over her chest as a small shiver wracked her shoulders.

"What is it? Seren? What's the matter?"

I continued to stare at the space where her hand now clutched over her heart.

"Delphine … how long has that cut been healed?"

She blinked up at me, confused and bleary eyed, until, at last, understanding dawned on her. She fumbled to pull the sheet back down, and there was no mistaking the surprise on her face when she saw the scar now running down the center of her sternum. No small trickle of blood remained, that marker of the moment I nearly came for her too late.

Her lips parted, but at first, no sound came out. She rocked forward on her hips until she was able to trace the scar herself with the free hand no longer supporting her weight, as if feeling it might somehow make some sense of what we were both seeing.

"I … I hadn't noticed."

Her eyes finally flickered up to mine when she said it, and though that concern on her face now echoed in her voice, she still clearly had no idea why that might concern me. And why would she?

Maybe I shouldn't be concerned, either.

Maybe I was wrong. Maybe there was some other explanation for it.

Either way, there was only one way to find out—and I had to find out, now.

I stood suddenly, reaching for the silken trousers I'd left to pool at the bottom of the bed.

"Seren?"

The sleep was finally starting to drain from Delphine's voice, and it was all I could do to force myself not to fall back into the bed and relish the last moments before our first morning together ended. But I couldn't. This couldn't wait.

"I need you to think very carefully, Delphine, are you sure you can't remember the last time it bled? When was the last time you changed your dressing?"

Delphine shook her head. "I … I don't remember," she said. "It's become a habit. I swore I redressed it yesterday, but I can't remember. Honestly."

Her eyes lifted back up to mine.

"Is something going on? Have I done something wrong?"

I stopped then, kneeling on the edge of the bed. I dug one hand into the hair at the nape of Delphine's neck as she tilted up her face towards mine.

"I don't know yet," I admitted, refusing to lie to her. "I need to speak with the other kings. But I promise you, it's nothing you've done. I just have to get some answers before it's too late."

I was half risen from the bed when her next question made me pause, again.

"Too late for what?"

I looked up towards the stars, counting the pinpricks of light outlined between the panes of glass that formed the dome over my bed chamber. "I don't know yet," I admitted.

Delphine fell quiet as she watched me finish dressing, her own hand pulling the silk sheets tighter to her chest, bundled up over her healed wound as if it might protect her. I didn't dare create a portal until I'd spoken to Tarrack, until I'd discovered the full ramifications if my hunch was true, so I found the emergency hatch in the bottom of the floor and tugged it open.

Only, it didn't budge.

I swore aloud again, and Delphine flinched. She pulled her knees up beneath her, pulled the sheets ever tighter.

I should have expected it. The hatch hadn't been used in … well … millennia.

I planted my feet on either side, back and legs straining with the effort as I threw the full strength of my body into pulling it open until, with a deafening screech, it finally did. A dark stairwell spiraled down into darkness below.

"Seren … "

This time, for the first time, the way Delphine said my name was tinged with fear, not just concern. I whirled back, thinking she must have finally figured out why I was so eager to leave, when I saw the reason for it.

As if we needed any further complications.

There, on the ground where my portal was opened last night, an amulet glittered on the ground—where Delphine had pulled it through.

Using Seeker magic.

I swore, straightening with a sigh and then holding out my hand to the shivering half-fae in my bed. "I suppose you'd better come with me after all."

29
DELPHINE

THERE WAS NO TIME, APPARENTLY, FOR ME TO LACE UP YESTERDAY'S dress. Seren loaned me one of his robes, and ignoring the fact that it positively swamped me, pulled me after him through the narrow trapdoor.

It wasn't the first time I'd been dragged through the Starlight palace, but there was a new urgency to this. Where Itris had tugged me with vengeance, Seren pulled me onward on the brink of panic. He was usually so calm, so careful, so composed —I didn't like this new side of him, not because he was scaring me deliberately, but because he was trying so hard not to.

I was able to stay silent while I was being led, practically blind, around and around the narrow staircase smelling of a thousand years of must, but I could only hold the questions making bile rise in the back of my throat so long. I held out until the stairwell opened into more familiar passages, passages where the light of the stars and the glowing orbs actually allowed me to see where my next step was going to fall—and no further.

"Seren," I said, the sound of his name broken between my breaths. "Seren, what does this all mean? The amulet … "

"We don't have time for this."

Like our hurried journey, the way his hand gripped my wrist a little too tight, the very cadence of his voice sounded off. I knew his mind was elsewhere, but I had my own reeling thoughts, questions that needed answers.

Answers that, according to the pace of my heart threatening to beat me into an early death, couldn't wait to ask.

"It means I'm a Seeker, doesn't it?" I continued, ignoring him and getting to the point. "It means we're … we're … "

I'm not able to say it. Fortunately, Seren doesn't make me.

"It may mean we're of the same line," Seren admitted in answer. "But maybe not. I may have stood too close to you last night. The glamour that pulled the amulet through the portal may have been mine, despite our precautions."

Despite his half attempt to console me, that bile bit at the back of my throat again. "But maybe not."

"But maybe not." Seren's hand pulled me ever faster. I have to take two steps for every one of his.

He'd not so much as balked at the sight of the amulet. I knew he'd never been afraid of the lineage that might have tied us together, that it didn't matter to him, to fae. But it mattered to me. So, despite the fact that Seren seemed determined to ignore this, I refused.

"Why'd you ask me to come with you if you didn't want to give me any answers?"

He stopped then, finally turning to face me. He placed one hand on each of my shoulders to steady himself as much as me.

"Because the last thing I was going to do was leave you there, in my room alone, to fall apart."

Warmth spread through me, something that melted away some of the overwhelming fear.

"We have to try again," I said, my determination paling in comparison to that which I saw flashing in his eyes. "We have to do the test, we have to know for certain."

"We will, Delphine. But we have to do something else first."

"What could possibly be more important? I let you take me to your bed. I need to know, Seren, if it was a mistake."

He flinched, visibly flinched. But he didn't give in, despite himself.

"Mistake or not, Delphine, this can't wait."

He paused just long enough to draw in a deep breath of his own. "We'll do the test again, if we can. First, we have to see if we have enough glamour left to do it."

Shock hung in the air between us, and this time, and for one of the first times, he offered more information voluntarily—with no deal, and without any more prying. Like his pace, his urgency, it scared me, too.

"Because if time is passing, Delphine … then it can only mean one thing. It means that when the realms collided, they never broke apart. It means we're subject to the curse that ruined Avarath, that drained it of its magic. It means that all this time, since I brought you here, the glamour has been hemorrhaging out of Elysia like a river run through a broken dam."

He swallowed, hard. "We must see Tarrack first, before we do anything else. We must see what kind of damage I've wrought."

"We, you mean," I said, my voice smaller, still. "What damage *we've* wrought."

Seren stopped again, fury once again rising in the back of his voice. "No, Delphine. Not we. *Me.* I'm the high king of Elysia. If there's something wrong here, then I, and I *alone*, am to blame."

TARRACK KNEW the moment he saw us that something was wrong.

The brief glow on his face faded as his gaze shifted first to Seren, then to me, and then, slower still, back to the high king. Seren didn't make him wait to ask what it was that weighed down the both of us so heavily.

"Delphine's cut has healed," he said, dryly.

"But that's impossible."

Seren pressed his lips together. "I thought so too until now."

Tarrack nodded once, understanding dawning on him with the same gravity that pulled at Seren and me. "I'll prepare the tests, but it'll take some time."

"Then there's none to waste."

Tarrack paused.

"Shouldn't we alert the other kings? Surely they deserve … "

"Not yet, not until we know for sure. We don't need to raise the alarm unless—" It wasn't until Seren was halfway through hissing his response, however, that it became apparent what Tarrack had been trying to tell us. Or, more like, warning us.

It turned out we weren't the only fae who'd thought to pay Tarrack a visit this morning.

Itris stepped from the shadows of the nearest vessel, both her grandchildren in tow.

She took one look at us, her haughty gaze raking over me a little too long, taking in the way my borrowed robes threatened to slip from my shoulders to pool on the floor.

Tarrack chewed the inside of his cheek. "Shall we begin? Or should we waste more time while the two of you try to think up idle insults? I myself have a few I've been saving for such an occasion."

His eyes flickered over to Itris and away quickly, but not so quickly as to be missed. It was obvious who these saved insults were for.

"No need for that," Seren growled, and even though I was very interested to find out just exactly what it was Tarrack had to say to his sister, I had to agree. Right now, we needed to discover if the glamour was intact. Seren, to find out if his magic was slipping away. Me, so I could discover once and for all if the man I'd just fucked was my great-great-great-grandfather, or something of the sort.

Tarrack danced around us in a swirl of robes, readying at least half a dozen different vessels of all sorts. The rest of us looked on in increasingly uneasy silence. Itris was all too happy to glare at me, unblinking, but her grandchildren kept their eyes downcast in embarrassment. I was happy to see that Elvie showed at least a little shame about how she turned me in last night, even if in its own way, it was for the best. I was tired of being betrayed by the fae I was too quick to consider my friends, but at the same time, I was getting so used to it that I wasn't sure if I could really hold it against her.

Let the other fae hold their grudges. I had enough to worry about without adding another one to the mix.

The air began to thrum as each of Tarrack's vessels began to channel his magic. Whispers broke out around us, crystals and pools of water cast shimmering reflections across the ceilings and walls—and with each moment that those whispers grew louder and the reflections brighter, Tarrack's face grew more serious.

Eventually his footsteps slowed and then, at long last, stopped altogether. His face was stony as he let the room fall into dark silence.

Then, slowly, and with his Adam's apple bobbing in his throat, he turned to Seren and nodded once.

"It's true. The realms … they never broke apart."

His eyes dropped then, staring at some invisible space between us. "The magic, it's already dying."

I expected Itris to gloat. She'd been right, after all. I was their undoing, just as she's warned.

But even she was silent.

Eventually, Tarrack nodded again, his hands working anxiously in front of him. "I'll call the kings."

"Make sure to send the news with servants, and instruct them not to use any magic to get here. From here on out, in fact, no one is to use *any* magic, not until we find out at what rate the glamour is being lost."

"I'll go spread the word," Itris said, finally stepping forward. She wore the same stoic look that the other two kings did. "I'll be faster than any servant. Every second counts now."

She bowed her head went to leave, motioning for her grandchildren to follow, but Elvie lingered.

"Wait," she said, hesitantly. Her eyes flickered from Itris to me, and then finally, to Seren. "The cards. I read Delph's cards, and I thought they were strange. I saw death. The death I saw, could it have been the magic?"

Elvie seemed almost surprised when not only Seren suddenly snapped to attention, but so did both the other kings. Itris no longer seemed so desperate to leave.

"What cards did you see?" Seren asked, and then, when Elvie started stuttering over her words, he demanded she show him instead. The moment Elvie plucked the last card from her deck, however, completing the tryptic that had led to her betrayal of me in the first place, all three kings took a step back.

"No," Seren said, his head tilting back, his whole body

leaning away from the cards laid out as if that way he could somehow escape them. "No, that isn't the magic dying. No, that only means one thing."

It was Tarrack that said it, Tarrack that broke the sickening tension.

"That means a fae is dying," he said, quietly. He glanced at Seren and Itris with worry. "Soon."

Seren's voice had practically dropped to a whisper. "You said … "

"I know what I said," Tarrack interrupted him. His hands twitched nervously in front of him. "I must have read things wrong. This news, with the realms shifting … "

"You have to read them again." The determination returned to Seren's voice in an instant.

"But the magic … "

"Damn the magic," Seren snarled. He stormed halfway across the first chamber to a small, intricate vessel in the middle of the room. "This is a life we're talking about. If we're losing a fae, then we have to know."

This time, Tarrack's work kept him glued to the front of that single vessel. It was smaller than most of the others in the room, a contraption made with mirrors and curved glass that could be moved and fixed by brass arms.

He read the device once. Twice. Three times.

He would have probably read it a hundred times more if he could, but it would have given him the same results.

True horror masked Tarrack's face when he looked back up.

"A Starlight Fae is going to die, and they're going to die tonight."

30
DELPHINE

TIME WAS PASSING.

The magic was disappearing.

A fae was dying, a Starlight Fae, no less.

There was much to prepare for—first and foremost, it seemed, was a funeral.

If ever there was something to put my own dilemmas into perspective, that would be it. I hadn't been long in Elysia, but the solemnity of the court weighed nearly as heavily on me as it did the fae all around me.

Even Ayre, surly as she usually was, had fallen into a new kind of silence.

She'd arrived in my room draped in as much black fabric as she had bundled in her arms. It took much longer than usual to dress when we discovered none of the gowns would fit without the magical tailoring I'd taken for granted up until now. The dresses were all too large, swamping me nearly as much as Seren's borrowed robes had earlier. It took several trips—trips much longer than usual now that the doors and staircases all seemed to lead exactly where they were actually supposed to—

before she found something dark and slightly faded from the bottom of some forgotten heap of funeral gowns.

I could only imagine how quickly the rest of the palace was falling into chaos if her labored breath was any indicator. She, more than most, was used to life without the glamour, and she was already exhausted.

From my tower window, I was able to watch the new flurry of movement throughout the palace and beyond. A kind of chaotic energy raced through the air, marked with the dark gloom that turned the already solemn faces of these fae into masks of sadness. Strange looks haunted them, memories of death so suddenly remembered when they'd tried so long to forget.

Tarrack and Seren had been unable to divine the fae that was to die, but they had been able to calculate the moment of death before sending out the missive that had so quickly turned the palace on its head. All fae were slated to attend the funeral, a tradition that extended even to the prisoners so newly returned to their cells—with one exception.

An exception that Seren had allowed me without so much as questioning me.

Ayre stopped to rub her temple where a small bump had formed a bruise in the days following Waylan's visit. Each time she'd come back up to the tower, her drawn brows had kitted a little more together. Now, they were pulled so tight it was a wonder the blood vessels beneath them hadn't broken yet.

At long last, she broke the equally tense silence that had stretched between us all afternoon with a swear.

"I don't know how much more of this I can take," she snarled, fingertips pressing harder and harder into the bruise until I felt guilt pounding in my own temples. "This whole place, it's like a tap running dry. Every time I think it's finally finished, that we've finally seen what it'll be like now that they've cut off all the glamour, something else gets taken away."

I found my eyes flitting down to the small bracelet on her wrist. "Does that mean … "

Her eye roll was welcomingly familiar. "Don't worry, some magical objects are imbued with their own power. It's not that the magic is gone, besides, not yet. The palace has just ordered no one to use it, not until they've discovered how much there is left to go around."

She stopped then, hands finally falling down to her sides as she stared at the massive piles of black gowns at her feet that would need to be returned. "I just hope they bring back the portals. I'll be the next fae to die if I'm expected to climb these unholy tower stairs much longer. How many towers can one palace have?"

Too many, that's how many.

Ayre finally caught her breath enough to leave when a sudden second swear tore from her lips.

"I nearly forgot," she said, dropping the enormous pile of faded black silk back onto the cold tower floor. She dug into her pocket and withdrew a large velvet bag. "Seren ordered these for you."

Dark gemstones I recognized glittered from between the drawstring folds.

I stopped Ayre once more before she could leave. Seren's jewels had given me an idea.

"Can you do a favor for me?"

"I don't have time for any extra favors today," she snapped back. "These fae have never learned how to so much as wipe their own asses without magic. I've already been ordered straight down to the funeral hall once I'm finished here … and I already know exactly what that means."

She stared down at her hands. "So many candles that need to be prepared. So many to be lighted. I'm going to have burns and blisters for weeks."

I imagined the dark passages. I'd grown so used to the starlight orbs that passed through the halls here, and shivered at the thought of how dark the corners of this place would be without them.

"Well, wouldn't this give you a good excuse then? A reason to stay busy and avoid the funeral hall a little longer?"

Ayre shot me a glance then that was as close to appreciation as she was capable. "I'm starting to like the way you think."

GUARDS WERE SUPPOSED to be sent up to fetch me later, for my own protection, but I had no intention of waiting around for them. I waited just long enough for Ayre to make one last, final trip up to my tower before I followed her echoing footsteps.

I couldn't be left alone with my thoughts—they were too much and far too many—so I turned to the only fae that might still be sane enough to offer me some semblance of comfort, no matter how misguided. They were, of course, the only fae here who knew what it was to live in a realm where magic was already long gone.

A fae realm, anyway.

The silver cloak pulled up over my head hardly matched the black funeral colors filling the chaos of the corridors, but I was more worried about being recognized for myself then I was about making a fashion faux pas. All anyone knew was that a Starlight Fae died tonight, not who—or where—that fae might be. At present, I was all too aware of the fact that my presence drew enough increasingly unwelcome glares that I was somewhere near the top of the list most likely to end up dead.

Fortunately for me, Tarrack's map seemed to have been imbued with some of that same magic in Ayre's cuff. I never would have dared wander the palace without it, especially now that the few routes I'd once memorized had changed completely over the course of the last few hours. It seemed most fae had grown as used to the shifting staircases as they were in devising the time of day from a sky without a sun—too used to it. They were lost without it. For once, I was the only one who wasn't.

It meant I got to the prison not a moment too soon, either.

Seren was a sight to see in his black robes. Though he was hardly the fae I came to see, one glimpse of him standing before the crystal of Nyx's cell, and I was unable to look away. My heart raced at a pace that would have surely betrayed me if I didn't do it myself a moment later, when I saw why he wasn't the only figure gathered stubbornly before the glass.

Not only did two guards stand at Seren's shoulders, but so did both Tethys and Armene. They'd already been re-released from their cells and now stood begging with the last fae still stubbornly refusing to budge from the other side of the crystal.

"It's just for a night, Nyx," Armene said, and even though I couldn't see his face, I could imagine the annoyance on his face from the tone of his voice. It was subtle enough that Nyx was very unlikely to notice—even though I could already imagine the way Armene's teeth would be gritted and his lips pulled back as he tried to keep himself from lashing out at yet another one of the Woodland Prince's unbreakable *principles.*

"All this over a stupid bracelet? Really, Nyx? I'm sure you look fine in silver. Who even cares about—"

A loud, keening wail drowned out the rest of Tethys' own plea.

"*I* care," Nyx screeched, his figure flickering frantically between the broad shoulders of the onlooking fae. "Don't you think I'd know if I looked good in silver? I don't look *good* in silver."

He was pacing across the back side of his cell, the roots and vines swaying out of his way with every step.

"You have to stop that," Seren snapped, shoulders tensing further. "It's not about the funeral anymore. You have to wear the bracelet if you won't stop using our magic."

"It's not *your* magic," Nyx countered, the tone of his voice so close to that of a petulant child that he actually made himself flinch. That, or he caught a glimpse of his own reflection in the crystal and once again imagined what it would look like if he gave in and so much as let the offending silver touch his skin. He froze in step, unmoving, as slowly—ever so slowly—the plants around him began to wither and die.

"Fine," he said, only once the last of the roots had turned into a shriveled mess on the ground. He swallowed, hard, his face as horror-stricken as I'd seen it the day he saw his blackened forest. "I won't use magic. Just … just don't make me wear that damned silver bracelet."

"Not even for me?"

The small gathering of fae all turned on their heels in surprise at the sound of my voice—well, almost all in surprise. If Seren felt the same as the rest of them, he was doing a good job of hiding it.

"Ah, yes, I was wondering when you'd turn up."

I stopped, my own surprise taking hold of me for a second. "But Ayre said you'd send guards … "

"Knowing how little you trusted them? Especially now?"

Seren fixed me with a look that left my mouth dry.

How well he knew me, already. *Too well.*

Not to let the attention be drawn away from him too long, Nyx was quick to press himself up against the crystal confines of his cell and let out a long, pointed sigh. "I can't, Delphine, I've already told you … "

Nyx's magical garments had disappeared with the withering of his magic, leaving him stark naked on the other side of the glass. Even with the pained expression on his face, he truly was a perfect specimen of a fae. He left me averting my eyes and still somehow unable to look away, all while the words that had been about to tumble out of my mouth completely dried up.

Seren, meanwhile, let out another flustered huff that had nothing to do with the nakedness that didn't seem to affect anyone other than myself—except maybe Tethys, who was appreciating Nyx almost as much as I was trying not to.

"Come, Delphine, if the prince wishes to miss out willingly, that's his own right," Seren said, though he wasn't so good at keeping the displeasure from his voice as he was from his face. "We're wasting our time here."

"Not even if it wasn't … silver?"

I held up the fruits of Ayre's last favor—a spool of thin, golden wire—for Nyx to see.

Now I had Nyx's attention, his true attention. The disappointed curve of his mouth turned into one of abject joy as a glint returned to his eye that I'd only had a few chances to truly see. It was a glint that died with his blackened forest.

"At least pretend to have a little decorum, Nyx. You don't have to be devastated, but you should at least look a little bit less like you're about to go to a wedding instead of a funeral. You're a prince, for goodness' sake."

The Prince of Sands eyed Nyx with narrowed eyes, his own lips pressed together as he took his friend in with no small amount of disappointment—an expression *he* wasn't afraid would mar the handsome tanned planes of his face. And it didn't. It strangely suited him.

"Of course I'm devastated," Nyx said, though there wasn't so much as a hint of the emotion etched into any inch of his excited body. "I just don't like the way it looks on me. Not like that gold is going to look, anyway."

He eyed the spool of wire greedily, watching with rapt attention as I wound the wire around the silver bracelet loop by steady loop.

He wasn't the only one, either.

From over my shoulder, the air was soured by the distinct sound of Caldamir's scoff.

I'd almost forgotten he was here, too. *Almost.*

I didn't want to look at him, but I couldn't avoid it, not when every other eye turned from me to look on as the Mountain Court prince finally got up from his place against the wall to press his hands up against the crystal with a sneer.

"You're seriously going to leave me in here? At a moment like this? It's my right to mourn with my people, too. This is a betrayal."

Before I could answer, Seren crossed the small space between the cells to stand nose-to-nose with the prince. "You should have thought of that before you tried to murder one of your own people. You'll stand trial for what you've done, sooner rather than later. This might be a betrayal, but it was her right to betray you after all you've done to her."

That was the moment that Caldamir's eyes slid to meet mine. I wished I'd looked away in time, that I'd averted my gaze before I saw the contempt he held for me.

But it wasn't contempt for me that I saw, and somehow, that was worse.

It was hurt.

Something shifted in Caldamir's tone. It softened, slightly, as did the slope of his shoulders as some of the fight finally slipped out of him.

"Easy to commit a crime like this when you'll never have to stand before a court and face them."

Seren just blinked back at him, calmly. "You're right, Caldamir, that is where we differ," he said in reply. "You'll have to stand before the court. And I … I *am* the court."

That sneer had returned to Caldamir's face. "Easy to say when the courts haven't met in five hundred years, and as far as any of us know, they never will again. Are you really going to leave me here to rot forever and still deny me my most basic mourning rights?"

"Rights? You have no rights," Seren scoffed. "And you're wrong, again. The courts have already convened again. You'll stand trial for your crimes sooner than you know. There's no more waiting, you're finished with that … and so am I."

He turned from the prince and held out his hand to me. "Delphine, come with me. The guards will escort your princes out after us, but we can't tarry any longer. We have a funeral to attend."

31
DELPHINE

THE FUNERAL HALL FLICKERED WITH SHADOWS, BOTH FROM THE dark smudges of fae dressed in black and from the soft smoke of a thousand candles.

The pathway leading to the hall had wound through the city I'd yet had time to explore and beyond, up the sheer mountain walls opposite the palace where that pressing nothingness met Elysia. We were joined in our procession, slowly at first, and then in increasingly growing numbers. The crowds of fae thickened the closer we drew to the funeral hall, each dark shape adding to the tide of bodies until they spilled out beside us into the high-ceilinged hall.

It had been carved into the landscape of the mountain, one long edge leading out to a balcony skimming the brim of the night sky. The ceiling was carved so high into the depths of the mountain that without the light of the orbs that had, up until today, floated through the dark corners of the realm, the hall's ceiling simply disappeared into blackness.

It was, in a way, a cold, starless sky of its own.

More than heaviness hung in the air. Dread. Fear. Disbelief.

No one spoke above the soft murmur of a whisper. No one lingered too long in one place.

If it weren't for Seren at my side and the three princes trailing at our back, I would have felt naked without the shadows of my silver cloak. But here, with the newly proclaimed high king, no one dared more than a glance my way.

Seren had made his opinions of me clear, and despite the uneasy shift inside me each time I looked up at the fae I'd once again let too close, I was grateful for that. Without that, I was almost sure to end up the fae we all waited to see die. All it would take was one fae brave enough—or foolish enough—to see if they could tempt the fate that drew us here.

Unlike human funerals, fae funerals didn't actually bother to wait until after the fae had died to gather. There were no words spoken in remembrance, no great show of sadness. Instead, the fae of Elysia simply gathered together, waiting until the moment that immortal spark died, and together, they witnessed it. Not the body, viewed long after it had already begun to rot—dressed and stuffed like some kind of morbid doll propped up for show. No. They viewed the death. They shared in that last spark of life together, and together they watched it fade.

It was one of the many great gifts of the Starlight Fae.

Like the Pool of Indecision that had first drawn me to them, and like the bracelets encircling the three princes' wrists, it was an unyielding kind of magic. It didn't ebb and flow with the glamour Seren was so suddenly scared of losing. It was as fixed as the stars shining from the balcony where only the other six kings waited.

Or so, Seren had tried to tell me.

It was one of those things that I knew I had to witness for myself to truly understand, and whether fortunately or unfortunately for me—that moment was already upon us. A coldness had taken hold of me that I couldn't shake, the dreaded feeling that what I was about to witness was going to change me.

And not, necessarily, for the better.

Seren had promised to show me what it was to be a Starlight Fae. I didn't think even he knew, though, just how thorough that instruction would be.

The only eyes that dared linger on me for more than a moment, let alone with disdain glimmering within, were those of the kings on the other side of the balcony Seren now steered me towards. The guards barring entrance to the rest of the court shared a brief glance, but though they shifted uncomfortably beneath the plates of their armor, they didn't dare contest the high king as he brought me out to stand at his side. Enough of the sigil-bearing guards lined the hall to form a small army, their watchful eyes turned towards the crowd.

It was strange to have them on my side again, protecting me instead of being the ones hunting me. Seren was right. I'd yet to learn to trust them, and I wasn't sure I ever really would.

Then again, it wasn't the first time I'd told myself that about a fae, and look where I was.

I stole one glance back at the princes before I let Seren lead me through—feeling one small stab of pride that I'd managed to coax Nyx from his self-imposed prison. Of course, I was far from forgiving any of the princes for what they'd tried to do to me, but time was a strange thing. The more of it that distanced me from that dreaded moment under the mountain, the more it faded. The sharp memory of it instead turned into something made of soft, broken instances that when threaded together were impossible to forgive, but separately …

Separately, I wasn't so sure, anymore.

The night sky was so close here that it threatened to swallow us whole. We stood not just beneath it, but *inside* it, the black silks melding into the darkness and pulling it near.

Though part of me feared Seren's touch and the affect it still held on me, I found myself drawing closer to him as we came to stand before the other kings of Elysia. If I were to let him go, I felt as if I would be sucked into that inky blackness, never to return. The sky here was my pool, and the fae at my side, the king holding me tight, was my tether.

Tarrack was the first king to bow his head, the others following only a moment after. Whatever they felt for me, their reverence for their high king remained the same.

Or, if it didn't, then they were skilled at hiding it.

"You've made it just in time," Tarrack said, his voice unusually hoarse when he returned to his full height. "We should prepare ourselves."

Seren bowed his head, the heat of his breath stirring the hairs at the back of my neck. "Stand very, very still when it happens. Don't move, no matter what you see."

My lips parted, eyes lifted to search his out, but there was no time for explanation.

Together, all seven kings stepped to face the darkness, their heads slowly craning up to peer into the depths of the black sky. They stood in a line, each one just outside of reach of the other. The moment their heads tilted back, a deep hush fell over the fae gathered at our backs. They pressed closer too, the sea of them moving to peer up through the arches lining the edge of the sky. We were surrounded, a sea of darkness threatening to swallow us from one side, a crushing sea of fae on the other. Even the guards struggled to keep their eyes on the crowd, and I couldn't blame them.

Not when that all black sky began to change, and suddenly, it wasn't black anymore.

We weren't even standing in Elysia.

I stood with Seren alone clutched at my side, in a place I recognized all too well.

I stood in Alderia—and not just anywhere.

I was home. *Truly home.*

32
DELPHINE

If this was a trick, it was a very convincing one.

A cruel one.

The cruelest of all.

There were times that coming home to this cottage had filled me with dread, but never a dread like *this.* It struck me to my core, froze me to the spot even when every instinct in my body begged me to flee. I might have too, if it weren't for the tightening of Seren's arm around mine.

I wanted to look at him, to see if I could see any trace of what the *hell* was going on in his face, but I couldn't. Not when I saw what was before me, here, in the place I'd once called home.

More familiar than the low ceiling crisscrossed with beams overhead were the tightly huddled bodies before me. It took me a second to recognize them only because they were the last faces I expected to see today—and more than that, because despite the fact that I knew them, the two most important ones among them were missing.

Ixora.

Draigh.

Nerys.

My stepfamily stood before me, huddled so close that their shoulders touched. Someone was murmuring something on their other side, but I couldn't hear what it was. I ached to call out to them, but I knew, somehow, that I shouldn't. It was a second later, before I'd fully begun to wonder where my brother and father were, that I realized why that was.

And where at least one of them was.

Something that murmured voice said made Nerys' shoulders slump, one hand coming up to cover her mouth. She turned away, breaking away from her children to reveal who it was making soft, broken utterances from her other side.

It was my father.

I barely recognized him or maybe *refused* to recognize him. It was him, but it wasn't him at the same time. It was his body, but … but it wasn't right.

It was too hard and too soft at the same time. The skin too cold and too blue. The eyes, half-hooded, blinking too slow.

It was his body, but it wasn't right because he was dying.

I should have felt sorrow at the sight, but instead, all I felt was a horrible emptiness. I stared at the shallow rising of his chest, the parting, quivering lips that whispered words I'd never hear, and all I felt was … nothing.

My father lay dying in front of me, and it meant nothing to me.

As if sensing this, too, Seren tightened his hold on me again, and I finally allowed myself to look up at him. He was too enraptured in what he saw before him to notice, and for once, I got a glimpse behind that perfect mask he wore.

The horror I saw on his face only made the guilt in me grow.

Seren, who'd never so much as met my father, let alone been sired or raised by him, felt more affected by the sight of him like this than I did. Still, as much as I tried, I couldn't make the seed of sorrow sprout within me as the moments dragged on and the last whispers of my father faded. I knew without drawing nearer that the words he whispered weren't for me. I knew his regrets, if he felt any, wouldn't have to do with me. I doubted his memories, the ones that were said to flash before your eyes in that final moment of passing, even remembered me.

Maybe I was cold, heartless, and as cruel as the trick playing out in front of me.

Or maybe, just maybe, the reason I felt nothing for my father was because I knew this *wasn't* a trick. Maybe the reason I couldn't bring myself to feel sorrow or pain or loss was because I was too afraid. Afraid of what it meant.

I felt, rather than witnessed, the moment my father died in front of me. I was too busy staring beyond at something I couldn't see—that no one could—at the source of the panic rising in me.

I stood stunned, in shock, as the figures before me deflated at the sight of his passing.

Nerys leaned against the back of a chair, one hand pressed to her stomach as the other weighed hard against the wood to steady herself. Her eyes closed, and for a moment, I saw genuine pain on her face.

She waved a hand towards my step siblings, the next words cutting through any sympathy I might have felt for her, causing that panic to boil and bubble over, consuming me.

"Someone get me pen and paper. We have to write to your brother. It's time he came home."

It's time he came home.

It was never my mother who was fae, never my mother who passed her cursed genes onto me.

It was my father.

My father was fae, and that meant one thing, and one thing only. One thing that mattered.

That meant that there was one more fae trapped in Alderia. That meant that my brother Sol, my golden haired, sunny brother, was fae too.

My brother, my *unprotected* and unsuspecting brother could end the curse over Avarath … and all of faerie had just learned exactly where to find him.

I tore my arm from Seren and stumbled forward, breaking the spell at once.

Elysia crashed in on me in an instant. The blackness. The bright pinpricks of light. The silence. It was all too much, or would have been if hands weren't reaching out to tighten around me again. All around us, for a moment, the whole of the Elysian court remained transfixed on the unseen vision before them. It was just Seren and me again, just for a moment.

And in that moment, I saw my own terror mirrored on his face.

"Delphine …"

"Seren, did you mean your promise before? Your promise to protect *all* Starlight Fae?"

The question, blurted out above his own worried voice, caught him off guard.

"Of … of course," he started, only for me to cut him off again. I knew how little time I had.

"My brother," I said, or really breathed, since it was nearly impossible to get out the words, "my brother is fae."

He blinked at me for another second before understanding began to dawn on him.

"You promised to protect all Starlight Fae," I said, again. "If you meant that, then you'll protect my brother. You'll protect Sol. You'll go get him like you got me."

All around us, the court had begun to return now, too. I heard it in the rustle of their silks, in the soft sighs of their voices, the scrape of shuffling feet. Confusion tinged their voices. Relief too.

After all, it wasn't really a fae that had just died. It was just another half-human.

It was just another stranger, like me.

It was hard to mourn the loss of something that you never knew was yours to begin with.

"Delphine …"

It was the second time Seren said my name and I refused to hear him finish speaking the words I knew I wasn't going to like.

"You promised," I hissed at him. "Or are you really so quick to go back on your word?"

Tarrack was the first to recognize that something was off. The brief flicker of relief on his own face faded at the sight of me and Seren. I tried to straighten up before anyone else noticed, but I was too late.

The other kings had noticed too.

"What's going on?" Itris asked, storming over to stand beside us. "What's happened?"

"That fae was Delph's father," Seren said, answering for me.

"Well, I guess we know where she got it from then," Itris said. "Not that it mattered which side really."

"But it does, because I have a brother," I blurted out, unable to resist myself. It wasn't exactly a secret. It wouldn't be long before two and two were put together, and if Seren wasn't going to come through on his promise to protect his own court, then I wasn't above begging the other kings of Elysia. "He's out there, in Alderia. If anyone finds out, he could be used to wake the king of Avarath."

I expected the same fear I felt to alight in the kings' eyes, but instead, all I earned was one of Itris' smirks.

"Please, Delphine," she said, eyes narrowing. "Don't tell me you think so low of your own court that you'd think one of us would betray you?"

The words, spoken with so much vile condescension, had barely left her lips when I felt it. When we *all* felt it.

It rushed in all around us, through us, bled us dry.

It was silent, breaking, wracking … and I knew, without having to be told, exactly what it meant.

Fury tore through the kings as quickly as fear did through their subjects. The quiet, solemn crowd fell into panic just as a guard forced his way through the barricade barely keeping the sea of them from spilling out into the balcony.

"Your majesties!"

The guard's voice was as filled with that same fear as rumbled through the rest of them.

Seren pushed forward to face him. "Tell me, now."

The guard's face paled, and it took him a moment to find the words. When he did, they turned that already pale skin a violent green.

"It's one of the princes," he whispered. "He's gone. He took the magic … and he fled."

I saw Seren open his mouth to say it was impossible, but then I saw him falter. I followed the line of his gaze to what the guard held in his hand, and in that moment, I understood, too. I understood too much.

My own skin paled, the blood draining from my body to pool in the feet cementing me to the stone of the balcony.

I recognized the golden bracelet … and I recognized the perfect, severed hand it was still attached to.

Sure, it wasn't a Starlight Fae that betrayed me.

It was another fae, this one's betrayal far worse.

It was Nyx.

There was only one place he would have gone, and if the kings of this realm wouldn't take me after him, then I would go myself. I didn't have magic, but I had something more powerful than the deal that bound me here.

I had a favor owed me, and a favor from a demon was a powerful thing indeed.

A NOTE FROM THE AUTHOR

Thank you once again for the overflow of support and excitement for The Veiled Realm series. Here we are with book two, and I hope you've loved it as much as you did the first part of Delphine's story. Book three, A Veil of Moonlight and Madness, will release some time mid summer, 2022.

Looking forward to continuing this journey along with you!

With Love,

ALSO BY ANALEIGH FORD

The Veiled Realm

A Veil of Truth and Trickery

A Veil of Stardust and Savagery

A Veil of Moonlight and Madness

Academy of the Dark Arts

Dark Witch

Asylum Bound

A House So Dark

A House So Mad

A House So Cruel

The Forgotten Affinities

Absorb

Adapt

Abandon

Made in the USA
Middletown, DE
07 January 2025

68911454R00163